M000080916

# Praise For
## THE BLUESUIT CHRONICLES

"*The War Comes Home* would make an excellent TV series. The book features police work from the vantagepoint of the policeman, emphasizing the exposure to the danger of police work, as you carefully work around the restraints set forth in the law. I know the public does not realize what the cop is up-against, and this book sets forth that scenario without fault. The major bestseller *The New Centurions*, by Joseph Wambaugh, is a book I will never forget, and your book is equal to his." ~Patrick Lowe, Anderson Island, WA

"The first installment of The Bluesuit Chronicles, (*The War Comes Home*) is a compelling start to what is sure to be an epic saga. A former Golden Gloves boxer and Army medic returns home from Vietnam to a very different America than the one he left. The drug craze of the early seventies takes a heavy toll on the Boomer generation, and the social fabric begins to unravel, nail-biting action, romance, and intrigue, based on actual events." Rated Four Stars.
~ Red City Reviews

"An exciting, read, riveting action, romance and moving scenes. *The War Comes Home* took me back to the Bellevue I knew in 'the good old days.' Impossible to put down." ~ Cynthia Davis, Bellevue, WA

"*The War Comes Home* follows the activities of two city police officers, Hitchcock and Walker, as they prepare and then head out for the nightly patrol of their Neighborhood streets. Hitchcock feels a strange foreboding that there will be danger that evening, and someone will die. The two police officers spend the evening patrolling areas looking for drug dealers, prostitutes, and other criminals.

This manuscript is extremely well-written. The author has infused the prose with an interesting mix of dialogue, inner thoughts. The characters are nicely developed, the dialogue is genuine and flows organically. The reader is immediately drawn into the story and wants to learn more, not only about the officers, but what awaits them as they begin their nightly patrol." ~ Editor at Bookbaby

# Praise For
## THE BLUESUIT CHRONICLES

"Having grown up in Bellevue in the '60s and '70s, I bought the entire series for my husband for his birthday. He is completely engrossed in them. Thank you, John, for writing them, it's hard to get him to relax, and the books are doing it with laughter and 'do you remember' comments. We are eagerly waiting for the next book to come out."
~ Jeanie Hack, Bellevue, WA

"From the moment I started reading *The War Comes Home*, I couldn't put it down. I was captivated by the balance of action and drama that John Hansen expertly weaves throughout this fast-paced historical fiction. I'm looking forward to reading the next one."
~ S. McDonald, Redmond, WA

"Book Two of The Bluesuit Chronicles series, *The New Darkness*, continues the story of Vietnam veteran Roger Hitchcock, now a police officer in Bellevue, Washington. The spreading new drug culture is taking a heavy toll on Hitchcock's generation. Some die, some are permanently impaired, everyone is impacted by this wave of evil that even turns traditional values inside out. Like other officer, the times test Hitchcock: will he resign in disgust, become hardened and bitter, corrupt, or will his background in competition boxing and military combat experience enable him to rise to meet the challenge? Romance, intrigue and action are the fabric of *The New Darkness*."
~ Amazon.com

"*Valley of Long Shadows* is the third book in The Bluesuit Chronicles… Returning Vietnam veterans who become police officers find themselves holding the line against societal anarchy. Even traditional roles between cops and robbers in police work have become more deadly…The backdrop is one of government betrayal, societal breakdown, and an angry disillusioned public. The '70s is the decade that brought America where it is now.
Four Stars Rating ~ Red City Reviews

# Praise For
## THE BLUESUIT CHRONICLES

"By the time I finished reading the series up through Book Four (*Day Shift*), I concluded most men would like to be Hitchcock, at least in some way. What sets him apart is the dichotomy of his makeup: he grew up with a Boy Scout sense of honor and right and wrong, yet he isn't hardened or jaded by the evil and cruelty he saw when he went to war, though he killed in combat. As a policeman he *chooses* good and right: to do otherwise is unthinkable. He is a skilled fighter, yet so modest that he doesn't know he is a role model for others around him, and women feel safe with him. I know Hitchcock's type—two of my relatives were cops who influenced my life."
~ Tracy Smith, Newcastle, WA

"Book Five (*Unfinished Business*) moves to show how difficult it is for Officer Hitchcock to do right. Bad people are out to get him for his good work. He is a threat to their nefarious activities. There is even a very bad high-ranking policeman who puts Hitchcock and his family in extreme peril. Organized foreign crime is moving into his city, he works hard to uncover the clues to solve this evil in his city. I'm still waiting to find out what restaurant owner Juju is up to and who she works for. Great series and story. Another fine book by John Hansen. Yo! ~ T.A. Smith

"I've read all of John's books and rated them all 5 stars, because those stars are earned. I worked the street with John as a police officer for years and what he speaks of in his books is real. John is an excellent author; articulate and clear, always bringing the reader directly into the story. I like John's work to the point that I've asked him to send me any new books he writes, I'll be either the first or almost the first to read all of them. I lived this with John. He's an author not to be missed. You can't go wrong reading his books. I strongly encourage more in the series." ~ Bill Cooper, Chief of Police (ret)

# Praise For
## THE BLUESUIT CHRONICLES

"John Hansen has written another great read. *Unfinished Business* is filled with conspiracy, corruption and crime, much of which is targeted at Hitchcock. From the beginning of the book, I was hooked. The author has a gift with words that drew me into the story effortlessly— I could not put the book down. I have read all in the series and I look forward to reading more of John Hansen's books." ~ S. McDonald

"A viewpoint from the inside: I worked with and partnered with John both in uniform and in detectives, and like him I came to the Department after military service. This is the fifth (as of this date) of five books in this series. I have read and re-read all five books, and for the first time, recently, over a two-day period, read the entire series in order. All five books were inspired by John's experiences, during many of which I was present. John is an extremely gifted author, and I was transported back to those times and experienced a full gamut of emotions, mostly good, sometimes less so. His use of humor, love, anger, fear, camaraderie, loyalty, respect, disapproval, devotion, and other emotions, rang true throughout the books." ~ Robert Littlejohn

"The whole series of The Bluesuit Chronicles brought back a flood of memories. I started in police work in 1976. This series starts a couple of years earlier. The descriptions of the equipment, the way you had to solve crimes without the assistance of modern items. John made me feel that I was there when it was happening. This whole series is what police work is about. Working with citizens, caring about them, and catching the bad guys. Officers in that time period cared about what they did. It wasn't all about a paycheck... We knew our beat and the people in it. I am not saying we were perfect; however, we were very committed to our community. That being said, I can't wait for the next book. Please read the whole series. Once you start you won't stop."
~ Garry C. Dixon, Ret. LEO-Virginia

# Praise For
## THE BLUESUIT CHRONICLES

"Received Book 4, *Day Shift* on a Wednesday. Already done reading it. Couldn't help myself. Was only going to read a couple chapters and save the rest for my upcoming camping trip. LOL. 3 hours later book finished. Love it. 2 Thumbs up!!! ~ Alanda Bailey, Kalispell, MT

"Retired Detective John Hansen is a master writer. He brings to life policing in the Northwestern U.S. during the '70s, a transitional period. One has to wonder of how much of his writings are founded in personal experience vs. creative thinking. Either way, his stories are thoroughly enjoyable and well-worth purchasing his original books in this series, his current release, as well as the books yet to come." ~ Debbie M.-Scottsdale, AZ

"I urge you to complete your 'to do' list prior to reading *Unfinished Business*, as once started, I could not put it down. It was always, 'one more page' and soon I was not getting anything else done, but it was well worth it. The author has an amazing way of drawing the reader into each scene, adding to the excitement, sweet romance, raw emotion and revealing of each fascinating character as the plots unfold. I highly recommend this book to anyone who wants a truly good read. Looking forward to the next book from this highly talented author." ~ Cynthia R.

"I received the 5th book in *The Bluesuit Chronicles* and started reading and per usual, didn't stop until I finished the book. I am a huge fan of John's stories. I grew up in the general area that the stories are set in. Also, in the same timeframe. John's books are always fast paced and entertaining reads. I would recommend them to any and all." ~ A. Bailey-Kalispell, MT

Also by John Hansen:

The Award -Winning Series: The Bluesuit Chronicles:

*The War Comes Home*
*The New Darkness*
*Valley of Long Shadows*
*Day Shift*
*Unfinished Business*
*The Mystery of the Unseen Hand*

Published & Award-Winning Essays and Short Stories:

"Losing Kristene"
"Riding the Superstitions"
"The Case of the Old Colt"
"Charlie's Story"
"The Mystery of Three"
"The Prospector"

Non-Fiction Book:
*Song of the Waterwheel*

# Unfinished Business

Book 5 of The Bluesuit Chronicles

# JOHN HANSEN

Unfinished Business
by John Hansen

This book is a work of fiction. Names, characters, locations and events are either a product of the author's imagination, fictitious or used fictitiously. Any resemblance to any event, locale or person, living or dead, is purely coincidental.

Third Edition
Revised and Reprinted - Copyright © 2021 John Hansen
Original Copyright © 2017 John Hansen

No portions of this book, except for book reviews, may be reproduced, stored in a retrieval system, or transmitted in any form by any means—electronic, mechanical, photocopying, recording or otherwise, without the written permission of the publisher.

Cover Designer: Jessica Bell - Jessica Bell Design
Interior Design and Formatting: Deborah J Ledford - IOF Productions Ltd

Issued in Print and Electronic Formats
Trade Paperback ISBN: 978-1735803043

Manufactured in the United States of America

All rights reserved

# Unfinished Business

# JOHN HANSEN

*To Patricia, my bride, my passion and joy.*
*Our love story is still being written.*
*~ J*

"We sleep soundly in our beds because rough men stand ready in the night to visit violence on those who would do us harm."

~ Winston Churchill

*Unfinished Business* is dedicated to the memory of Chief Donald P. "Van" Van Blaricom, who rose through the ranks of the Bellevue Police Department from Patrolman to Chief, building and shaping the Department at every level of rank he served in. More than anyone, Van made the Bellevue PD the model agency it is to this day. Rest in Peace, Chief.

# CHAPTER ONE
## Fighting Back

*May 1971*
*Bellevue, Washington*

THE ATTACKER LYING supine on the carport floor at Hitchcock's feet didn't react when Hitchcock nudged him hard with his foot. His lips were parted and bleeding. He appeared to be Chinese, about Hitchcock's age–early to mid-twenties, wearing a high-collar green polyester disco shirt, black bell-bottom slacks and Beatle boots, close-cropped military haircut. Six feet tall, leaner than himself by twenty pounds–about one seventy-five, every ounce like a steel spring.

A cool breeze carried the sounds of approaching police sirens as blood-curdling howls from the other invader and Jamie's growling erupted again from the lawn beyond the carport and cabana, interrupting Hitchcock's bewildered thoughts. *Got to check on Jamie and the other intruder...*

The second he unsnapped the handcuff case on his

duty belt, the human panther seized his uniform pant leg at the knee and vaulted upward in a fluid arc. His boot whooshed past Hitchcock's head, missing by an inch. Like a cat thrown out of a door, he landed in a fighting stance, hands swirling, ready to strike.

A lightning left jab, perfected by over a hundred boxing bouts, powered by hundreds of pushups a week, zipped between the assailant's hands, smashing his lips again.

As the assailant stepped back to regain his balance, Hitchcock closed in. Twisting from his waist, he shifted his weight into a right hook that circled around the attacker's raised hands and crushed his nose. He fell backward. The back of his head hit the concrete with a loud crack like a bowling ball.

Blood flowed from the assailant's nose as he rolled to one side and made a feeble effort to stand, but his legs buckled. He sank back to a supine position on the concrete. Two split-second trips to the deck had been enough.

As the sirens grew louder and the terrified cries of his infant stepson in the cabana erupted again, Hitchcock remembered his wife said the intruders were breaking in to get her before he arrived. He seized the fallen assailant by the front of his bloody shirt with his left hand and lifted.

Limp, arms dangling, mouth hanging open, the assailant stared blankly at the cocked fist aimed at his face. Suddenly a woman's voice broke through.

"Roger, stop!" The voice and the small hand touching his right arm were Allie's. "We're okay, honey. The police are almost here. We're safe. He's finished. Let him go."

The thought that his wife had seen the second fight stopped him cold. His blonde, breathtaking little wife said she is safe. He released his grip, letting the semi-conscious attacker slump back to the concrete.

"I'm going back inside to Trevor," she said, touching his arm again as she left.

The sirens were seconds away now.

Hitchcock bent down and tapped his forefinger on his assailant's forehead. "Lucky you! The police will be here in seconds. Stay down and I'll *try* not to hurt you worse!"

† † †

TWO BLACK-AND-WHITE '71 Plymouth Fury police cruisers roared up the tree-lined driveway. Walker and LaPerle bailed out. Hitchcock told them what happened. Walker took the assailant's arm. "I'll help you to your feet now," he said. He cuffed the suspect's hands behind his back and fished his wallet from his pants pocket.

"The driver's license in your wallet is for Jinjie Zhang. That you?"

Zhang, swaying on his feet, eyes shut, replied with a nod.

A third round of ragged shrieks came from the lawn

on the other side of the cabana, more fiendish than before, and the dog's growls took on a new ferocity.

"Stay with the prisoner!" LaPerle shouted as he and Hitchcock ran to Zhang's confederate.

Walker retrieved a card from his shirt pocket. "Okay, Mr. Zhang, you are under arrest for Second Degree Assault, and Attempted First Degree Burglary." He read the Miranda warnings to him. "Do you understand these rights as I read them?"

Struggling to stay on his feet, head bent, eyes shut, blood dripping from his nose and mouth, Zhang nodded again. Walker steadied him by the elbow. "Is that a yes, Mr. Zhang? Speak up."

Dried blood had cemented Zhang's lips. He worked his jaw and pushed his tongue between them to speak. "Yes, I understand. May I sit down, officer?" he croaked. "I am dizzy. I might fall."

"Sure thing. I'll help you to a patrol car."

Walker patted Zhang down for weapons, then escorted him by the elbow to his cruiser and guided him into the back seat.

Another siren sounded in the distance. "That's the ambulance. They'll be here in a few seconds," Walker assured him. "They'll check you out."

JAMIE DETAINED THE other would-be hitman face-down on the lawn. His body quivered as his bloody hands protected his head and neck. Hitchcock approached his dog from the side, took his collar in hand, and patted his shoulder. "Out! Good boy."

Unlike his well-dressed Asian partner, this one was white—his skin was a sickly pallor, his dark, shoulder-length hair was greasy, scattered beard stubble grew through acne scars and puss-filled pimples. Evil, beady eyes and grime under his fingernails made for a rabid, hyena-like persona. His jeans, flannel shirt and denim jacket stank. Hitchcock smelled cigarette and body odor on him from four feet away.

"You're under arrest for Attempted First Degree Burglary. Spread your arms and legs out, palms up and turn your head to the left," LaPerle ordered.

"I can't—the dog!" He whined, his voice cracking.

"The dog's under control. Cut the sniveling and do as you're told."

"Look at my leg! And my hands!" The back of the suspect's left pant leg was ripped and bloody at the knee. Blood drenched the shredded left sleeve of his jacket, hand and wrist.

"That's what you get for trying to escape when I left to check on your partner," Hitchcock scolded. "I *did* warn you."

"You deaf?" LaPerle shouted. "Spread your arms and legs, palms up. Turn your head to the left. NOW!"

The suspect obeyed.

"Are you armed?"

"If I had a gun, both you oinkers and that dog would

be dead! I got rights!" He shouted, his mouth spraying saliva. He winced and whimpered as LaPerle knelt one knee on his back.

"Whoof—you stink, sonny! But don't worry— they've got hot showers and clean clothes where you're going," LaPerle said. He cuffed the suspect's hands behind his back and helped him to his feet, revealing what he had underneath him.

"Well, well, well, what have we *here*?" LaPerle said, grinning as he picked up a six-inch long, fixed-blade knife, the prison made kind. "You weren't armed, eh? LIAR! Did you really think you could pull this on us and live? What else are you hiding?"

A pat-down search yielded a long flat-tip screwdriver and a pair of surgical gloves in the inside pocket of his denim jacket.

"You have the right to remain silent..." LaPerle began reciting Miranda warnings as the cuffed suspect continued squirming.

"You stupid pigs! I'm bleeding! I got rights! I need medical help!"

"Your free ride to the hospital is almost here," LaPerle said. "Sit on the ground if you're hurt so bad, and shut up."

"Someday I'm gonna kill me a pig!" The suspect cleared his throat and blew a gob of spit and green phlegm on LaPerle's uniform.

LaPerle's face reddened as he spun him around,

seized him by the back of his collar and marched him toward the driveway.

"Can't I say goodbye to Mrs. Hitchcock? Woo-hoo! I almost had me a cop's wife!" he cackled as he shook his filthy hair. As LaPerle half-dragged him past the cabana, he stuck his tongue out and licked his lips at Allie on the other side of the sliding glass door, holding her crying son. "I'll be back for you!" He shouted at her.

LaPerle grabbed the back of his hair and wrenched his face away from Allie as he shoved him to his patrol car.

Hitchcock stepped into the cabana, his face dark with fury. "Are you and Trevor all right?"

Allie trembled as she hugged him; Trevor clung to his leg, tears streaking down his cheeks. He scooped his three-year-old stepson into his arms.

"That white guy's got demons," she said, her voice trembling.

"Take a deep breath, let it out, then tell me what happened."

Allie placed her hand on her chest. After two deep breaths, she spoke at the speed of adrenalin. "Jamie went on alert when they appeared at the door-I never heard a car-they came from out of nowhere—they tried to get in when they saw me—I had locked the sliding door earlier-thank God-the white guy leered at me, put his hands on the glass—licked his lips-licked the glass-mocked me—made grunting sounds. He tried to pry

7

open the latch–I dropped the stick into the track–shouted–go away. They beat the glass–I let Jamie out–called station."

He handed Trevor back to her and strode to the patrol car where Zhang sat. He ripped the rear door open and leaned in.

"I know I'm the reason you two are here," he said, seething. "Because I wasn't here, you two cowards attacked my wife and child instead. The officers here are the *only* reason I don't kill you both. If either of you come near my family again, *nothing* will be able to protect you. If anyone or any*thing* bothers them in *any* way, if they have an accident, if anyone follows or threatens them, it will be your fault and I will hunt you down. *Nothing* will be able to stop me. Understand?"

Zhang stared ahead, saying nothing. Hitchcock grabbed the front of his bloody shirt and shouted in his face. "I'M TALKING TO YOU!!"

He turned his head to Hitchcock, eyes down, and gave a solemn nod, a sign of submission in his culture.

Hitchcock realized this was a hit job gone wrong. Acres of thick forest surrounded the house and the cabana at the end of a long, unmarked, private dirt road. Yet the would-be assassins knew where to find his home. They knew his name and that Allie is his wife.

Realizing what they would have done to Allie if he had not arrived, he shook Zhang hard by his shirt. Hitchcock shook him hard. "Who sent you here? Tell me!"

Zhang glanced at Hitchcock, then lowered his eyes. Through swollen lips caked with dried blood, he said, "I *can't*. I am sorry, very sorry, Officer Hitchcock."

"So, you both know my name! Spill it! Who sent you here?" Hitchcock shouted.

Zhang looked down, saying nothing.

He cuffed the side of Zhang's head with his open hand as he got out and slammed the door. The other suspect was thrashing and screaming incoherently in the back of LaPerle's cruiser as Hitchcock returned to the cabana.

SERGEANT BREEN ARRIVED, then an ambulance. Medics examined the suspects while Hitchcock and LaPerle showed Breen the tool marks on the doorjamb, the knife and the screwdriver taken from the second suspect.

"After the hospital, book 'em for Attempted First Degree Burglary, the Oriental for Assault Second. Keep 'em separated for the dicks," Breen ordered LaPerle.

# CHAPTER TWO
## The Third Man Question

WILLIAMS, THE NEWEST detective, tapped on the sliding glass door. "Excuse me for interrupting, Roger, but we've learned the suspects are from Seattle. This area is all woods. No neighbors, no place to stash a car, not even a street sign on the road."

"Their car is probably at Hyak Junior High," Hitchcock said. "The trail behind our cabana goes straight to it. The one who fled ran toward it before our dog got him."

Williams nodded toward the main house across the patio. "Anyone home there?"

"They're wintering in Palm Springs."

"Did anything unusual happen recently? Like strange or hang-up phone calls, people in the area?"

"As a matter of fact, our dog followed a strange new scent around the main house and the cabana as soon as he got out of our car yesterday," Hitchcock replied. "I went with him as he followed the scent to the school. I thought someone was casing the place for a burglary, so

I phoned in a report. Records gave me a case number."

"Okay then," Williams nodded, "after I dust your sliding door for prints, I'll head to the school to see if their car is there."

"You'll know where I'll be," Hitchcock said, half-joking. He winced as he stood to remove his jacket and gun belt.

"Honey, are you hurt?" Allie asked.

"The Oriental guy kicked me before I dropped him the first time. Felt like a lead pipe. Lucky me, his second kick missed my head, or I wouldn't be talking now."

"Let me have a look," she said. He removed his gun belt and lowered his pants, exposing his bare hip.

"Roger!" She gasped.

"Just a bruise."

"No way. Your hip is already turning purple." She stepped outside to the patio. "Detective, please come in. Roger's been injured."

"You should go to a doctor right now," Williams said, staring at the bruise. "My camera's in the car. Prosecutors will want photographic evidence."

"Take your pictures quick. I'm taking my wife and son out for ice cream."

"Ice cream? How can you be thinking of ice cream after all this?" Allie squealed.

"After what's happened, a little time away from here and a sweet treat will help Trevor and us too."

"We're taking Jamie with us?"

"Of course."

"The prosecutors will also want a medical report of your injury," Williams interjected.

"All right, you guys, I'll go to the ER, but *after* ice cream." He winced as he straightened his leg. "We have aspirin in the bathroom, baby. I need six, please."

† † †

THE ONLY CUSTOMERS in Farrell's Ice Cream Parlor were two couples in a booth. The women ogled Hitchcock's athletic frame and chiseled features. The men gawked at Allie's beauty and hourglass figure until their wives elbowed them.

They savored the silence and change of scenery as much as the hot fudge sundae they shared. Trevor devoured his chocolate ice cream cone, forgetting his fears. Allie wiped his chin and hands with a wet napkin, then looked at her husband.

"Those guys almost got to me, Roger. If you hadn't arrived when you did, I'd be dead. I needed a gun, but I didn't have the combination to the safe. As a cop's wife, I should expect this sort of thing, I guess, so I should learn to shoot."

Her spunk amazed him. Most women he knew would be catatonic after an ordeal like this.

"I'll show you how to open the safe and teach you to shoot every gun I own. We start on my days off next week." He paused for a second. "We should move, Allie.

What if Doc and Ethel had been home today?"

"The sooner the better."

Trevor fell asleep. Hitchcock scooped him into his arms. "You drive. My hip is stiffening. I need more aspirin."

"Uh-uh. Next stop is the hospital, Mr. Tough Guy," she said as she started the Wagoneer.

† † †

THEY RETURNED TO an empty driveway. Trevor awoke and started crying "No bad men, Daddy" when Hitchcock carried him inside.

"Shhh, bad men all gone, little man. You're safe with me and your mommy now."

He handed Trevor to Allie, built a fire in the fireplace and got out his guitar. "A little music will soothe us."

"I'm surprised you feel like playing after this."

"Nothing like soft music and a nice fire to take the edge off a tough day," he said.

Allie cuddled Trevor while Hitchcock softly strummed old folk ballads and sang lullabies until Trevor drifted into the deep slumber of the very young. They placed him in his bed and laid down, holding hands, gazing at the ceiling, listening to the fading crackle and pop of the fire, as Jamie settled into his blanket at the foot of the bed.

A minute of silence passed before he asked, "How

much of what happened in the carport did you see?"

"The whole thing. I thought he was out cold. I was shocked when he attacked you."

He shook his head. "My job is to protect you from such things. I don't want you to be exposed to what I see all the time on the job. I feel I've failed as a husband."

She kissed his right hand and smiled. "Not so, my man. Seeing you in action I know I am safe with you. Now I understand why you qualified for the Olympic boxing team when you were in high school."

The phone rang.

"Detective Sergeant Jurgens here, Roger. I got called in on your case. Thought you might want an update."

"I'd appreciate it."

"We're not at the bottom of it yet, but these two are from Seattle. No history here at all. The Oriental guy, Zhang, had your name, address and directions to your home on a piece of paper in his pants pocket, which rules out any claim they were just wandering around. They came to get *you*."

"I thought so," Hitchcock said calmly.

"My contact at Seattle PD says Zhang is an advanced martial artist. Lives with his mother, grandmother and siblings in the International District. His father was a highly decorated general in the Chinese nationalist army. Died fighting communist forces on the mainland. His family came here from Taiwan when Zhang was a child. Of late he hires out as an enforcer to street gangs in Chinatown, but he has no criminal history. Rumors are he's also a debt collector for hire. I ran checks on him. Nothing."

"Hmm," Hitchcock mumbled, struggling to grasp the gravity of Jurgens's revelations.

"Before I go on, I should say how amazing we are that for all Zhang's training and competition matches, and street fights in Chinatown, he was no match for an experienced boxer."

Hitchcock didn't comment.

"But I digress," Jurgens said after a pause. "The white guy, Andy Stanford, is a different story. He lives in the Fremont District, which is a hotbed of radical activists these days. His rap sheet includes prowling, attempted abduction, burglary, assault, assaulting a police officer, resisting arrest, interfering with a police officer. He's a regular in the Seattle Jail and a rabid cop-hater."

"Of the two," Hitchcock cut in, "I figure Stanford will be back as soon as he's out of jail. He's a vicious 220-operates on emotion, no regard for the consequences."

"You got that right. New evidence indicates they came with other intentions besides knocking you off."

"New evidence? What—"

"Williams located Stanford's car on the dead-end dirt road above Hyak Junior High. He found marijuana and hardcore pornography in it. He walked the trail back to your place, where he found a canvas bag holding several feet of rope, strips of cloth, duct tape and a pair of cheap handcuffs stashed behind your cabana. Looks like they planned to abduct your wife after they got rid of you."

Too shocked to speak at first, "What else?" he asked.

"Williams found a lot of cigarette butts in the brush not five feet from your bedroom window."

Alarmed, Hitchcock asked "How many?"

"Nine. Five Salem, four Marlboro. The amount and the fact that some are older, indicates they've been watching you for some time."

"I was back there almost two months ago, checking the grounds because we're so isolated here."

"And?" Jurgens asked.

"No cigarette butts were there—at all. The two in custody, did either of them—?"

"Stanford had a pack of Salem's on him when he was booked, and several empty packs of Salems were in his car. No Marlboros."

"What about the Oriental?"

"Apparently Zhang doesn't smoke, as he's an athlete," Jurgens replied, "and he wouldn't have needed directions to your place if he had been there before. The Marlboro butts indicate Stanford cased your place with a different accomplice. They spent a lot of time watching you through your bedroom window."

Goosebumps covered Hitchcock. "While I was working nights..." he mused aloud.

"Most likely. Ever hear of anyone smoking both Salem and Marlboro? I haven't. There are no Marlboro cigarette buts or packs in Stanford's car. So, someone other than Zhang is involved."

"Where are they now?"

"Stanford's in the slammer. Had to have shots for rabies and tetanus, needed thirty stitches after tangling with your dog. We booked him for Attempted First Degree Burglary. Even with all those stitches, the booking officer needed help controlling him."

"And the other one?"

"Zhang?" Jurgens started chuckling. "X-rays revealed a mild head concussion, plus a broken nose, loose teeth and split lips. He's in Harborview for twenty-four-hour observation under police hold until the brain swelling goes down. Tomorrow the prosecutors will charge him with Attempted First-Degree Burglary and Assaulting A Police Officer. Both will be held without bail until arraignment."

"Uh-huh. Sounds good," Hitchcock said drowsily.

"Lastly," Jurgens said, "Williams lifted several identifiable palm and fingerprints from the outside of your sliding glass door. If the prints match either of the suspects, with tough bargaining by our side we'll find out who put them up to this."

"Thanks, Sarge. I'm ready to pass out. We'll talk later."

He wondered if he should tell Allie as he hung up.

She touched his shoulder.

"Tell me what a 220 is, honey."

"Cop slang for a crazy person. Back in the thirties, the County hospital contracted with Seattle PD to transport violent psycho patients from one facility to another in the safety of their patrol cars. The City of Seattle charged the County two dollars and twenty cents for each transport."

"Huh. How about that. I never thought of cops having traditions," Allie said, stroking his hair.

"Umm-hmm," he replied.

"What did you learn from the phone call, honey?"

Not wanting to tell her about the binding equipment the suspects brought to the scene, he said, "Oh no you don't, time for sleep."

"Come on, tell me…"

AT THE STATION, Sergeant Jurgens ran a thick hand through his thinning dark hair as he typed a confidential memo to his superiors:

> *Two Seattle men attacked Officer Hitchcock's residence today. One had Hitchcock's home address in his pocket. The writing indicates another involved party. The suspects are in custody. Attached are the statements of Hitchcock and his wife and incident reports.*
>
> *Stan Jurgens, Sgt.*

# CHAPTER THREE
## The Next Morning

LIEUTENANT ROWLAND BOSTWICK came to work early as he always did to read reports not intended for his eyes. His bone-chilling resemblance to Heinrich Himmler, the commandant of the Nazi death camps explained why he never married–or even dated. Like Himmler, Bostwick was short and flabby, had a double chin, a scraggly mustache, and wore round silver wire framed granny glasses. He gave women the creeps just by showing up.

His heart took a jolt when he read Sergeant Jurgens's memo in Captain Delstra's inbox. With trembling hands, he copied the statements of Hitchcock and his wife, the arrest sheets and officers' reports and returned them, he hoped, unnoticed by anyone.

When the desk clerk wasn't looking, he took the evidence room key from the duty sergeant's desk drawer, and searched desperately through the stacks of evidence envelopes for the one that contained the note.

Ernie Brown, the timid, slender, bookish civilian

evidence room custodian, appeared in the doorway. "Good morning, Lieutenant. Can I help you find something?"

Startled, Bostwick stared at Ernie, open-mouthed and speechless. His face reddened as he forced a smile. "Oh, uh, no-no-no, young man, heh-heh-heh," he stammered. "I–I just happened to notice the door. The door–I saw it open! Open from last night, I guess. Must've been a wild shift last night, eh? Just an honest mistake–thought I would just, uh, close 'er up for you, heh-heh-heh."

Ernie saw the evidence room door was closed just minutes earlier. He gulped and blinked at Bostwick through thick, coke-bottle bottom glasses. Like other civilian employees of the Department, Bostwick's very appearance made Ernie feel accused.

The drastic change in Bostwick's behavior, the fear in his eyes, and his fake joviality made Ernie's heart pound. No more the cold stare, now his beady eyes were furtive, his laugh was a nervous titter. As if this weren't enough, Bostwick lied about finding the evidence room open.

Ernie felt his flesh squirm in his clothes as he realized he had inadvertently caught a member of the Brass red-handed at something illegal. Just what he didn't know. Worse, Bostwick didn't sign the logbook as required of everyone who enters the evidence room, regardless of duration, rank or reason.

Ernie's voice squeaked as he said, "Please leave it open, Lieutenant, I have work to do here."

"Of course, of course, of course you do, young man. Heh-heh. Top of the day to you—do carry on, now."

Ernie fixed his eyes on the floor, wondering what would become of him, his wife and children. "Thanks, Lieutenant," he murmured, fearing eye contact might make Bostwick suspicious.

† † †

FEAR GRIPPED BOSTWICK as he closed the door to his office. Ernie's untimely arrival foiled his search for the note. In minutes all evidence from the weekend, including the note would be moved to the larger property room located over a mile away, to which he had no access.

As members of the Brass began arriving, Bostwick left his office door ajar to overhear discussions about the attack. He faked reading new case reports as he listened to conversations between the deputy chief and captains Delstra and Holland about the attack by two men on Hitchcock's home.

His heart pounded when he heard Captain Holland, across the hall in Captain Delstra's office say "The attack on Hitchcock's home was a disastrous failure. Both suspects are in custody. One of them is bound to talk given the prison time they're facing."

Unable to manage hearing any more of the details,

Bostwick hastily stuffed the unauthorized copies of the report inside his uniform shirt. Without telling the duty sergeant where he was going or when he would be back, he went to his unmarked car. His heart sank when he saw the other evidence custodian's van arrive to transfer the evidence to another location, where it would be forever beyond his reach. Woozy with fear and a strong sense of doom, he left the station, headed for Eastgate.

† † †

TWO HOURS LATER, throbbing pain in his hip awakened Hitchcock. The cabana was quiet. He had the day off because of his injuries. Jamie slept on the floor next to his side of the bed. Allie had dropped Trevor off at his mother's house on her way to work.

That two strange men came to his isolated home to attack him and his family and the cigarette butt evidence that he had been under surveillance for an unknown time set his mind reeling again. He couldn't get his head around who would want him dead this badly.

It hurt to move from the waist down. He washed two Valiums down his throat with cold coffee. He slathered peanut butter on two slices of toast. A light rain began falling and the Valium eased his pain as he left the cabana, taking Jamie with him in his Wagoneer.

He drove to LaPerle's lair, a small '40s vintage rambler tucked away on a side street south of the downtown core. The white '59 Ford 1-ton 4x4 with stake sides, bed loaded to cab height with firewood parked on the side meant Frenchie was home.

The smells of coffee, woodsmoke, gun oil and the dry warmth of a woodburning stove greeted Hitchcock when LaPerle opened his door.

"Been expecting you. Coffee's fresh," LaPerle said, grinning as he opened the door. Blue, Frenchie's aging Bloodhound, sniffed his pant leg and wagged her tail at the scent of Jamie.

"You're getting' to be quite the mystic, Frenchie. Keep it up. I hear there's money in it," Hitchcock quipped as he helped himself to a cup of coffee.

"You're needing practice ammo for your woman, I'm guessing."

Setting his coffee on the battered wooden sea chest LaPerle used as his coffee table, Hitchcock used both hands to ease into the deep cushions of the sofa.

"Ahh, so this is what old age will be like," he sighed as he settled in.

"If you live long enough," Frenchie smirked.

He winced as he leaned forward to pick up his coffee. "Ah, you're a prophet *and* a mind reader? The boys and I'll pass the hat to buy you a crystal ball for Christmas. Yeah—I need a lot of practice ammo. Plus, a box of your custom defense loads for Allie. She said she would've shot 'em both before I got there and leave the bodies for me and the boys to pick up if she knew how to open my safe. She wants to learn to shoot."

LaPerle burst into laughter. "Damn if you didn't marry good!"

Settled into in his brown leather overstuffed chair, feet on the frayed matching ottoman, a Pall Mall cigarette in one hand, and a steaming mug of the stout coffee he called "a cuppa Joe" in the other, Robert LaPerle was about to turn thirty. He was of French descent, Cajun, to be precise, hence his nickname. A former logger from the deep woods of southwest Washington, with bad teeth from packing his gums with snoose and smoking, his arms and forearms were over-developed for his round-shouldered, medium-size frame. Like Otis, LaPerle was a hunter and expert woodsman whose Army service record in the early years of the Vietnam war was classified.

Frenchie's girlfriend was a mystery too. A plain, quiet type, a banker by profession. Despite her svelte figure, she hunted deer and elk and tramped and camped the forests with Frenchie. Though she skinned and dressed his kills, cooked for him and slept with him in a tent as an Indian woman would, yet Nordic was her blood, platinum tresses, sky-blue eyes, and translucent skin which sunburned easily.

At after-hours drinking sessions, officers were only half-joking when they asked him: "Okay—tell us—where and how did you find her?" or "If she has a sister, I'm getting a divorce!"

Normally a man of few words, today Frenchie

wanted to talk.

"Yeah, I'll *bet* she wants to learn to shoot after what happened. Probably the best call I ever went to," he said, smiling at the memory of it. "Between you and your dog, those two got what they deserved—injuries, pain, and jail. Your dog sure impressed us—did you train him?"

"Didn't have to. His former profession was junkyard dog."

LaPerle smiled appreciatively. "You're limping today."

Hitchcock nodded as he sipped his coffee. "Your powers of observation rival Sherlock's. Yes, Watson, the Oriental got the drop on me. His one kick felt like a lead pipe. He must know Karate or one of those other kids from the Far East."

With an admiring chuckle, LaPerle said, "The battle was classic East versus West. Zhang had no fight left in him after tangling with you. Wouldn't talk when I found your name and directions to find your place on a note in his pants pocket."

"I imagine he wasn't talkative, seeing he'd had such a rough day and all," Hitchcock quipped, grinning at his own humor.

"The written directions to your place I found in Zhang's pocket tells me they were hired to take you out, and that there's a third man must be in the equation to instruct the two we arrested. I'm thinking the Oriental was to make the strike, put you down and the white punk had the knife in case his buddy needed help. No doubt about it."

Hitchcock nodded as he listened. "Allie and I figure they'll be back."

"Maybe I'm wrong, but I doubt Zhang will. They're both from Seattle, by the way. No history here."

"So I'm told."

"Any idea who sent them?"

Hitchcock shook his head. "We'll be prepared if they come back."

"As you should. From Stanford's behavior in the booking room, my guess is he *will* be back, but after he saw you destroy his partner in seconds, next time he'll ambush you or set fire to your house while you're all asleep."

Hitchcock grinned and lifted his cup as a toast. "Best wishes to you too."

"The Oriental kid was respectful; I'll give him that. Seems losing so badly destroyed him on the inside. I doubt he'll ever try anything like this again. Against you, at least."

"He was probably that way because of his head injury. The back of his head smacked the cement hard when he fell."

"Mebbe—mebbe not. He understood his rights at the scene, and he gave clear answers to the medics and the ER docs."

"What happened after they left the hospital?"

"I enjoyed every minute of it," LaPerle replied, smiling. "They were in so much pain, if I hadn't been called to the scene, I would have *paid* to go. One of the dicks came in to interrogate. He didn't talk to Zhang because his uneven pupils indicated a head concussion, so they took him to Harborview from our ER for twenty-four-hour observation."

Hitchcock grimaced with pain as he started to laugh.

"The docs at Overlake did so much stitching on Stanford that he resembled a skin quilt," LaPerle chuckled. "I couldn't stop laughing at him."

Hitchcock smiled. "Aha, no wonder he wouldn't talk to the dicks, Frenchie. Good job."

"Anyway, Stanford wouldn't say anything even to Detective Meyn. I figure whoever sent them will send someone else in the future."

"So do I. Do you think they'll lay low for a while?"

LaPerle took a last drag on his cigarette, exhaled a long plume of smoke and dropped the butt into his ashtray of the moment, a brown beer bottle.

"My opinion, nothing more," he qualified as he watched the butt hissing in the bottle, "is yes – Stanford will be back, but only after a considerable wait. One other thing, though."

"What?"

"While we were at the ER, I asked Zhang if he knew

Stanford's last name or where he lived. He didn't. I asked Stanford about Zhang. He knew nothing about him – only his last name. They're too opposite to be friends. One is clean-cut, well dressed, well groomed. The other is a young Skid Row bum."

"Which tells you what?" Hitchcock asked.

"Somebody put 'em together for this job. Remember what I said about a third man. Finding out who he is will be the key to what's going on."

"Makes sense. I'll pass it on to the dicks."

LaPerle put his coffee down and got up from his chair. "So, you need practice ammo. A thousand-round case?"

"A thousand rounds for starters. Light loads Allie can learn with. Also, find me a lady-size .38 revolver. Allie has small hands."

"I got five hundred rounds of .38 in lead wadcutter, light practice stuff I can sell you now. I'll load another five hundred this week."

"Sold."

"Save the spent cases so I can load 'em again."

"Sure."

"I just took in a lightweight Smith & Wesson .38 your wife might like. Take it home. If she's comfortable with shooting it, sixty bucks."

"That's almost the new price, Frenchie."

"I sold it new-in-box, unfired. The customer changed his mind later when I showed him a used Smith

I took in."

"Why the move from new to old?"

"More stopping-power. This customer needs it. He's a shopkeeper. He traded up to a .44 Special in like-new condition."

"I wish they'd let us carry .44 Special. More stopping power than .38, mild recoil."

"It will never happen," LaPerle scoffed. "The Brass and the City are afraid of the press. They care more about public relations than our safety."

"Ain't that the truth," Hitchcock said as he hefted the short-barreled, compact five-shot stainless steel Smith & Wesson, Model 60, in .38 Special. It felt light and well balanced in his hand. He made sure the cylinder was empty and smiled when he tested the trigger.

"Ah, about four pound pull on double action, two on single," Hitchcock said approvingly. "Sold. We've been married less than a year and already Allie hides the checkbook when she knows I'm coming here."

LaPerle laughed. "Yeah, I'll bet."

He handed LaPerle the check and slipped the new revolver into his jacket pocket. "She didn't hide it this time when I told her I'd be coming here. She wants a gun of her own. If she doesn't like this one...well," he shrugged, "a man can't own too many guns. I'll get something else for her. From you, of course."

"Of course."

Hitchcock turned to go, then stopped. Married

officers, himself included, lingered long to savor male rusticity when they visited LaPerle's place. It was the innate longing for a time they were born too late for, that they were better suited for; an earlier, earthier time, not so long ago when men hunted, farmed, ranched or fished to feed their growing families that Hitchcock felt when he visited LaPerle's place. LaPerle's woodstove, fish and animal trophies, rifles, pistols and ammo-makings lying about drew men of a certain cut of cloth, men who hid yet hungered for the backwoodsiness that forever called to them.

Hitchcock, having long felt he was born a hundred years too late, set the box of practice ammo down. "Got time for another cup before I go?"

SUNSET MEMORIAL CEMETERY was empty except for an old man on a riding lawnmower. The sky was cloud-covered as usual, and the scent of fresh-cut grass permeated the air. Hitchcock knelt at his father's headstone. Within himself he balked at the notion of meeting his father through a hunk of marble, but he accepted it on the remote possibility that it could be true.

"I'm married now, Dad. Her name is Allie. She's warm and beautiful, inside and out. People naturally warm up to her. It amazed me how quickly Mom, Jean and Joan accepted her. You'd approve of her standards too, like Mom did: She made me wait until after our wedding. Her little boy by an earlier marriage is named Trevor. Her husband left her. To her boy, I'm dad."

He stopped to gather his thoughts. A soft wind came up, chilling the air.

"Yesterday I caught two men trying to break in to get Allie and Trevor. I defeated the one who attacked me, our dog stopped the other. As we waited for the police to arrive, I almost resumed beating him. He'd be dead if Allie hadn't stopped me. I'm shocked at myself, and afraid for my family. I don't know who my enemies are, Dad, or why..."

# CHAPTER FOUR
## A Tip from The Barber

FROM THE CEMETERY, Hitchcock drove around until he ended up at the barber shop in Bellevue Square. He walked into a traditional man's world: Black-and-white checkerboard linoleum tile floor, mirror-covered walls, worn leather waiting chairs, chrome ashtray stands, side tables covered with sports and girly magazines including *The Police Gazette.* Masculine smells of cheap cologne and cigars, cigarettes, glass jars of the blue antiseptic liquid they soak combs in, shoe polish from the wooden shoeshine chair, and hair tonic hung in the air.

"Hey-hey! Here's the champ!" the barbers cheered as he smiled and headed for Hamilton Shields, his barber since junior high. Shields, in his late thirties, lounged in his barber chair, reading the sports section of the *Seattle Post Intelligencer* through horn-rimmed glasses, his dark hair slicked straight back. He always thought Shield would be perfect for Brylcreem television commercials.

"You won't find anything worth reading in that rag, Ham," he quipped. "There's nothing in Seattle for sportswriters to write about, except why the Pilots left after only one season. We're years from having a major league team in anything except basketball.'"

Shields smiled as he snapped the white sheet with the collar at one end. Hitchcock grinned as he settled into the deep brown leather chair with chrome hardware and a leather strop hanging on one side.

"How do you want it, Roger?"

"Tight on the sides, just a little off the top."

Hitchcock noticed Shields didn't talk or join in the latest sports news and gossip like he usually did.

"Something wrong, Ham?"

"A word with you outside," Ham mumbled as he brushed hair clippings from Hitchcock's shoulders.

On the sidewalk, Shields lit a cigarette with a stainless Zippo lighter bearing a brass Navy emblem.

"What's bothering you?"

"An hour before you came in, I gave a haircut to a young guy who could be the blue-hood rapist you guys are looking for."

"Has he been here before?"

"Never. He matches the sketch and the description of the rapist in the newspaper to a tee."

"How?"

"About your age, mid-twenties, clean-cut, six feet, but not lean like you. He's pudgy, over two-hundred, thick in the middle. Soft fat."

"What did he say?"

"Not a word except how to cut his hair. Ice cold. Paid cash, plus a tip."

"I don't suppose you got at least his first name?"

Ham put his cigarette in the corner of his mouth as he fished a piece of paper from his pants pocket. "He left in a new or fairly new Olds 442, metallic gray, mag wheels. I got the three numbers of the plate." He handed the paper to Hitchcock. "Glad you came in. I'd rather talk to you than someone I don't know."

Hitchcock read the numbers. "Thanks. I'll take this to the dicks right away."

He left the barber shop feeling cooler around his neck and ears. After he dropped off the plate number and Ham's information at the detective office, he drove to the neighborhood behind Bellevue Square where the homes were mostly small, sturdy structures built in the '30s and '40s.

A tidy, white two-story on a one-acre lot, a large apple tree in the front yard, single-car detached garage in the back, caught his eye. He wrote down the realtor's phone number on the sign in the front yard and went home.

# CHAPTER FIVE
## Allie Prepares For
## Another Attack

AGAINST BACKGROUND NOISES of sporadic gunfire and rangemaster commands on a bullhorn at the Issaquah Sportsmen's Club, Hitchcock schooled Allie on gun safety. "Always check every gun you handle to see if it's loaded, every time you pick it up."

She nodded.

"Face downrange when you inspect your gun. Is it loaded?"

She opened the cylinder, looked, then closed it.

"Relax, face the target with your feet shoulder width apart. Hold the gun out at arms' length with both hands, right hand gripping it but not so tight that your hands shake. Left hand wraps around the right. Now do what I just told you, do it three times, slowly."

Allie followed his instructions. Her brows were knit, and her jaw was set as she went through the drawing, aiming, snapping the trigger three times, slowly.

"Don't be so tense, just relax," he said, "focus on the front sight," he said. "The top of the front sight should be level with both sides of the top of the rear sight. Keep the front sight on the target. *Squeeze* the trigger straight back, steadily, so it goes off when you don't expect."

"You mean like a surprise?"

"Exactly. Practice aim and trigger pull at home with an empty gun every day. Aim at a spot on a wall or door; slowly pull the trigger while keeping your sight picture. Do this between twenty-five to thirty times each day. After a while, the movements become second nature, you won't flinch and throw off your aim when you use live ammunition."

AFTER A HALF hour of repeating the drills in slow motion, Allie pumped all five rounds into the chest of a man-sized silhouette paper target ten feet away.

When the range master called cease-fire, Hitchcock marked the bullet holes with a pen and moved her target back another five feet. At the commence firing command, Allie reloaded.

"Take your time getting in position and aiming, breathe normally. We're in no hurry," he said. Each time Allie put five rounds in the chest area of the target, he moved the target back until she fired five rounds without a miss at twenty yards.

"Great shooting! You can ride with me anytime."

"I already do!" she said with a playful slap on his

shoulder.

He grinned. "Yeah, that you do, baby. You've had enough shooting for your first time."

"I have to use the ladies' room."

"No regular facilities here–just outhouses."

"Well, this is my first time at a gun range, so using the outhouse makes for a complete experience."

"You understand outhouses are crude woodsheds set over holes in the ground, there's nothing to flush and you wash your hands with well-water from the hand-pump on top of the pipe in the ground over there, right?"

"Yes! This is really a trippy place! Now don't keep me any longer!"

He laughed. "I'll be here."

"Wait for me in the clubhouse. I want to see it too."

The clubhouse was a genuine turn-of-the-century log house, recently wired for electricity but still lacking indoor plumbing. A stone fireplace dominated one wall of the main room which was filled with heavy, rustic handmade pine tables and chairs. Allie smiled when she walked in. Men were lounging and chatting amiably.

"I can *feel* the history of this place, honey!"

"Let's go into town for a couple schooners."

"Yeah? You buyin'?"

"I always do," he said, smiling and slipping his arm around her waist.

THE UNION TAVERN was the oldest such place in Issaquah's Historic District. The place was dark and rustic inside; wide-plank wood floors, tongue-and-groove yellow pine walls and ceiling. No matter how clean the janitors made it every morning, decades of tobacco, beer, and cheap wine had left their stamp.

Three logger types were leaning on the bar, resting their heavy lug-soled laced boots on the brass foot rail, rolled-up sleeves of tattered flannel shirts draped over burly shoulders and bulging arms, schooners in hand. Their heads turned as one when blonde, everything-in-the-right-place Allie walked in.

Hitchcock grinned at them and gave a friendly "howdy boys" as he and Allie passed by. The three men nodded and returned their attention to their beers as Allie and Hitchcock slid into a booth, side-by-side. A friendly-faced barmaid, slim, in her forties, red bandanna over her hair, apron over her jeans, came over.

"What'll ya have, you two?"

"Iced tea, unsweetened, for me," Allie said.

"Schooner for me."

"Rainier or Oly?"

"Rainier."

"Comin' up. I'll be needin' a peek at your ID, miss, before I can serve you anything."

Hitchcock held his hand up. "Hold on, miss," he said in a confidential tone, motioning the barmaid to come close. "I got a confession to make," he said in a low voice, "She's my wife...sorta. She's sixteen, a runaway. We eloped to Idaho without her parents knowing. We lied about her age and got hitched yesterday. We snuck back into town minutes ago. We're tryin' to decide what to do."

With one hand on her hip, she gaped at Allie, then at Hitchcock, her mouth open. "Are you–"

"Oh, Roger!" Allie laughed. "Don't listen to him. I'm his wife and I'm twenty-one. He thinks it's funny when I'm asked to prove my age. I get checked everywhere so I don't mind." She reached into her purse and took out her wallet. "Here's my driver's license."

Doubt changed to laughter after she checked Allie's driver's license. "Ya sure sucked me in, mister!" she exclaimed with a sardonic grin. "A schooner and an iced tea comin' up. You better keep an eye on your gorgeous little wife here. In case you didn't notice, the three bears belly-up to the bar almost fell over when she walked in. Men's eyes will follow her wherever she goes."

His eyes beamed at Allie. "Mine always do."

The barmaid returned with their drinks. "Take care of those youthful looks of yours, miss. They don't last forever. Take care of your handsome hubby, too, he's a catch."

"Thanks, I do, and I will," Allie replied with a smile.

He leaned toward her after the barmaid left. "How are you feeling?"

"Alcohol doesn't appeal to me today."

"I mean how do you feel now about guns, and shooting?"

"Oh—I'm surprised at how much I enjoyed it. I want to shoot often."

"Would you be able to shoot someone if you had to?"

She scoffed "I had my three-year old son with me when those guys tried to break in. I was in fear for my life and Trevor's. If I had a gun then, those two would have left in a hearse, no sweat. If they come back, they're dead meat."

He sat back, amazed at the cold steel beneath her beauty. "Okay," he nodded. "Lessons will continue."

"Amen! And I want the little gun I shot today."

"I bought it with you in mind. You need a holster now. Ever played pool?"

"You married an Irish girl, laddie."

# CHAPTER SIX
## Of Cop Killers and Other Bad Men

*The Squad Room*
*3:45 A.M.*

HITCHCOCK SLURPED VENDING machine coffee to wake up as Sergeant Breen came to the podium. "The good news first: Ten more days to shift change—that's it."

"The rest is bad. First up, the blue-hooded-sweatshirt pervert struck again. Same description, same M.O. as before. The victim is a single mom in a basement bedroom with her baby in a crib next to her. She woke up to her baby screaming and there he was, standing over her, holding a knife, exposing himself. He fled when she screamed and threw the clock on her nightstand at his face."

Hitchcock squirmed. *Sounds like the man who escaped custody from me on a naked prowler call a year ago.*

Sergeant Breen continued. "Next, the prosecutor's office filed charges on the two scumbags who tried to break into Roger's home with one count each of

Attempted First-Degree Burglary and a second charge of Second-Degree Assault was added to the one who attacked Hitchcock."

Breen paused.

"This is from the latest issue of the *Western States Crime Conference. A* gang of three commercial burglars, confirmed as wanted out of California, all convicted felons. Jack Donohue, aka 'Gravel Jack,' white male, D.O.B. 5-10-37, bald, blue eyes, five-ten, and 180, six-page rap sheet; next is Lee Willard James, white male, DOB 8-7-39, brown and brown, five-seven and 150, and Robert "Bobby" Scanlon, white male, DOB 6-21-39, brown and blue, six-foot-two and 210, gray and blue.

Clive Brooks, who always worked the downtown beat, spoke up. "I arrested Gravel Jack for possession of stolen property three years ago. He's always armed and is skilled with explosives."

Sergeant Breen continued. "Gravel Jack and company have been known to pick up a fourth person, a local, as a guide. They're expert safecrackers, use expensive custom-made tools, and are known to be armed and often violent. Gravel Jack was tried twice for murder and got off on a technicality both times. According to the bulletin they're heading to the Seattle area from San Francisco. No vehicle description is available at this time."

Breen paused for a second.

"The second threat believed to be headed our way

is even more dangerous. Two armed escapees from the Georgia State Penitentiary are headed here. Lonnie James Slocum, white male, DOB 9-20-47, 5'9" 165, blond and blue; serving life without possibility of parole for Burglary First Degree and two counts of Murder One. Virgil Quentin Howard, white male, D.O.B 5-19-41, five-eleven 185, brown and hazel, was also serving life without possibility of parole for Armed Robbery and one count of Murder One. They escaped by killing a guard six weeks ago."

The officers shifted uneasily in their seats, but no one spoke.

Breen had more.

"They captured a sheriff's deputy who stopped them, named Cunningham, on their way across Texas," Breen said, looking at the bulletin. "They handcuffed and tortured him for two days. They marched him to an open field and executed him with his own gun. They were last known to be driving a blue '63 Ford Fairlane four-door, bearing Georgia plates Mary Charles Mary Seven One Eight. They're believed to be heading to Washington, where Slocum's cousin lives in Mount Vernon.

"Slocum's rap sheet includes homicide, armed robbery and burglary. He was sent up for life for killing a man who caught him breaking into his house, then raping and murdering the man's wife. Slocum also served time for a string of armed robberies in

Louisiana."

"Shoot 'em on sight," Walker muttered, breaking the grim silence. Others mumbled their agreement. Sergeant Breen continued.

"There's a third man with Slocum and Howard but he's unidentified so far. Each of you, keep and study the mug shots and descriptions, because both gangs are headed our way."

As the squad gathered their gear, Breen had more to say: "*Before you hit the street, I will read this just in from Wisconsin: 'Officer William Miscannon, a 33-year-old police officer of nearly four years' service, was shot and killed at 1:38 a.m. on September 18, 1970, while he sat in his patrol wagon parked on Junction Avenue and Dorr Street. He left behind a wife and four children. Officer Miscannon was in his wagon with another officer when a late model Cadillac pulled up behind them. A man stepped out of the vehicle and walked up to Officer Miscannon's side of the wagon. According to an article in The Blade magazine, Officer Miscannon asked the man, 'What's going on?' The man responded, "This is what's going on," before pulling out a silver handgun and shooting Officer Miscannon in the head at point-blank range. He was taken to Mercy Hospital where he died shortly after his arrival.' End of report."*

Breen paused to allow the details to register with his men before he continued.

"*Never* let anyone walk up to you while you're sitting in your patrol car. Any time someone pulls over and starts to approach you on foot, get out, order them to stand at the back of their car. If both subject's hands aren't visible, order them to show their hands. If they don't comply, draw your weapon, keep your distance, call for backup. I'll handle the complaints. The important thing is, you'll be alive.

"The City closed our range over four years ago and has provided nothing since. We're carrying guns without training or qualifications. The higher-ups still think nothing will ever happen here, even after the shooting Hitchcock and Sherman were in last year.

"The range at the Issaquah Sportsmen's' Club is all we have as a place to shoot. It's available only to law enforcement free on Mondays. You'll make yourselves and others safer if you use it regularly. The Department still supplies practice ammo monthly. I'll be conducting weapons inspections without notice. Anyone I catch with a dirty gun will be sent to the station to clean it before returning to duty. Now hit the bricks and stay sharp."

A sullen mood hung over the squad. They already knew bad people were drifting into town from Seattle and elsewhere to escape the scrutiny of larger, more experienced police agencies. They hated the heads-in-the-sand apathy of the City elites and the attitudes of "it can't happen here" that persisted even in the Brass even after Hitchcock and Sherman's bloody shootout last year. The town weekly, *The Bellevue American*, again quoted the City Manager's frequent references to the Police Department as "a necessary nuisance," in a recent article.

Sergeant Breen, ever the cop's cop, used squad room briefings to protect his men by heightening their alertness of the dangers they face by reading recent accounts of murders of officers in the suburbs. He secretly protected his men further by discreetly pairing officers who had actual combat experience with officers who didn't.

# CHAPTER SEVEN
## Shifting Shadows

ALLIE WAS ON the couch reading to Trevor when he came through the door, late from helping Walker on the Brock case. He smelled chicken noodle soup on the stove as he kissed them both.

"How was work today, hon?"

"Quiet. In a few days I rotate to the noon-to-eight shift with Sundays and Mondays off."

"Decent hours and days off at last. More time together," she sighed.

He unloaded and wiped his service revolver with a silicone cloth, put it in the safe, and changed clothes as he talked. "We can date on Friday nights and go shooting on Mondays."

"We'll have evenings together, for a change too, but there's something else on your mind."

He nodded at her. "They might come back after they're out of jail."

"If they do, I'll be ready," she said bravely.

"I don't want you to go through that again."

"Those two didn't know us from Adam. Someone wants you out of the way, honey."

"I know."

"Find out whoever hired them before they make another run at us," Allie said.

"Easier said than done. I was wondering if you're open to moving," he said.

She shook her head. "Our roots are here. Stay and fight."

† † †

AS SOON AS Hitchcock left for work the next day, Allie loaded her gun with Frenchie's defense loads, left Trevor with her mother, and drove past the addresses of Zhang and Stanford. She copied the license numbers and descriptions of the cars parked there.

She wrote the car descriptions on three-by-five cards and taped them next to Stanford and Zhang's mugshots on her refrigerator door at eye-level. She used the mugshots as targets in her daily dry-fire practice. She continued to shoot at the gun range until she could draw from the holster and fire five rounds in the kill zone of a life-size police silhouette target fifteen feet away in three seconds.

† † †

THE KITCHEN PHONE rang. Hitchcock picked it up on the second ring.

"Morning, Roger. Steve Miller here."

"Hi Steve. I see you're still writing for the *Bellevue American*, so what's up?"

"I'm calling as a friend."

Surprised, Hitchcock hesitated. "Yes?"

"This is very important for you to know."

"This is a switch."

"It is. Someone unknown posted enough bail to release Zhang and Stanford. They were released less than an hour ago."

Hitchcock froze. He liked and trusted Miller, but press involvement on something involving his family was unwelcome.

"Zhang and Stanford?" he echoed.

"C'mon, Roger. The two who attacked you and your family."

"How'd you find out about this, Steve?"

"Reporters routinely attend bail bond hearings. To learn of something as serious as this with no mention in the daily recap at the front desk suggests something is being swept under the rug. What can you tell me?"

"I'll talk only on your solemn agreement of confidentiality because of security concerns for me and my family."

"Agreed."

"And I'm not being recorded?"

"Correct."

He gave Miller an abbreviated account of the attack.

53

"As I recall, you live in a secluded area of Wilburton Hill in a rented cabana. Did this happen there?"

He hesitated, wondering how Miller knew where he lived. If he knew, so did other reporters. "Okay – yes – it happened at our home."

"How did they know where to find you?"

"Wish I knew."

"Why do you think they attacked you?"

"Ditto."

"At the risk of sounding far-fetched, do you think these guys were hired thugs?"

"Ditto again. The dicks are looking into it."

"I'm personally digging into it."

"We're friends, Steve. We started our careers at the same time."

"But?"

"No offense, but I'm uncomfortable with reporters compromising our privacy and risking our safety just for a story. Except for you, I don't trust journalists. My family's security is already uncertain enough now that these guys are out on bail."

"Understood," Miller said, "but sometimes a private third-party can find out things the police can't. Another eye on this is more likely than not to enhance the safety of your family."

"I hope so."

† † †

SLEEP BECAME MORE difficult for Allie after

Hitchcock told her about the call from the reporter. Every sound in the surrounding forest awakened her. During the day, the sound of a car or truck coming down the lonely gravel road made her jumpy. At night she kept her revolver on her nightstand.

"Our approval for a home loan came through today and the house I think would be right for us is still available," he told her the next morning.

"Take me there."

† † †

HITCHCOCK REPORTED TO Captain Delstra's office after shift briefing the following day. "Sergeant Breen said you wanted to see me, Captain?"

Delstra gestured to the chair across from his desk.

"First off," Delstra began, "how are you and your family holding up after what happened?"

"We're doing okay. My wife's a strong girl from a working-class family. The men are in construction and big game hunters."

"Glad to hear it," Delstra said, smiling. "If you need anything, counseling or time off, just say the word."

"Thanks, but we're fine."

"What we discuss next is confidential."

"Yes, sir."

"Mark Forbes came to see me on his own initiative. He told me about the boxing "lesson" you gave him at the Boys' Club and what he disclosed to you about his agreement with Bostwick," Delstra said.

"His signed confession is in my safe."

"I need it."

"I'll get it to you right away."

"I'm pleased with the way you protected the Department's interests, and Forbes's by giving him a second chance. Most people would have thrown him to the wolves. I'm pleased that Forbes came to me wanting to clear his name at the risk of being fired."

"Mark came back to Patrol a changed man, Captain. He's a real team player now. He puts citizens and us ahead of himself."

"So I've been hearing," Delstra said, smiling as he lounged in his chair.

"I'm convinced the change in Mark will last because it cost him so much. His wife left him holding the bag on the house, two car payments and her credit card bills. To avoid bankruptcy, he sold the house and both cars, bought a junker and moved with his two kids into his mother's basement."

"To his credit, he didn't ask for leniency when he told me about his secret deal with Lieutenant Bostwick," Delstra added. "I gave him another chance because you did. We don't know yet where this is going, but the written confession Forbes gave you is vital to our investigation of Bostwick. I want a written statement from you too."

"Yes, and I'll get you Mark's confession right now, Captain."

# CHAPTER EIGHT
## Dread of Discovery

WITH HIS DOOR closed, his phone unplugged so he wouldn't be disturbed, Lieutenant Bostwick sat at his desk, mulling over Mark Forbes's sudden transfer from the coveted Warrant Detail back to Patrol without notice. It had a nuclear impact on his plans. Whatever Forbes's reasons were, it made him aware that he wasn't as aware of the events around him as he thought.

He overheard talking in the hall between the deputy chief and Captain Delstra. He strained to listen but with his door closed, he could only hear fragments of conversation. When he heard the names of himself, Forbes and Hitchcock mentioned in the same breath, his dread of discovery almost broke him.

His phone rang as soon as his trembling hands plugged it in.

"This is Lieutenant Bostwick."

"Christopher Morton, reporter for the *Seattle Post Intelligencer*, sir."

"Yes, I recall our recent *private* discussions. To what

do I owe the opportunity to speak to a member of the press today?"

"Are you still in charge of the Patrol Division?"

"I am," he lied, his tone arrogant.

"Good. I'm calling about two Seattle men, Jinjie Zhang, an advanced martial artist rumored to be an enforcer for street gangs in the International District, and Andrew Stanford, a convicted felon and activist in anti-police demonstrations."

Bostwick felt his heart pounding. "Those names aren't familiar to me, but go ahead," gulping as he lied again.

"They're charged with attacking the family of Roger Hitchcock, a police officer in the Patrol Division, at their home. Someone unnamed posted their unusually high bail, pending trial. An attack on a police officer at his home is very alarming. Certainly, you must have inside information."

Caught off-guard, Bostwick replied, "Sorry, Mr. Morton, but I'm not privy to everything going on around here, especially in the Detective Division."

"But, Lieutenant, at the bail hearing the prosecutor objected to bail because they suspect someone hired the defendants to attack the officer at his residence. Here at the *Seattle PI* our investigation into corruption in the Seattle Police is winding down. An attack like this suggests corruption on the part of the officer."

"I wouldn't know," Bostwick replied, his voice

shaking.

"You don't know about it?" Morton asked, sounding disbelieving. "Then it *certainly* bears looking into by a high-ranking official such as yourself. This could be a cover-up, don't you think? It smacks of organized crime and police corruption."

"Again, I wouldn't know," Bostwick said.

"But Lieutenant," Morton persisted, "as you oversee Hitchcock's division, you surely must–"

"I'm sorry, Mr. Morton. I cannot comment on whatever investigations the Detective Division may be involved in. I can't be of any help to you at this time. Goodbye now."

He hung up the phone. *Now what? What happened to Hitchcock was without my knowledge. I would have prevented it if I knew of the plan beforehand–or would I? Either way, the deed is done.* He let out a deep breath, shaking his head. Then he remembered: *The note—that note is the noose around my neck.*

The only course of action left was to plunge ahead with his scheme. He was in a race against time to destroy the note in time to prevent evidence examinations that would tie the note to him from ever coming to light. Unless his fortunes improved, and improved fast, he, the prince-in-waiting once destined to become the next police chief, was a man in a rowboat trying to reach shore with broken oars.

And the tide was going out.

# CHAPTER NINE
## The Fowler Clan

THE NOTE INSIDE the hand-addressed envelope in Hitchcock's inbox read:

> *Roger, please come to Randy's baptism at*
> *9:00 a.m. this Sunday. Neighborhood Church,*
> *625 140th Avenue NE. Bring your wife too.*
> *We would like to meet her.*
> *Love, Barbara, Connie, Randy, Jim*

"Who is Randy, honey?" Allie asked when she read the note.

"A childhood friend. We played in Little League together. My dad coached the team."

Allie brought him a cup of coffee as he settled into his leather easy chair.

"What are they like?"

"Randy's dad often showed up at our games falling-down drunk. Couldn't hold a job," he grimly recalled. "Randy's mom, Barbara, worked two jobs to keep food on the table. My dad treated Randy and his mom for injuries from her husband's beatings. Dad never charged for his work and paid their prescriptions himself. She never reported it to the sheriff's office."

"How sad. I wish I could have met your dad," Allie said.

"Randy spent a lot of time at our house when we were in junior high, but when his father disappeared, and was later found to have committed suicide, he fell in with the wrong crowd. He dropped out of school. I didn't see much of him after that."

"What happened afterward?"

"Randy was unemployed, living at home, doing nothing. After my dad died, I talked Randy into joining the Army with me on the buddy system. It crushed him when he failed the physical. I found him hooked on heroin when I came home three years later His sister Connie had been into the drug scene, but got off it cold turkey. Randy's brother Jim, the baby of the family, got Randy and Connie into a different kind of church thing."

"Church thing?"

"Like what my dad got into before he died," he said.

"What was it?"

He shrugged. "Never saw it myself, but I guess it's more intense than regular church. I see changes in Randy that I never thought possible."

"Like what?"

"Overnight he quit drugs and drinking, he quit

blaming others for his failures. In the process he gained weight of the right kind, got a full-time job at the neighborhood gas station. He's working on a general education degree, a GED it's called, to make up for not graduating from high school. He even pays most of the family's bills."

Allie gazed at him with empathy in her eyes. "That's a lot of positive change, but my heart is heavy for this poor family," she said as she touched his hand. "I'm proud of Randy for the progress he's made. Even with God's help, coming off drugs isn't easy. I feel like I already know him, and you, my love, are a guardian angel for him."

He took a sip of coffee. "I don't know why," he said, "but since we were kids, I've felt responsible for Randy. I'm not sure where he's going with this, or how long it'll last. I mean—is it real, or a foxhole conversion? Either way, he's my friend."

† † †

THE NEXT SUNDAY morning, Hitchcock, Allie and Trevor sat with the Fowlers in the second row of bench pews at Neighborhood Church. Randy appeared happy and healthy as he entered the baptismal pool in a swimsuit and white T-shirt with a tall, athletic-looking young pastor. Randy proclaimed Jesus Christ as his Savior, folded his arms across his chest and held his nose as the pastor tilted him under the water. The congregation applauded when he came up smiling. In the lobby after the service, Hitchcock squeezed Randy's arm as he shook his hand.

"Thanks for inviting us, Randy. You've come a long way in a few months, and I'm as proud of you as your family is."

"I wouldn't be here if you hadn't saved my life with that wild one-hundred-mile-an-hour ride in your patrol car to the hospital," Randy grinned.

"Meet my bride, Allie, and my stepson, Trevor."

Randy blushed when he shook hands with Allie.

"Hi, Allie. Never thought I'd be talking to Roger's wife one day. Thanks to him I am here today, serving the Lord."

† † †

"I'M GLAD WE went to Randy's baptism," Allie remarked as she prepared a late breakfast. "It was an important day for him and his family. I could tell they admire you very much. And what's this he said about you saving his life and a wild ride in a patrol car—at a hundred miles an hour?"

"Randy told the story about right," Hitchcock said. "I went to a drug overdose call at his house. He was clinically dead. I revived him with CPR. We didn't have an ambulance service then, the city contracted with Flintoff's Mortuary in Issaquah, fifteen miles away, to use their hearses to transport injured people to the hospital. So, I—"

Allie put her hand over her mouth as she burst into laughter. "A hearse? No way! This can't be for real!"

"It's true. There've been injured people waking up on the way to the hospital and freaking out to find themselves in a hearse," he said, chuckling.

"Material fit for a comedy! Honestly, imagine trying to talk an injured person into getting inside," Allie said, still laughing. "I can just hear the argument—'No, please! I'm not dead!'"

"To finish my story," he broke in gently, laughing with her, "we had no time to wait. I got him breathing again, put him with his mom in the back seat and sped to the hospital, Code Three—as in lights and siren. He was turning blue again when we arrived. But God was with him. He completed the rehab program."

Allie let out a deep breath after her laughter. "What a great story. You should write it down. I liked the service today, too, honey."

"Yeah, I gotta say, the peace in the eyes of the older couples really blew me away. It seemed I could see forever in their eyes."

"You were seeing a glimpse of eternity."

"Maybe, but their conduct was nothing like the church I grew up in."

"How so?"

"People raising their hands in the air during the music, or the prayers flipped me out. And talking during the sermon, saying 'amen' and 'that's right' and 'preach it,' and other stuff. Seemed rude and distracting."

"Well, honey, Neighborhood is a typical, lively Pentecostal church, the kind I grew up in, and where we were married, by the way."

"It was? Guess I wasn't paying attention."

"Hah! You had something else on your mind, huh?"

"Confession is good for the soul. My attention was on you and what would happen as soon as we left."

She smiled at him, a loving glint in her eyes. "Me too."

The phone rang.

"Stan Jurgens, here, Roger. Sorry to bother you on your day off, but something unusual just happened which concerns you. Meet me at the station right away."

"What's going on?"

"Not on the phone. Meet us in the Patrol Sergeant's office—now."

# CHAPTER TEN
## A Chance Encounter

AS HITCHCOCK DROVE to the station, three white men in a blue '63 Ford Fairlane, bearing Georgia license plates stopped next to Traffic Officer Lee Kendrick on the road shoulder, working radar on the frontage road above the 520-405 interchange.

Kendrick felt his blood run cold when the man in the front passenger seat rolled the window down. He was in his thirties, with bushy ash-blond hair, beard stubble, flannel shirt. Everything about him was hard and lethal. Kendrick's gut told him if he reached for his radio or got out of his car, he would be dead. For the first time in his five-year police career, he unsnapped his holster.

"Hey, officer, can you tayle us whur the Fawg Hawrn rest-runt is?"

The driver and the man in the back seat bore the same stamp of deadliness as the man asking directions. Even as dishwashers none of them fit the Foghorn, a white tablecloth, candle-lit, seafood restaurant located on a pier over Lake Washington.

Kendrick had spent his entire career in the Traffic Division. He had never made a criminal arrest. Now his internal red flags were frantic. *These men are cold-blooded killers. I feel it in my blood. There is nothing to stop them for. Their speed on the radar screen was below the speed limit.*

He hoped the men in the car didn't notice the fear in his voice when he replied. He swallowed hard as he said, "Sure. Stay on this road. You'll go under the freeway. Turn left at the signal. You will pass the Burger Master drive-in on your right. Turn right at the next stop sign. Stay on that street for about a mile. As you reach the town of Kirkland, The Fog Horn will be on your left, on the lake."

The man said thanks and the car left. He copied the plate number and called it in to Records. Kendrick felt relieved as he watched them drive away. He never read Patrol bulletins. Catching crooks never interested him. Accident investigation was his niche a skill he could carry into the private sector, making better money working for insurance companies after he retired. He worked radar between accident calls. It was nicer and safer than Patrol, weekends off, no late hours except for certain holidays.

The radio crackled.

*"Records to Five Zero Five, be advised the computer is momentarily down."*

A minute later: *"Records to Five-Zero-Five, okay to*

*broadcast?"*

Kendrick felt a lump in his throat when he heard the tension in the records clerk's voice.

"Go ahead."

*"We have a hit on Georgia license Mary Charles Mary Seven One Eight, a blue 1963 Ford Fairlane four-door. Two subjects associated with said vehicle are wanted for Escape, Murder and Kidnapping: Lonnie James Slocum, WMA, D.O.B. 9-20-47, serving twenty-five to life for Murder One. Virgil Quentin Howard, WMA, D.O.B 5-19-41, serving life without possibility of parole. Consider armed and extremely dangerous."*

Fear and nausea gripped him. His hands became cold and clammy. Just this much from Records was bad enough. *I just came close to being executed just for being a cop,* he realized.

He forced himself to push fear aside. He pressed the red button under the dash to release the shotgun with the folding stock. He switched to F-1 and called in the information to Dispatch, requesting help in finding the suspects.

Adrenalin and a do-or-die resolve filled Kendrick as he flipped the switch on his console and sped Code Two along the route he had given the killers, accepting that he would probably die if he caught up to them.

The three west side Patrol units sped to the area. Dispatch notified the Kirkland Police. Records sent out a teletype to all Western Washington agencies. Within minutes the Seattle FBI office called the station, but the Slocum gang had vanished.

† † †

HITCHCOCK SAW TWO uniformed officers roar out of the station parking lot in an unmarked squad car and head west over the 405 overpass on Main Street as he arrived. Detective Sergeant Jurgens and Detective Joe Small were waiting for him in the Patrol sergeant's office.

"There must be something big going on for you guys to be here on a Sunday. What's up?"

"Plenty," Sergeant Jurgens said. "Some wanted cop-killers are in town. The hunt is on to find them. But we called you in for something else. Come with us."

"What is it?" Hitchcock asked as he got into the back seat of a black Ford Fairlane with brown vinyl seats.

Neither detective answered him.

# CHAPTER ELEVEN
## Helter-Skelter?

THE DETECTIVES' SILENCE and where he was sitting made Hitchcock feel like a prisoner. Something bad was up. His stomach began churning as the car entered the tree-lined gravel road to where he used to live. *This has got to be bad. Has something happened to Doc and Ethyl?*

He couldn't stand the silence. "Again, what's this about?"

"You'll see," Small said with a slight look back.

Two marked patrol cars and a white late model Buick station wagon were in the driveway. Hitchcock recognized the maroon Cadillac El Dorado of Doc and Ethel's son, Lew, in the carport. Everyone stood in front of the sliding glass door of the vacant cabana, talking in hushed tones.

He froze when he saw it. Written in blood in big letters on the sliding glass door was the message:

DIE PIG

Lew Henderson, thirty-one and heavy-set, stood,

ashen-faced, arms crossed, looking down at his dead German Shepherd lying in a puddle of dried blood.

The dead dog and the message on what once was the front door of his home brought to mind the grisly slayings of the pregnant actress Sharon Tate and the LaBianca couple in Los Angeles at the hands of the Charles Manson" family."

Sergeant Jurgens touched his arm. "Zhang and Stanford got out on bail two days ago. They wouldn't know you've moved. Lew says his dog was almost a twin of yours."

Hitchcock was too stupefied to comment.

"Lew says he's a light sleeper and would have heard his dog tangle with an intruder," Jurgens added.

"So, you think they came back for revenge and killed Lew's dog thinking he was mine?"

"Looks that way," Jurgens replied. "We'll check with the prosecutor, but I believe the circumstances, and the behavior of the suspect your dog chewed up, should be enough for an investigative arrest."

"Now what?" Hitchcock wondered aloud, unable to take his eyes off the dead dog.

Sergeant Jurgens gestured at the man examining the dead dog. "Dr. Tallman here is a new veterinarian in town. He'll autopsy Lew's dog and forward the samples to the state lab for testing."

"And then?"

"Whether or not the prosecutor says we have

enough probable cause for an investigative arrest, we'll hunt 'em down, starting with the one your dog chewed up, Andy Stanford."

† † †

AT THE STATION, Hitchcock copied the arrest sheets of Zhang and Stanford and checked DMV for all vehicles registered to them. He explained the situation to Allie as he took her and Trevor, with Jamie, to his mother's home ten blocks away.

"Aren't you coming in, honey?"

"I'll be back soon," he said.

† † †

"IS STANFORD'S CAR still in impound?" Detective Small asked Sergeant Jurgens as he gathered his evidence kit from his desk.

"Paid cash yesterday."

"Uh-huh. Which poor mom-and-pop store did he stick up to pay the impound fee?"

"The bright side is that without bad guys like Stanford we'd be driving delivery trucks or pumping gas to pay our bills, Joe."

Small shook his head. "Things ain't so cut-and-dried anymore, Stan. The public is liking us less and less these days, no matter how well we protect them. Everyone's whining and calling us names, questioning everything we say."

"Okay, Joe, but before you quit and join the fire

department so people will like you, go where we found Stanford's car last time. Check for fresh tire tracks and footprints. Photograph and make plaster casts of any you find. Canvas the immediate neighborhood when you're done. Somebody saw or heard something last night. I'll join you as soon as I run this past the on-call deputy prosecutor to see if we're clear to make an investigative arrest."

† † †

DETECTIVE SMALL PARKED at the edge of the short dead-end dirt road above Hyak Junior High School's athletic field. Last night's rain made the clay soil the consistency of putty—perfect for the legible tire tracks he saw leading from the pavement for about fifty feet, ending where the dirt road ended. The car left a separate set of equally clear tracks when it backed out. The freshness of the footprints showed the driver exited and re-entered the car within a short timeframe.

After he spent his roll of color film and updated his photo log, Small loaded a canister of black-and-white film for better contrast and switched to a close-up lens to record the tire tracks and shoe prints in greater detail. He included a ruler in the photographs for scale. He assembled wood frames around the footprints and tire tracks. He mixed and poured a batter of Plaster of Paris into the frames.

Sergeant Jurgens arrived.

"Well, Sarge, what did the on-duty legal-beagle

say?"

"We need more corroborating evidence to place Stanford at the scene before we can make an arrest."

"You mean a police officer's secluded home is attacked a second time within hours of the suspects' release from jail, a dog resembling the officer's dog is killed, and die pig is written in blood on the door, yet we can't make so much as an investigative arrest?"

"I don't like it either," Jurgens said, "but we need to find someone who witnessed the suspect or his car in the area within the last twenty-four hours, or we find blood on his clothes or in his car. Any one of those will make the case for an arrest."

"C'mon Stan—let's put the grabs on Stanford now."

Jurgens shook his head. "We gotta find and preserve evidence before it disappears, including witnesses as soon as possible."

Small pointed to the plaster casts. "The clarity of the tracks couldn't be better. We'll have identifiable tire tracks and shoeprints to work with. For what it's worth, only one person got out of the car."

"Did you follow the tracks?"

"The casts aren't dry enough to be moved, and I won't leave them until they are," Small answered.

Jurgens sighed. "Find me on the trail to the cabana as soon as you finish up."

A BREATH OF cool wind rustled the trees above Stan Jurgens as he slow-walked the trail to the Henderson place. From growing up in a family of hunters and woodsmen in rural Eastern Washington, followed by years with the US Border Patrol, he had experience in the craft of tracking.

He picked up a trail of heel-in-first tracks and short strides which meant the suspect walked to the Henderson place. On the other side of the path, freshly overturned leaves, broken twigs, toe-in-first impressions in a zigzag pattern and a longer stride showed the suspect ran back to his car in a panic.

Using a stick, he gently lifted wet maple leaves out of the way, looking for drops of blood or fallen items. He turned quickly at the sound of footsteps behind him. It was Joe Small, with camera in hand.

"Find anything, Sarge?"

Jurgens pointed at the faint disturbances in the ground and the leaves. "The disturbances of the leaves show the suspect walked in on the north side of the trail. The zigzag pattern on the south side tells me he was in a panic. He ran, slipped and fell on the leaves at least twice. If it was Stanford, he'll have dirt on the knees of his jeans which will match the soil here."

"C'mon, Stan," Small scoffed, "how can you tell so much from piles of wet leaves?"

"Pay attention, city boy. The leaves on top have been lying here since last fall. The leaves on the bottom are older. They compress as they decompose, so they can be separated only with effort. The direction of major displacement is eastward from the Henderson place, toward where their car was parked. The tracks are toe-in first and the stride is longer, which indicates running not walking."

Jurgens paused to look at Small. "It's like following breadcrumbs."

"I stand corrected, Hansel. How far have you followed the tracks?"

"Only up to where we are, Gretel," Jurgens grinned. "Take pictures of the piles of leaves I show you and an overall shot of this tunnel through the woods. We'll have to hurry to follow the rest of the breadcrumbs before dark."

They followed and photographed the footprints from the back of the cabana to the tire tracks, then split up to knock on doors of houses overlooking the dead-end road above the school.

† † †

SMALL HIT PAY dirt at the first home. "Yes, Detective. My husband and I came home late last night from a party. Minutes after we settled in for a night cap in the living room, a car drove down the road below us and stopped," Claudia Tompkins said.

"What time was this, ma'am?"

"Late," she said as she turned her head down the

hall. "Scott! The police are here!"

A puffy-faced, balding man in his late forties appeared, wearing a horn-rimmed glasses and gray sweatshirt. A hairy pink paunch bulged over his gray sweatpants as he waddled down the hall like a woman in late pregnancy.

"Scott, this is Detective Small from the police. He's asking what time it was last night when the little white car parked on the road below."

Scott scowled at Small's trendy blond semi-Beatles hairstyle and long sideburns.

"Did you ask him what this is about, Claudia?" he asked, staring at Small as if he was a mannequin.

"No, dear. He showed me his police ID, though."

"Teenagers park on the road below us at night all the time. Why the interest?" he sneered.

"A home on the other side of these woods was the scene of an attack last night, sir. The suspect's tracks lead from the house through the woods to the dirt road below you where the white car was. The family wasn't home, but the dog was killed. Butchered. I'm trying to establish the time this car arrived."

Scott stared at Small, expression blank, mouth open in disbelief. "Why should we believe you? This is Bellevue, not Seattle. Nothing happens in Bellevue."

Small dropped his gaze to look for a moment at Scott 's bare belly. He resisted the temptation to pat it and ask, "what're you going to name it?"

The wife broke the silence.

"For heaven's sake Scott, do you really think a police detective would be here on a Sunday night to make this up? Someone mutilated an animal at our neighbor's—horrible! Tell the detective or I will!"

Small stifled an amused grin. *So, the little woman wears the pants here.*

"Okay, okay," Scott said, playing the irritated big shot. "We came home a little after midnight. We changed clothes and came out to the living room for a nightcap. As Claudia brought me my martini, a small car entered the dirt road below us and parked. Then the lights went out."

"Then what happened?" Small asked.

"I saw the driver door open, and someone got out."

"Can you describe the person?"

"He was young, thin build. He was alone and he walked toward the woods."

"About how long after the car arrived did you go to bed?"

Scott glanced at his wife. "About twenty to thirty minutes."

"Sounds right to me, too, Detective," the wife volunteered.

"Car description?"

"White. A foreign compact. Whiny motor," Scott replied.

Small flipped to a fresh page of his notebook. "What

time did the car leave?"

"We went to sleep. It was gone by morning."

Small handed his notebook to Scott. "Is this what you said?"

"This is a statement?" Scott asked.

*Just sign it, Sherlock.* "Yes, sir. I wrote down what you said for accuracy. Is it correct?"

Scott read it, mouthing each word. "Close enough."

Small tried to hand his pen to Scott. "Initial the beginning and the ending of the writing, and sign at the bottom, please."

Scott didn't take the pen. "What's this for?"

"To protect both of us as to what you told me."

"Hmm...maybe I should ask my attorney first."

Claudia groaned loudly. "Sign it, Scott, or I will!"

"All right, I guess it's innocuous enough."

"Thank you. I have no more questions. Is there anything else you can think of before I leave?"

Scott raised his forefinger. "We won't have to go to court, will we? Don't want our names in the papers."

† † †

A SEATTLE POLICE car cruised past where Hitchcock sat in his Wagoneer, across the street from Stanford's address. Stanford's white Datsun B-210 was in the driveway. He wondered how he would explain himself if the officer contacted him.

Darkness descended. Lights came on in the house.

He left to find a restroom. Nothing had changed when he returned. At 9:30 the lights in the house went off. After ten minutes he crossed the street, glancing in all directions. His feet made crunching sounds as he snuck up the gravel driveway and shined his flashlight into Stanford's car.

The interior was littered with trash. On the center of the front passenger seat was a large fixed-blade knife, lying on newspaper, with what appeared to be blood on the blade and the newspaper. *Pay dirt, but now what?* He'd told no one what he was doing. The nearest pay phone is four blocks away, but he didn't have phone numbers for any of the detectives. He could be arrested for prowling. As silently as he approached, Hitchcock left.

# CHAPTER TWELVE
## The Deepening Frenzy

*The Bull Pen*
*Monday, 8:00 A.M.*

CLOUDS OF CIGARETTE smoke, overflowing ashtrays, burnt coffee, clacking typewriters, overriding phone conversations and tired four-letter grumbling brought the bull pen to life. The long weekend of callouts sapped the detectives' energy.

The room fell into silence as Captain Holland picked his way through stacks of evidence envelopes and open briefcases on the floor. He wasn't smiling as he faced his team.

"Doctor Tallman, the vet, called," the captain said. "The blood samples from Lew Henderson's dog tested positive for strychnine, the most common chemical in rat poison. It was also in the raw hamburger the doc found in the dog's gut.

"So," Holland continued, "in addition to the blue-hooded-sweatshirt rapist, we've got another psycho on the loose, and here's more bad news: I went over the case with one of the senior deputy prosecutors. I didn't like what I was told, and neither will you, which is no felony can be charged at this point. All we have are two misdemeanors: Criminal Trespass and Animal Cruelty. If the suspects are either of the two who attacked Hitchcock's place, they'll be charged with violating the terms of their release on bail."

A stir of anger wafted across the bull pen.

"Am I to understand, Captain," Detective Meyn asked, "the prosecutors are saying a bad guy can go to the home of someone he doesn't like, kill an animal belonging to the family and use the animal's blood to write a threat on the house, and we can't arrest him on probable cause?"

"Not quite," Holland replied. "I asked the same question. If the intended victim had been home at the time the threat in blood was written on the door, then the act would rise to Second Degree Assault because the ability to harm or cause fear of harm existed. But in this case, the place was vacant."

As a sullen silence permeated the bull pen, Captain Holland's secretary stepped in and handed him a note. He looked up at his men after he read it. "Thanks to Joe's good work yesterday the prosecutor says we can arrest Stanford, but only on a warrant."

A murmur of approval floated around the bull pen.

"We're gonna track down the bastards who did this

and the people who put 'em up to it," Holland said.

He turned to Jurgens. "Send someone to eyeball the house and car for the affidavit."

Jurgens pointed at Small, who grabbed a set of keys and left.

Captain Holland added, "I'll call the Patrol Commander at the Wallingford Precinct to request a uniformed officer assist in arresting a suspect in their city. If Stanford is there, detain him on probable cause until we have the warrants."

Holland's secretary appeared. "Pardon me for interrupting, Captain. You have a call holding from Seattle PD. They said it's urgent."

# CHAPTER THIRTEEN
## Going After Stanford

A NATIVE OF North Seattle, Detective Joe Small drove straight to Stanford's address. He radioed Sergeant Jurgens: "I'm here, Stan. Stanford's white Datsun is in the driveway. The house is an old 1930s dump."

*"Judge Hadley will want something a little more definitive for a search warrant than a 1930s dump, Joe,"* Jurgens snapped.

"Okay, we got us a small one-story house with tan clapboard siding, a green asphalt shingle roof, the house number is posted next to the front door."

*"Anything else?"*

"There's a detached single-car garage in the back."

*"Meyn and Williams are on their way. We're getting an SPD unit to assist you. An impound is on the way. Follow the tow truck when it takes Stanford's car to the station."* Jurgens said.

Before Small could acknowledge Jurgens, Stanford dashed out of the house, arms loaded with clothing and a battered suitcase which he threw into the passenger side. He backed the Datsun out of the driveway and sped away.

Small keyed his mic: "Stanford just fled the house. He's eastbound on North Thirty-Ninth Street. I'm following."

Detective Meyn came on the air: *"We're minutes from you, Joe, North Forty-Fifth Street, crossing Latona. Radio, call SPD Dispatch; advise them we're following a suspect we are trying to arrest on a warrant in their city."*

Small: "Suspect turned right, southbound on Daytona Avenue. He's about six car-lengths ahead of me—may be headed to the bridge. Need a marked Seattle unit to make the stop."

Dispatch: *"We have SPD Dispatch on the line. What's your location, direction of travel and suspect vehicle description?"*

Small: "Suspect turned left on North Thirty-Sixth Street, which becomes Fremont Avenue. Vehicle is an older white Datsun B210."

Small felt beads of nervous sweat trickle down his chest as he weaved in and out of traffic. Angry drivers honked as he narrowly missed clipping or sideswiping other cars to keep from losing Stanford in traffic.

Even at slow speeds Small didn't dare take a hand off the wheel to radio his direction and location.

A car ahead of Stanford cut in, forcing him to stop at a red signal, giving Small time to grab his mic. "Suspect is about to cross the Ship Canal on the Fremont

Bridge. Three cars between us."

Dispatch: *"Radio copied. Notifying SPD."*

Meyn: *"We're a couple blocks behind you, Joe."*

Small: "Signal changed. Suspect now crossing the Fremont Bridge. He turned left, now headed south along Lake Union toward the downtown."

Traffic moved. Two cars ahead moved right, leaving only one car between Small and Stanford.

The last car between them suddenly switched lanes as the traffic signal at Mercer Street changed to red. Stanford stopped, with Small right behind.

Stanford stared at Small from his rearview mirror. Even at this distance Small could see hate in his eyes. He lowered his head. *Where are the cops when you need 'em?*

A second later Stanford sped uphill on Westlake against the red light. He busted through two more red signals. At the top of the hill, by *The Seattle Times* building, he turned right and disappeared downhill into the downtown core.

Small cursed as he grabbed his mic. "Suspect made me while waiting at the signal at Mercer Street. Busted through three red lights to get away. Last seen headed into the downtown—I'm returning to the station."

Meyn turned to Williams. "Let's find the other guy—Zhang. Maybe Stanford is with him."

Williams held up his notepad. "Got the address. Let's go."

ZHANG'S APARTMENT WAS on the second floor of a dank-smelling four-story building in Chinatown. An elderly Chinese woman answered the door. They smiled and showed her their badges. She bowed politely and waited. Meyn smiled again at her. "Hello, ma'am, we would like to speak with Jinjie, for a minute, please."

"Jinjie—he gone."

"Where he go?" Williams asked in pidgin English, for which Meyn elbowed him.

"Taipei," she scowled as she slammed the door.

† † †

HITCHCOCK WAS LEAVING the house when Allie stopped him.

"Where are you going?"

"To the station."

"Why? This is your day off. What's going on?"

"You don't want to know."

"I'm your *wife*, in case you forgot. Tell me what's going on!"

"Okay, but you'll wish you hadn't asked. Saturday night, someone came through the woods to our old place, killed Lew Henderson's dog, who resembled Jamie, and wrote 'die pig' in blood on the sliding door. The dicks believe the person who did it thought Lew's dog was Jamie."

Allie covered her mouth as she gasped. "Who else but the creep Jamie chewed up?"

"That'd be my guess."

"Why were you gone so long yesterday?"

"I went to Seattle."

"Seattle? Why?"

"To find Stanford. I found his car at the address on his arrest sheet. After dark I walked up the driveway and shone my flashlight inside. I saw a bloody knife on a piece of newspaper on the front passenger seat. I didn't know how to reach our detectives, so I came home."

Allie stared at him, openmouthed with fear and surprise. "I don't like the sound of this, Roger. Won't you be in trouble for acting on your own? Shouldn't you have come home and stayed with me and Trevor and let the Department do its work?"

"I know first-hand how slow the Department is in resolving situations like this. Your safety and Trevor's come ahead of the Department's rules. I told everything to Sergeant Breen. Captain Holland and Captain Delstra aren't happy. I'm going in to face the music."

"Whatever happens, stay with me and Trevor when you're not working. Let the Department handle this."

"Yes, dear," he said half-teasingly.

"I'm serious!"

"I know. How about a kiss before I go?"

"Don't make me mad. Go and come back!"

"I love you," he said teasingly.

Allie folded her arms defiantly. "You come right back, Roger!"

# CHAPTER FOURTEEN
## A Mole, Blood, and Poison

A SEATTLE PATROL unit met Meyn and Williams at Stanford's address. The officer rang the doorbell. A slender, unkempt woman in her late twenties with straight, oily dark brown hair and acne scars opened the door.

"Good morning, miss. I'm Officer Dobbs and these men are Bellevue Police detectives. I'll let them explain their purpose."

"We're here to talk to Andy Stanford on some police business," Detective Meyn said. "Is this where he lives?"

"He did until he got a strange phone call about forty-five minutes ago," the woman replied.

"Phone call?"

"I answered it. A strange man asked for Andy."

"Then what happened?"

"Andy took the call, then packed up his stuff and left in a hurry."

"Do you know who the caller was?" Meyn asked.

"No clue," she shrugged, "he had a strong accent

that sounded Oriental."

"What did he say?"

"He sounded desperate. He said, '*I must speak to Andrew Stanford right away!*' "

"I said, 'he's sleeping.'"

"He said, 'This is an *emergency*. Wake Andy up *now!*'

"I awoke Andy. I told him a strange man with a foreign accent is on the phone with an urgent message. He bolted out of bed as if I said the house was on fire. He listened, said 'okay' and grabbed all his stuff. As he left, he told me the police are coming for him and he wouldn't be back."

"Are you the landlord here?"

"I am. This was my parents' house. They died a couple years ago in a car accident. I rent out rooms to make ends meet."

"I'm sorry for your loss. We have a warrant to search Andy's room."

"You won't need it. This is my house. I'll let you search."

"Thanks, but legally you can't permit us to search a room someone is renting from you. Even though Andy said he was moving out, the case is stronger if we search under the authority of the court."

† † †

MEYN AND WILLIAMS were shocked to see *Los Angeles Times* news clippings of the Tate-LaBianca slayings, the trial of Charles Manson and his so-called family were thumb-tacked to the walls of Stanford's bedroom. Magazine articles about the bizarre, murderous cult and its leader were in the nightstand drawer. Williams photographed them in place before gathering them.

When Meyn swept the top shelf in the closet with his hand, he found a carton of rat poison.

"I'll get the landlord," Meyn said.

"That's the brand I bought because our next-door neighbor piles kitchen trash in their backyard," the landlady said when Williams showed her the carton.

"They don't use the waste disposal service?" Meyn inquired.

"They're a bunch of animals next door," she scoffed. "They haul their trash to the dump after it's been left in open piles for a month. Draws rats like you wouldn't believe. The City and the Health Department have cited them eight times that I know of. Because of them I've had rats in my house and have to keep rat poison on hand."

"Where do you keep it?"

"In my garage. Never in the house," she replied, staring at the box. "Looks like Andy found it and helped himself, but what for?"

"I need to be sure this is yours; not something Andy bought. Please show me where in your garage you keep yours." Meyn asked.

He returned minutes later.

"The landlady's rat poison is missing from where she kept it," he told Williams. "She said it's the brand she always buys, so it appears Stanford took it to kill what he thought was Hitchcock's dog and didn't put it back."

Suddenly they heard a large truck outside. "Is that the garbage truck I hear?" Meyn asked the landlady.

She nodded.

† † †

"LOOKS LIKE YOU guys scored," Sergeant Jurgens said when Meyn and Williams returned with full paper sacks and manila evidence envelopes. Stanford's collection of Charles Manson memorabilia shocked him.

"The captain ain't gonna like this, Stan," Meyn said.

"Won't like what?"

Meyn told Jurgens about Stanford being tipped off by a strange phone call and splitting just before they arrived.

Stunned, Jurgens asked: "Who could have snitched us off?"

"It's gotta be somebody here in our building," Meyn said. He told Jurgens about the rat poison. "If Stanford's prints are on the box and it's the same stuff that killed the Henderson dog, case closed."

Sergeant Jurgens slowly nodded, digesting the information. "Good work, as always, Larry. Anything else?"

"We grabbed piles of receipts for meals, gas and other stuff. The dates and times will help us retrace Stanford's steps, maybe find him."

"Nice job, boys," Jurgens commented.

"That isn't all, Stan," Meyn announced.

"No?"

"The best is yet to come. As we were about to leave, we heard a garbage truck coming down the street. We hurried out and dug through the landlady's trashcan. Remember Hitchcock said he saw a bloody knife wrapped in newspaper inside Stanford's car?"

Jurgens leaned forward in his chair. "Uh-huh."

Meyn held up a bloody sheet of newspaper. "We found *this* in the landlady's trashcan, but no knife. She was shocked when we showed it to her. Bet you lunch at The Barb that the lab reports will state the blood on the newspaper and the blood of Henderson's dog are a match."

"I'm impressed, Larry. What else you got?"

"We went to Zhang's apartment in Chinatown, looking for Stanford. An older Chinese lady told us Zhang is in Taiwan now, Taipei specifically."

Captain Holland had been standing by, listening. "Well done, Larry." He turned to Sergeant Jurgens. "We need to find out who told the suspect we were coming for him, Stan."

"According to Stanford's landlady, the person who called to warn Stanford had a strong Oriental accent,

Captain," Jurgens said. "No one in our building has an accent. The tip had to originate from someone in our building."

"It's getting so we don't know who we can trust. I have no ideas how to do it, but find out who it was," Holland muttered to Jurgens.

† † †

HITCHCOCK RETURNED HOME from the station and flopped into his brown leather chair. Allie brought him coffee and stood, waiting.

"Well?"

Instead of answering, he sipped his coffee and stared into space, sadly shaking his head.

"Talk to me!" Allie demanded.

"I face the firing squad at sunrise," he said with his best straight face.

"Stopped teasing or you'll find out I can punch hard, too!" she shouted. "Tell me what happened!"

"Not much," he said with a coy smile. "I got royally chewed out by Captain Delstra, then by Captain Holland for possibly compromising the investigation and the charges..."

"And...?"

"No sweat, baby. Captain Delstra said because it was my family and home that was attacked, they let me off with a verbal warning; nothing will be in my personnel file. I had to promise not to act on my own again, which I did."

"Thank God, honey. No more jokes or teasing. Please," she said with a sigh of relief.

He paused. "Okay. No more jokes, but I can't promise no more teasing. And there's more..."

"Don't keep me in suspense."

"They both jumped bail."

"Oh, no."

"That's a good thing."

"Why is that good?"

"They're on the run instead of lurking around here, and full-time bounty hunters, professionals who hunt bail jumpers will take up the chase. They'll do nothing else until they've got 'em both. Not only are Stanford and Zhang up to their eyeballs in trouble with the law, whoever sent them against us isn't happy with them, either. And will want their money back."

"Will they stick around here?"

"They're young, single and unemployed. They've got eons of prison time hanging over their heads. I don't think they'll risk going after me again. They're on the run."

"Where can they go?" Allie nervously asked.

"The logical place is Canada; three-hours away."

"I won't relax until those two are locked up."

He slipped his arms around her. "Keep up your weapon training."

# CHAPTER FIFTEEN
## Down in the Boondocks

IT WAS PARTLY sunny at the South Precinct when Seattle Police Officer Brent Roberts began his noon to 8:00 p.m. shift. No calls were holding when he radioed himself in service.

His beat was the industrial area south of the downtown core, where the Duwamish River empties into Puget Sound. He patrolled there between calls, looking for and finding stolen cars, fugitives, and dead bodies in the heavy brush of scattered patches of undeveloped land under bridges, between industrial buildings and fenced equipment yards west of the Rainier Brewery, south of the West Seattle Draw Bridge.

A brief ray of sunlight enabled his eye to catch a glimpse of white high in the brush on the other side of West Marginal Way. It wasn't there yesterday.

He pulled over for a better look. Another ray of sunlight between moving clouds revealed the white roof of a car deep in the tall brush. He saw fresh tire tracks and footprints on the narrow dirt road that went from the street into thick brambles.

Like Bellevue, Seattle patrol officers didn't have portable radios. Roberts keyed his mic.

"Two William Four, Radio, I'll be out of the car checking a possible abandoned vehicle under the West Seattle Bridge in the 3000 block of West Marginal."

Last night's rain had softened the clay soil to the consistency of thick paste, allowing for sharp detail. Fresh tire tracks went in, not out. Footprints showed two people walked out, but not in.

Figuring it was another false stolen car report in the brush, another vehicle stripped and demolished for the insurance money, Roberts carefully avoided stepping on the footprints and tire tracks as he made his way in.

He found a white, early '60s Datsun B210, its lower body riddled with brown rust spots, license plates removed but the glass, the radio and the tires were still intact. The dead brush piled on the roof was meant to delay discovery, which told Roberts this was not another insurance fraud case. The doors were unlocked. The interior stank and was cluttered with fast food wrappers and empty packs of Salem cigarettes. Finding no registration, he copied the vehicle identification number in his pocket notebook.

The rumbling of heavy trucks on the West Seattle Bridge above was deafening. Even with his door and windows shut, he had to turn up the radio volume to hear and raise his voice to report his discovery to

Dispatch.

He switched to Channel Two. "Two William Four, Records. I got the VIN number of an abandoned vehicle if you can copy."

The results would take time. The records clerk would write the information on a three-by-five card, clip it to "the clothesline," a pulley system used to send requests from Dispatch across the hall to Records, which phoned the request to DMV in Olympia, who would then write the response on the same card and send it back the same way.

Roberts returned to the Datsun to see what else he could find. Wearing surgical gloves, he sorted through the trash and stopped at the sight of dried blood on the front passenger seat and the floor below.

The reply to his inquiry came in as he returned to his cruiser: *"Per DMV, vehicle is a 1966 Datsun registered to Andrew Stanford, Seattle address of... outstanding no bail warrant for Attempted First Degree Burglary..."*

Roberts mentally put the pieces together before he keyed his mic to acknowledge the report. *Plates removed, blood on the passenger seat, brush piled over the roof, the footprints of two people walking away. It's starting to look like something more than a phony insurance claim.*

He requested his duty sergeant to contact him. As he waited, he returned to the vehicle again and stood at the rear, wondering what was in the trunk.

# CHAPTER SIXTEEN
## With One Eye Open

JAMIE'S THROAT RUMBLED when he heard a car stop in front of the house, followed by a man walking up to the house. His toenails clicked on the hardwood floor as he moved from the kitchen to the front screen door.

Tom Sherman smiled as he extended the back of his hand against the screen door to Jamie.

"You of all people don't need to stand on invitation, Tom," Hitchcock said. "Come on in."

"I'm letting your dog do his work. He takes his job seriously enough to check me out before he lets me in."

Jamie sniffed Sherman's hand, then looked up at him as if to say, "You may pass."

Sherman pulled up a chair at the kitchen table. Allie set a steaming mug of coffee in front of him.

"Thanks, and good morning, Allie." Turning to Hitchcock, he said, "Given the recent attack at your former place and us being on second shift now, we should start tomorrow morning."

"Agreed. What's the plan?" Hitchcock said.

"What are you guys talking about?" Allie asked, turning her head between her husband and Sherman.

"We're going to protect Jamie by poison-proofing him," Sherman replied with his usual smile.

"How?"

"We'll follow the Army training manual we used when I worked merchant security patrol with a dog before the PD hired me. How much time it takes depends on the individual dog, and you," Sherman answered, sipping his coffee.

"What do we do first?" Allie asked.

"We'll start with treats or other food items offered to him by people he doesn't know, with the handler using commands to stop the dog from taking it, including people filling the dog's dish or tossing food in front of him.

"Discipline through use of the leash and collar will be used when necessary. The one other person who feeds the dog should be incorporated into the process. More than one person should offer the food the dog is not to accept so the training is not fixated on one person."

"We'll need a couple volunteers," Hitchcock said.

"Right," Sherman agreed. "As Jamie improves, the process should be extended in both time and distance between the handler and him. A long lead would be used, if necessary, to apply compulsive discipline. Eventually the scenario will involve the handler being out of sight as food is thrown into the dog's area by someone uninvolved with the first process, meaning we will need to introduce new people as tempters."

"At least two other people," Hitchcock concluded.

"Three is better. Four is ideal. The risk of the Stanford or Zhang coming back is high as long as they're at large. If they haven't learned by now that they poisoned the wrong dog, they will. We should start right away so Jamie never takes food from strangers."

"I'm in. We're not sleeping well," Allie remarked.

"Why not mix something in the food to make the dog sick and put it in the dish?" Hitchcock asked.

"Putting something like cayenne pepper in treats as a deterrent has been tried, but one sniff usually tells the dog not to eat that particular treat and doesn't change the overall behavior. Most dogs will sniff the food first."

"How soon can we start?" Allied asked.

"Tomorrow at nine-thirty?"

† † †

HITCHCOCK STOPPED BY the bull pen after Sherman left. Detective Meyn, looking pale and washed-out from working long hours, was at his desk, dressed as always in a drab suit, drab white shirt, drab tie. He gestured for Hitchcock to have a seat.

"Zhang took a Northwest Airlines flight to Taiwan right after his release on bail, before the second attack on your former place," he said, "so that leaves Stanford."

"I wasn't worried about Zhang coming back, only Stanford," Hitchcock said.

"The state lab reports are in. Six of the prints from your sliding glass door are Stanford's. Only one is Zhang's," Meyn said.

"I'm not surprised."

"Stanford got a phone call that we were coming," Meyn said.

Hitchcock was too surprised to speak.

"He split seconds after Joe Small arrived."

"What happened then?" Hitchcock asked.

"Joe lost him in downtown traffic."

Hitchcock grit his teeth but said nothing.

"Someone overheard Small being told to get a description of the house where Stanford was living," Meyn added.

"Has to be someone in the building – on our floor or the court above us," Hitchcock said.

"Only in theory. I agree that Stanford having a connection with someone *here*, who would warn him, doesn't fit."

"What else do you know?" Hitchcock asked.

"The rat poison we found in Stanford's room matches the poison that killed Lew Henderson's dog. It's available anywhere, to anyone. If Stanford's prints are on the carton of rat poison we found in his room, we add to the charges."

"The old close the barn door after the horses have

left, trick," Hitchcock scoffed.

"Every bit of pressure we put on Stanford helps," Meyn replied defensively."

"What's your opinion, Larry—do you think Stanford is wacked-out enough to try again?"

"Stanford operates in dark realms. He's an admirer of Charles Manson, so the answer is unknowable."

Hitchcock cursed under his breath. Meyn heard him.

"Look, Roger—Stanford got chewed up bad by your dog. After stitches and shots, he went to jail on felony charges. It's no surprise that he jumped bail. With his prior record and this hanging over his head, he knows he'll die of old age in prison if he doesn't go underground."

"I get it that being torn up by a dog would be enraging for a wacko like him," Hitchcock said.

The pause was long and heavy.

"You're right, Roger—we can't rule out that he's angry and crazy enough to get revenge. But he's got to go underground to escape the people who hired him. They can't risk either of them being where prosecutors can offer deals and protection in exchange for information and testimony."

"There's something else, Larry."

"What's that?"

"What's the status on the two different brands of cigarette butts piled outside our bedroom window?"

Meyn bit his lower lip. "To be honest, with all that's going on I forgot about 'em. Unless Stanford changed brands, I agree the Marlboro butts indicate another person is involved."

"I think the Marlboro smoker came to our place first, then brought Stanford," Hitchcock said. "He probably put Stanford with Zhang. The handcuffs and the tape Williams found was their plan to abduct my wife."

"I'll submit the cigarette butts for blood type identification today. I'll get Stanford and Zhang's blood types from hospital records. If one blood type on the cigarette butts doesn't match the blood type of either of them, we have a third suspect to hunt for."

"Whoever tipped Stanford off might be the third suspect," Hitchcock said. "Our place was remote."

Meyn shook his head as he stood up. "An assassination attempt on a police officer at his home is a sign that certain people are desperate to stop you. Now that it failed, the people behind it are sweating bullets. They'll stop at nothing. There's no telling where it'll lead. I'll keep you posted. Watch your back."

# CHAPTER SEVENTEEN
## A Sobering Reality

*Shift Briefing*
*11:45 A.M.*

"AS IF WE didn't already know, the feds notified us today that the escapees from the Georgia state penitentiary are here," Sergeant Breen said, smirking and shaking his head. "Kirkland PD acted on our alert that the Slocum gang asked one of our officers for directions to The Foghorn. Expecting an armed robbery, they put two plainclothes officers inside and a stakeout team outside four nights in a row, but nothing happened.

"The morning after the last stakeout, the manager discovered the place had been broken into through the roof. The FBI learned the gang posted a rifleman on the roof while the other two bypassed the alarm and took their own sweet time cracking the safe and busting open cash registers."

The squad members stared grimly, but no one

spoke.

"I'm passing out new flyers with prison mugshots of the gang," Breen continued. "They've probably changed cars since their encounter with our traffic officer. Start backing each other up on traffic stops. Remember the Texas deputy they abducted and shot in the head with his own gun. Anybody who wants to can read the details in my office. Any questions?"

The men said nothing as they studied the faces in the bulletin.

"This is as close to shoot-on-sight as it gets in police work," Breen said. "Should you see Slocum or Virgil Howard, draw your weapon and radio for backup."

"Okay—Diss-*missed*!"

The officers didn't notice Traffic Officer Kendrick sitting in the Patrol Sergeant's office, reading and re-reading the account of the abduction, torture and execution of Deputy Clark Cunningham in Texas by Lonnie Slocum and Virgil Howard.

He studied Slocum and Howard's mugshots, remembering their voices. The driver had been Virgil Howard. The front seat passenger who asked him for directions to the Foghorn was Lonnie Slocum. He would never forget the death he saw in Slocum's eyes.

He visualized Deputy Cunningham stopping their car, being captured and going through two days of torture and humiliation, knowing he would never see his family again. Even as he knelt before his captors in the Texas dust, restrained by his own handcuffs, he must have hoped against hope he would be spared or rescued.

Since his encounter with the Slocum gang, Kendrick wrestled with the realization that almost two thousand miles away and three weeks after Deputy Cunningham was murdered, by an unexpected twist of fate, the killers crossed *his* path.

His close encounter with escaped convicts on a killing spree forced him to face unpleasant truths even his fellow officers didn't know—that he never checked anyone he stopped for warrants or ran the plates of the cars he stopped for traffic violations. Other times he had even backed down from writing a ticket out of fear of a fight.

He knew his fellow officers regarded him as a "nice man," a churchy fellow incapable of discerning danger; a man too passive and friendly to be dependable when a situation demanded a strong hand. They never said this to his face—they didn't have to. He knew they regarded him as a liability who shouldn't be in police work.

His fellow officers' opinions of him were justified.

Niceness was his code. He never understood the lack of importance so many officers put on being nice.

His thoughts came to his gun—what would he have done in a real gunfight? During three years of riding motorcycles in the rain, he never removed his gun from his rain-soaked leather holster. His negligence continued after he transferred to an accident investigation car.

Alone in the Traffic Division office, he unsnapped his holster. It took two hands to remove his gun because of green mold inside the leather holster. His heart skipped a beat when the hammer couldn't be cocked, nor the trigger pulled, and the cylinder was rusted shut.

He burned with embarrassment when the twelve rounds of spare ammunition in pouches on his gun belt were stuck inside. Green mold covered them when he pried them out with a screwdriver.

Shame hit him hard. He had been living in a bubble of his own making. He had to sit down to face his negligence. Humbled, Kendrick walked into Sergeant Bill Harris's office unannounced.

"I'm a liability to the guys, the public and myself, Bill. Look at my gun. I'm so ashamed. It's best for everyone that I resign."

Sergeant Harris stared at Kendrick's rusted gun and moldy ammunition. For a minute, he couldn't speak. "I share the blame for not holding weapons inspections," he finally said. "I won't let you resign, Lee. You're one of the best men here. Most of us wouldn't be so honest about something as embarrassing as this. Because of your integrity, I'll keep this between us. We'll turn the situation around, and learn from it."

Harris quietly replaced Kendrick's weapon and

ammunition. He arranged for three weeks of re-training at two hours a week with Lieutenant Ian Fletcher, the Department firearms instructor, and head of the pistol team.

† † †

SERGEANT HARRIS CALLED a division meeting the next day. He related the details of Kendrick's encounter with wanted cop killers.

"We could just as easily be attending his funeral instead of having this discussion."

The room became quiet. Harris continued.

"Working traffic, most of our contacts are with law-abiding people. Over time, we tend to forget that bad people move among the law abiding. Our guard slips when all we do is write tickets and investigate accidents to decent people."

Harris paused again. "Police funerals are on the rise. I don't want any of them to be here. From now on, each of you will read Patrol bulletins *daily* before we hit the street. Each of you is to check for warrants on every driver you stop. A review of the logs in Records showed me that we in Traffic aren't doing this. No more letting criminals slip through our fingers.

"Make sure your weapon is clean and loaded before you begin your shift. Practice with the fifty rounds you're allotted each month. From now on I'll be doing surprise weapons inspections."

# CHAPTER EIGHTEEN
## Always A Step Behind

*The Station*
*11:40 A.M.*

THE TAPE SEAL on the envelope in Hitchcock's inbox was broken. The note inside was from Patty in the Records Division: "Rooster requests Hitchcock call at the same number as before at a certain time."

He called Records. Patty answered. "Got your envelope. What time did Rooster call?" he asked.

"About an hour ago—"

"Did you seal the envelope?"

"Absolutely. Something wrong?"

"I found the seal broken."

"What? I sealed the flap and added tape before I put it in your inbox!"

"The tape was gone. Who did you see when you went to my inbox?"

"The usual Brass and a few Traffic officers."

"Who, exactly?'"

"Last name starts with a B," she replied.

† † †

THE WEATHER WAS cool and dry, and the radio traffic was sparse when Hitchcock rolled out of the station. He called Randy from the nearest pay phone. He answered on the first ring.

"Smith came by the gas station today. The game is changing."

"What time did you see him?"

"About two hours ago."

"What's changed?"

"He's got a different car now, had a chick with him – and a gun."

"Different car?"

"Blue Mustang. Cherry, a couple years old."

"License number?"

"I got it for ya. It's O-G-R-6-3-7."

Hitchcock scribbled the plate number down. "You gave me Ocean George Robert Six Three Seven, right?"

"Correct."

"Describe the girl."

"A kid. Fifteen or sixteen. Dark hair, skinny, real pretty. She was high – didn't say nothing."

"You recognize her?"

"She looked familiar, but..."

"But?"

"I can't place her."

"He had a gun?"

"A black revolver. Had it in his waistband under his

shirt. Showed me only the grip because of the customers. I asked if he's shot anybody. He said not yet but he's got a couple people he wants to shoot to get respect. Probably just talk, knowing him."

"Did he mention the kind of dope?"

"Smack and coke. Said business is real good."

"What did he want?"

"Me to work for him. Said the two guys with him can't be trusted. Promised me my own car, money, and a chick like the one with him."

"What did you tell him?"

"Told him no way."

"Did you tell him why? That you're a Christian now?"

"Started to, but I was too embarrassed. Afraid of being laughed at, I guess," Randy replied ruefully.

"Call me if Smith shows up again, or if you hear from him, but don't go anywhere with him. No spy stuff. You're back from the dead, literally. Focus on staying alive."

"Don't worry, Roger, I will."

† † †

HE RADIOED THE plate number Randy gave him to Records. Patty had it in seconds: *"License comes back to a 1968 Mustang coupe, blue. Reported sold a week ago, awaiting title transfer. New owner's name not on file yet. Former owners are Howard and Wilma Folger of Renton."*

"I need the former owner's address. Run both names for anything you can find."

*"Already ran the Folgers—no record. Their address is in Renton at..."*

He snuck out of the City to the Folger residence, a red brick ranch-style rambler on a large, landscaped lot. A tired, dowdy-looking woman in her early fifties answered the door.

"Yes," she said, concern in her voice. "I'm Wilma Folger. Is there something wrong?"

"There's been an incident involving the '68 Mustang you recently sold. The title still hasn't been transferred."

"Really?" Wilma gasped. "It was our son's Mustang. He died last year. Drug overdose. We put an ad in one of the Seattle papers. The young man who came paid cash. Didn't even try to negotiate. We signed the title and gave him a receipt. What kind of trouble is this?"

"The man you sold your son's car to is a wanted drug dealer."

"My goodness!" Wilma exclaimed. "We had no idea."

"How would you describe him?"

"Well, let's see...he was tall, heavy-set, with long dark hair, curly, like ringlets."

"He wasn't blond and lean?"

"Hardly. He's big-boned, slight beard. A logger type."

"Name?"

"I remember because it's unusual. Goforth."

"Goforth? Was anyone with him?"

"No."

"Any paperwork?"

Wilma shook her head. "He gave us the cash, we signed the title, he drove away—end of story," she said with finality as she closed the door.

The urgency to arrest Mike Smith before someone else died tempted Hitchcock to put Randy on the case. Randy was the only snitch he had, and he knew Smith, but given his drug history and past relationship with Smith, using him to track down Smith would be his death sentence. Not an option. He needed a new snitch, but there was no one on the horizon.

He felt helpless. *More people are gonna die if we don't catch Mike Smith.*

And Rome was burning.

# CHAPTER NINETEEN
## Marking Time

"EFFORTS TO TRACK Stanford down have been called off," Hitchcock told Allie.

"What? Why?" she asked fearfully.

"Captain Holland's orders—all leads have been followed to a dead end, nothing new. He only has five detectives, and they all worked on finding Stanford. New cases keep pouring in."

"I know they worked hard on it," Allie said. "How they handle all that pressure..."

"They all did, but it seems have taken the heaviest toll on Larry Meyn and Joe Small. They spared no effort to track down Stanford for our sake. They're having a tough time moving on."

Allie took the news in grim silence. "I guess it's up to the bounty hunters now," she said at last, staring out the kitchen window.

His time in Vietnam taught Hitchcock to be fluid, patient, to expect the unexpected, be ready to move on when unforeseen developments compel an operation to end and make new plans on short notice. His only worry was Allie. She had become distant, lost in a strange remoteness.

Dressed for work, he slipped his arms around her waist from behind as she stared out the kitchen window. She wrapped her arms over his.

"I don't feel safe anymore without you with me," she finally said, still facing the window.

"For now, the Department has done all it can. *We've* done all *we* can. Life must go on, baby. Living in fear isn't for us."

"I'm not wired for this like you are, I'm a woman."

He grinned and gave her a flirty squeeze. "Um-hm, so I noticed!"

She turned around in his arms and gave him a weak smile. She wiped away her tears and stepped back. "You're looking especially handsome in your uniform today. You'd better kiss me and go to work before I keep you here and muss it up."

As soon as he left, Allie checked that her .38 in her purse was loaded with Frenchie's hot defense loads. At work she kept a nervous eye on the parking lot, fearing Stanford was waiting to follow her home. She hoped the poison-proof training Jamie received was enough to protect him. She kept an eye out for anyone following her when she took Trevor to her mother-in-law's before going to work.

† † †

FEAR OF DISCOVERY, of being arrested and jailed plagued Bostwick without ceasing. Sleep and the ability to concentrate escaped him. He tired easily. Fatigue led to increased paranoia. He saw a knowing enemy in every face. Footsteps around every corner were coming for *him*. He dreaded going to work. His uniform he despised, for it stood for his failed plans. None of his schemes worked out as planned and now he had passed the point of no return. If only he could undo his deeds, he would. To survive is the only thing now. He must either get out while the getting is still possible. But then there was Juju, and his contacts...

# CHAPTER TWENTY
## Pressing On

"THE CORONER RULED Stacey Brock's cause of death as a homicide, and her mother Kate's death a suicide," Walker told Hitchcock. "The State Crime Lab confirmed the mother wrote the note found with her body. Problem is, her note only revealed the first name of the man who killed her daughter as Art. She left out the last name."

"It's still something to go on," Hitchcock said.

"I might have a break in the case. The parents of Stacey's friends say Kate Brock was the mistress of Art Brinkmann."

"What? The TV personality who always covers the hydroplane races?"

"The same. I need to sneak out to take a couple statements from the waiters at Hectors in Kirkland."

"Gotcha covered."

† † †

THE PROSECUTOR'S OFFICE informed the detective

division ruled that the witness statements Walker took, and Kate's suicide note were sufficient probable cause for an investigative arrest of Brinkmann.

After another week passed without word from the detectives, Hitchcock and Walker stopped by the bull pen where an intern from Seattle University was alone, playing hunt-and-peck on a typewriter. Walker did the talking.

"Do you know what happened with Brinkmann on the Brock case?"

The intern, a whiz-kid who at age twenty had already earned a bachelor's degree in accounting, didn't look up. His snooty mannerisms added to his comical persona: short, toothpick thin and prematurely bald. Plaid slacks and a white, short sleeve shirt with a bow tie which bobbed up and down with his oversized Adams' apple like the comedian Don Knotts when he talked. His first interview of a young bank teller on a check forgery case fell apart because she couldn't stop giggling.

"An investigative arrest of Mr. Brinkmann *wuz* made, offither," he said. "He wouldn't talk. He called his attorney, who came to the booking room right away. His attorney *wisely* told him not to answer any of our questions, which is what *I* would have told him to do."

Walker towered over Whiz-Kid. "Yeah? We only heard they arrested Brickman. Did he go to jail? Are charges being filed?"

"He didn't go to jail. They are waiting to hear from his *attuurney*."

"You mean the case rests in the hands of a defense attorney? Who's the lead dick in this case anyway?"

The intern shrugged without looking up. "None of this is up to me. I'm only an intern."

Never one to hide his disgust, Walker said, "We're talking the apparent homicide of a young girl and the suicide of her mother, not check forgery, Lisper."

Whiz-Kid blushed at Walker's insult. "Well, I *overhuurd* Mr. Brinkmann say his prints in would be found in Brock's house because he dated her for months. He told the detectives his marriage would be over if he cooperated. This isn't the only case I'm helping on," Whiz-Kid sniffed. "Now if you'll *excuuse* me..."

"Case over. The powers-that-be are gonna bury this one," Hitchcock predicted.

Walker nodded glumly. "There's a class of people in the country who don't go to jail."

† † †

HITCHCOCK ORDERED A cheeseburger at Art's the next afternoon. As soon as he sat down with a mug of coffee, the phone rang.

"Cop-shop's callin' ya, hon," Judy said in a low voice. He grumbled his way to the phone behind the counter.

"A subject named Rooster called the emergency line

reporting the subject you seek is at Robinswood Park right now in a blue Mustang," the dispatcher reported.

"Cancel my order, Judy, gotta run!" he said as he ran to his cruiser and sped uphill to the park, Code Two, thinking of fifteen-year-old Holly Goodrich, the runaway who ran with Smith, whose body turned up in the Mercer Slough, headless and half-eaten by coyotes, cause of death, heroin overdose.

As he reached the entrance to Robinswood Park, Dispatch came on the air: *"Emergency traffic only. Emergency traffic only. A private plane crashed into the residential neighborhood of Southeast Twenty-Sixth Street and One-Sixty-Third Avenue. Unknown injuries. Two Zero Six, respond Code Three."*

Hitchcock smashed the steering wheel with his fist and cursed before he acknowledged the call. He spotted a group of teenagers standing next to a blue Mustang deep in Robinswood Park as he sped past the park entrance.

† † †

A SINGLE ENGINE plane had crashed nose-first into the backyard of one of the homes. The slim, blond-haired man in the cockpit, appearing to be in his thirties, was the only occupant. He sat motionless, hands in his lap, head forward.

Hitchcock felt his carotid artery. No pulse. His neck and hands were cooling. No one else was hurt and no property was damaged. He obtained the names of witnesses and waited for the coroner and an FAA investigator from Boeing Field.

Robinswood Park was empty by the time he was relieved from the scene an hour later.

† † †

*THE BELLEVUE AMERICAN* dubbed the rapist "The Blue-Hooded Sweatshirt Rapist." The latest police composite sketch, complete with embellished details of the latest attack, which happened in the downtown core for the first time, was printed.

Clive Brooks, called "Officer Downtown" by his brother officers, took the attack personally. One of the most astute officers in Patrol, his analytical mind sought a pattern in the attacks that would lead to an arrest. The latest case showed either a change in the suspect's M.O. or, as Brooks believed, the presence of a new predator, a thrill-seeking copycat, had entered the fray.

The latest assault occurred in an apartment versus a house, and on the west side of the city instead of the less wealthy neighborhoods of Lake Hills and Crossroads on the east side. The detectives trusted Brooks with details they withheld from the press, details only the suspect would know.

Assigned to the downtown core as always, Brooks focused on apprehending the offender before another attack happened. He stopped by the detective office before shift briefing.

"Who's got the serial rapist cases?" he asked Meyn in a voice raised enough to override the din of clacking typewriters and phone conversations. Meyn put his hand over the mouthpiece of his phone. "Small," he said in a hoarse whisper.

Joe Small sat hunched over his desk, typing a report with two fingers. Watching him type was painful. His was the last of the old manual Royal typewriters in the division. Everyone else had the latest, the quieter IBM Selectric.

Small had loosened his tie and rolled up his shirt cuffs, exposing the muscle and veins in his forearms. His blond hair hung over his forehead. Crushed cigarette butts overflowed the ashtray on his desk. He forced a grin at the sight of Brooks. "Grab a chair, Clive, and tell me all about it."

Always the serious type, Brooks knit his brows into a frown. "All about what?"

Small kept up his torturous efforts at typing. "Oh, I dunno, your life, your wife troubles versus your girlfriend troubles, whatever floats your boat."

His hands on his knees, Brooks pondered Small's words before he cracked a smile. "Ah, a sense of humor. Well, the blue-hooded-sweatshirt guy struck in my district the other night and I was wondering—"

"Stumped, to be honest," Small interrupted. "The prints from the downtown case are at the state crime lab. After looking at them I'm not hopeful. The lab results from the previous two cases in Lake Hills came back insufficient."

"Insufficient?"

"Not quite enough detail to meet the twelve-point minimum the courts require to positively identify the person, or at least give us a list of possible suspects we could work with," Small said. "We still have no suspect vehicle descriptions, no neighbors reporting suspicious people. He'll keep going until we identify him, he stops for some reason, or Patrol catches him prowling around, hint-hint."

Brooks stared at Small.

"He'll gravitate to killing if we don't stop him," he added, staring back at Brooks.

"Are you getting FIRs on persons or vehicles from us?"

"Cleared 'em all."

"Do you think two different guys are doing this? One copycatting the other?"

Small lit another cigarette. "No doubt about it. The offenders are white males, six feet tall but there's an age difference of about twenty years," Small said as he exhaled a plume of smoke at the ceiling.

"Since the victim on the west side in an apartment, maybe the offender is a previous tenant or a guest of a previous tenant. All the victims are single. Knowing a victim's marital status and location requires a basis for obtaining that information. So far, we haven't a clue as to how they select their victims," Small said.

"Sounds like a lot of digging," Brooks said.

"I haven't checked neighbors in the complex yet. No time."

"Downtown apartment managers would love to help. They'll give me lists of past and present tenants."

"That'd be great, Clive. With all the callouts I'm getting at night I'm behind in my interviews, so I welcome your help."

"The owner of the apartment building where the last attack happened is a friend of mine," Brooks said. "She'll give me a list of past and present tenants."

Small's face broke into a broad smile.

"Clive, you sly devil-dog, you. I hear she's lonely and loaded. Nice catch!" He smiled, flipping his eyebrows at high speed.

Brooks blushed at the thought of his personal life being subject to gossip. Still, he knew Dottie, his live-in paramour, the owner of two downtown apartment buildings could be counted on to help stop a predator.

# CHAPTER TWENTY-ONE
## Unfinished Business

*The Next Morning*

HITCHCOCK WAITED IN a booth in the darkened, empty cocktail lounge of the Thunderbird Inn. The café and the lobby were full of customers. Eyes turned as Otis walked in.

Except for Captain Delstra, no one on the Department radiated command presence as much as Otis did. He was the "one riot, one officer" type. When he arrived at out-of-control scenes, order was automatically restored. His fighting skills, especially with the baton, were the stuff of locker-room legends. His service as an Army medic in Vietnam during the Eisenhower and Kennedy years was classified.

Wearing a white T-shirt and blue jeans, snub-nose off-duty gun bulging from an ankle holster, Otis was taller than Hitchcock by a couple inches, his thick dark hair, military cut, framed his boyish face. He was lean, sleek-muscled and strong in the manner of professional baseball players.

They held their silence until the waitress set coffees before them and left.

"This is a rare moment," Hitchcock remarked. "Must be important."

"I have something to say about what I see going on, so hear me out," Otis said, looking around to make sure no one was within earshot.

Hitchcock nodded with keen interest in his eyes, wondering what was up with his childhood friend and neighbor.

"In the Rangers," Otis began, "we were trained in the language and culture of the indigenous tribes in Laos and Thailand where we would be going to win their loyalty and train them to defeat the communists.

"By the time we shipped out, we had a working knowledge of the cultures and the history of the regions we would be in, which was the primary source of the world's supply of heroin and opium – the border region of Thailand, Vietnam and Laos. It's called the Golden Triangle because Chinese traders paid in gold for the opium the natives grew. The opium poppy was and is an acceptable aspect of their culture."

"The Golden Triangle," Hitchcock repeated.

"After the Chinese Communists defeated the Nationalists in '49, certain elements of the Nationalist Army settled in the Golden Triangle, where they entered the drug trade. They competed against poppy plantations in Iran and China until their governments shut them down during the '50s, which made the Golden Triangle the world's number one opium producing region."

Hitchcock nodded, wondering why the history lesson.

"When I was in the Triangle from '59 through '61," Otis continued, "I saw money from the drug trade being used by the CIA to fund secret missions and wars against communist insurgents."

"The Army never told *us* any of this," Hitchcock said in angry surprise. "Are you saying our CIA blesses the drug trade our other agencies fight, to fund secret wars over there while our soldiers and kids at home become addicted and die?"

Otis nodded solemnly.

Hitchcock sat back in dismay, staring at Otis. "Why are you telling me this?"

"Because you, more than the rest of us right now, are being targeted. Once you understand the big picture, you will know your enemy, you will be safer, your family will be safer, the people on your beat will be safer. History question: When Chiang Kai-shek fell from power in mainland China, where did he go?"

Hitchcock shrugged. "Taiwan," he replied.

"Right. After the communist takeover of the mainland, most of Chiang Kai-shek's forces went to the island of Taiwan where they set up a new nation which is friendly to the U.S., but they kept strong ties to their forces that settled in the Golden Triangle."

"To be expected..." Hitchcock acknowledged.

Otis paused to pour cream into his coffee, stir it, and take a sip. "With the war in Nam heating up," he went on, "we saw more use of heroin and overdose cases at home in which the heroin is from Southeast Asia."

"Guyon killed the people he thought would or could turn on him by giving them lethal overdoses of heroin from 'Nam. Since they were already known addicts, murder would be less obvious and hard to prove," Hitchcock interjected.

"After the Oriental kid who attacked you was released on bail, where did he go?" Otis asked.

"Taiwan. Specifically, the city of Taipei, I'm told."

"And Zhang, who lived in Seattle, went straight to your place, a secluded, unmarked location in a city unknown to him. In his pocket was a piece of paper with your name, address and directions, which the dicks believe was written by someone else, indicating he had never been to your place before, but Stanford, his partner, had."

"Makes perfect sense," Hitchcock said, wondering how Otis got this information.

"Here you are, a rookie patrolman, scoring felony drug arrests and record seizures of dope in Eastgate, the only district in the city with a small private airport located next to an interstate freeway which runs straight into Seattle."

"So, my drug arrests are interfering with a foreign drug ring?"

Otis leaned forward and lowered his voice. "The manner of execution and the staging of Colin Wilcox's body was a message."

"The VC did the same thing when I was there a few years after you. I saw the same scene on our patrols."

"No doubt you did," Otis said.

"But the dicks told me the way Wilcox died is typical of East Coast mob killings."

"Nothing against them, but they served during peacetime. They went to Germany if they went anywhere. What they're saying comes from crime bulletins, books and FBI conferences, a front they use to fish information out of us, the bluesuits, they call us. My experience is only in Southeast Asia, but I *saw* those executions, after the fact."

Hitchcock acknowledged, nodding. "I did too. The VC in-filtrated our camps, posing as workers," he recalled, "a young woman came from the nearest village, she was a real looker. For months she cooked, cleaned and did all kinds of favors for us, if you get my meaning. As we were moving out, she ran up behind one of our personnel carriers loaded with soldiers as it was leaving. She smiled as she handed up a nicely wrapped farewell gift to the guys. Then she ran. Within seconds the gift blew up, killing everybody. She disappeared. We always assumed the enemy was among us, but she took us by surprise."

"Unlike regular businessmen, drug lords operate with military strictness, they infiltrate and compromise their competition, they use extortion and blackmail to get what they want, and murder if they don't."

"I get that," Hitchcock said.

"You've crossed the line with those people," Otis said.

Hitchcock scowled. "What do you mean?"

"In any business," Otis went on "like the military, some losses are acceptable, but when the losses become frequent and large, survival becomes an issue, they suspect betrayal in their organization. They stop at nothing to find the traitor; they'll kill their own people on the slightest suspicion."

"How does all this relate to me?" Hitchcock asked.

"The top people think you've been too successful to be working alone. The size of your last few seizures makes them believe someone inside their operation is helping you."

"In other words, I'm breaking somebody's rice bowl."

"Exactly," Otis said. "They couldn't figure out who the leaker is, so they had to take you out to prevent further losses. Two Orientals wandering around Bellevue, a predominantly white town, looking for a hard-to-find address in the woods would attract attention. So they hired Stanford, a white kid with a criminal history, as scout and driver. Stanford, a known cop-hater, could be counted on to knife you the second the martial arts guy put you down. Then they would dispose of him"

"I figured that," Hitchcock mused.

"Being rank amateurs, they failed. I think it was divine intervention on your behalf."

"Divine intervention?"

Otis nodded. "It's like you've got an angel over your shoulder. Think about it: They arrived before you, instead of at the same time. They were seen by your wife, who deployed your dog and called the station. How long it would it take to discover your dead family if Allie *hadn't* called the station?"

Hitchcock paused at the thought of it. "You're right, with Doc and Ethel on vacation, discovery of our dead bodies would have taken a couple days. They would have gotten away with it."

"What's more," Otis said, "the Chinese kid probably had a cultural fear of big dogs, which is why he froze. *Then* you *happened* to arrive at *exactly* the right moment and from there a rapid chain of events unfolded. Stanford panicked when his partner attacked you and you cold-cocked him."

"So, what are you saying I, or we, should do?"

"You won Round One. The people behind the attack aren't going to give up and walk away. Round Two is coming. Be prepared. You're up against two separate factions."

"How so?"

"One is political. Their point man is Bostwick. Their aim is power. An effective police department is a hindrance to their plans."

"And the other?"

"Those who finance drug shipments. The factions run separately now, but they'll merge when it suits their common interests. Both factions believe the ends justify the means, so they're okay with bribery, blackmail and bumping off their enemies if that's what it takes. The losers are the common people who do the work and grow the food. I saw it happen over there."

Hitchcock nodded his head as he listened.

"The fact that they tried to take you out is an encouraging sign," Otis added.

Hitchcock went on alert. "How's that?"

"It means you're on the right track, you're so close that they were forced to play their hand," Otis said. "Think of it as like an onion. The outer layers are the expendable types, go-fers, homegrown people like Stanford. Mid-level operators direct them and enforce the rules. Mid-level operators were under orders when to find out where you live, do surveillance and send in Zhang and Stanford. The orders came from the people whose pockets you were hitting. The intel came from someone in our building."

Otis paused when the waitress came by to refill their

coffees.

"These people play for keeps. Because the mission failed, *you* are unfinished business. They'll set up another attack, but not for a while. To try again this soon would bring too much heat on them. They'll wait. They must dispose of Stanford and Zhang, and allow time for our guard to relax. Stanford is either already dead or soon will be because he acted on his own, putting everyone at risk by going back to your place for revenge. His body will turn up somewhere. That's the pattern. Kill or be killed."

A minute of silence followed Otis's words.

"This reminds me of 'Nam," Hitchcock said at last. "The enemy was invisible. They looked like anybody else. Out of the blue they hit, and you don't see it coming until it's too late."

"You need street-wise informants who know the drug scene." Otis advised. "Your Mata Hari was perfect, but people like her are often found out and die. Murder is the reason the drug world has a high turnover rate. With the right people helping you, maybe you'll learn who gave the order to set you up, but most likely you won't touch them even if you know, because they're outside the country."

Hitchcock fell silent. He stirred sugar into his coffee and took a sip.

"You have two choices," Otis continued. "You can stick it out or back off. Go into Traffic or something else.

They're watching you, so they'll know. They might let well enough alone if you back off."

Hitchcock leveled a hard stare at Otis.

"I *can't* quit, Joel. Problem is that my only snitch is too shaky to do anything but observe and report. We need a Narc Unit like other agencies have. Why the City won't let us, I don't understand."

"The city council isn't corrupt, Roger. It's just that they live in the past when the City was like the *Ozzie and Harriet* tv show. The mentality that closed our shooting range four years ago and never replaced it because they believe nothing happens here won't authorize an undercover narcotics unit either."

"So, it's a few patrol officers against organized drug outfits."

"Four of us, for sure. Plus a few others."

"Yeah, four of us," Hitchcock said pensively.

"In addition to informants with street savvy, to stay a step ahead you need an informant inside on the third floor."

"I had someone inside once, at the top," Hitchcock mused.

Otis grinned. "Yeah, you sure did. But she's past tense for you now. You're a married man, and she's slated to become our second judge."

Hitchcock's eyes widened. "*How* did you know about *that*?"

"You need to work on your naïveté, Roger." Otis

scoffed as he checked his watch. "Time to suit up."

"I can see you're not gonna tell me how you know about her."

"You're right. I'm not."

"Well, at least tell me who you suspect gave up my address."

"It would be only a guess."

"Come on, Joel."

"There are cop-haters in the City, even on the Department. Like cockroaches, they keep their views to themselves, they lurk in quiet, comfortable places, high in the ranks, acting like they're one of us but they're not. I know who some of them are, others I only suspect, so I won't say."

"None of this is very comforting."

Otis grinned as he stood and dropped a five on the table. "I should feel responsible for talking you into joining here instead of Seattle, but who would have guessed you would do this well?"

"Yeah, so well that I'm told by people in the know have told me I have a bull's eye on my back. Thanks, Joel," Hitchcock said, sarcasm in his tone.

"You're welcome, little brother."

# CHAPTER TWENTY-TWO
## Preludes to Adventure

LIKE A SMILE from above, a typical gray May morning became a clear, balmy, Bahama-like day. As the day wore on, the bright warmth drew office and shop workers outdoors for a few wistful peeks at the sun and feel its warmth.

Detectives remembered witnesses they had to interview and headed for the city's lakeside parks, hoping to find them there. Patrol and Traffic officers cruised the shores of Lake Washington and Lake Sammamish. Even Captain Delstra could take no more of staring at sunshine from his office window.

Across from the Bellevue side of Lake Sammamish, young moms with toddlers swarmed into the state park to enjoy the warmth of the sun.

Two hours later, the teletype machine in Records suddenly clattered to life after hours of silence. Something told clerk Patty Hooper to read it instead of waiting until more messages came in. She handed it to her supervisor, Police Matron Lola Maxwell. "It's marked urgent," she said.

Lola read it quickly and handed it back. "Captain Delstra needs to see this. If he's in a meeting, interrupt him."

"What about the chain of command?"

"No time. County needs help now."


A DOZEN OUTLAW bikers had taken over Lake Sammamish State Park. Wearing denim or black leather vests with gang colors on the back, Wellington boots and bandannas, they rode loud Harleys with ape-hanger handlebars. They laughed as they roared along the water's edge scattering young families like flocks of seagulls.

Delstra united his men with two deputies, two state troopers and an officer from Issaquah PD. They herded the bikers from the beach and the picnic areas to the gravel parking lot. Officers shut off the engines of any biker who refused to do so. County deputies arrested three on confirmed outstanding warrants. Onlookers cheered as tow trucks arrived to haul their Harleys away.

Delstra beckoned Tom Sherman to him. "We're gonna boot the rest of these pukes out of here in a few minutes. I want to make sure they don't enter our city on their way to Seattle. Set up a roadblock at the I-90 exit to 104th. Use your shotgun to show 'em you mean business. Shoot their machines if that's what it takes to keep them out of Bellevue. Go—go now."

Sherman sped Code Two to the last Bellevue exit. He left his overhead flashing light on and stopped on the gravel shoulder. He exited his patrol car and waited, holding his shotgun at port arms. Within minutes two bikers who had been at the state park arrived. Sherman blocked their path.

"I'm under orders to use force if necessary to keep you from entering Bellevue. Ride on."

The lead biker was grizzly and heavyset, but his fat was the hard gunnery-sergeant type, not desk-jockey flab. Crude prison-made tattoos covered his hands and forearms and the sides of his bull neck. Salt-and-pepper hair under a Nazi style helmet, beard of the same color, filthy jeans, he wore a silver wallet chain fastened to a belt loop. The back of his denim vest bore gang colors. A change of breeze direction blew the smells of body odor and grease across the ten feet to Sherman.

Two more bikers positioned themselves on either side of the leader, revving their motors.

"You can't do that," the outlaw leader said, testing Sherman's resolve.

*Click-clack!* With a cold stare Sherman jacked a round into the chamber of his shotgun and took aim at the front wheel of the lead biker's Harley. "I'm under orders to shoot your machines if you try to enter our city. Walk or ride to Seattle—it's all the same to me," he said as he flicked the safety off. "You've got one chance to leave before I shoot."

The only visible clue to Sherman's physical prowess when he was in uniform were the muscles and veins in his neck and hands. The rest of him looked gaunt under long sleeves. A former Army Ranger and war veteran, Sherman was soldier enough to shoot as ordered and let the chips fall where they will.

Without a word the lead biker raised his arm and pointed west. The four outlaws roared two-by-two back to the westbound I-90 onramp.

† † †

MEANWHILE, ONE HUNDRED sixty-five miles across the state, two young Bellevue entrepreneurs Rick Milford and Terry Gordon filled out applications to hold a rock festival in the desert between the towns of Odessa and Marlin in Grant County. Without waiting for permit approval, they publicized the event as *Sunrise 71* in the Seattle news outlets, set to occur June 18-20. They touted it as "the Woodstock of the West."

*The Odessa Record* pictured a sign taped on the window of a downtown business. The accompanying story reported:

> *The status remains indefinite as to the 'festival' announced for June 18-20 on the outskirts of Marlin. Law enforcement officials have expressed concern as to how to manage an influx of 50,000 or more people (apparently the*

*estimate of attendance had been scaled down from the promoters' figure of a week before). A formal application under a new state law (to hold the festival) was made to Grant County commissioners, but no action had been announced as of The Record's press time on Wednesday afternoon.*

Before the Grant County commissioners could meet, streams of hippie-type festival-seekers in hand-painted VW buses and old cars drifted into the town of Marlin like locusts ahead of the main swarm. Some pitched tents in city parks or on private lawns, while others slept in their cars.

Like closing the barn doors after the livestock left, the Grant County Commissioners finally refused to issue a permit to hold the festival, citing lack of adequate sanitation facilities and security.

Their decision was too little and too late. Swarms of rowdy festival goers had already overwhelmed the town, intent on a rock festival, permit or no permit, with more pouring in as the hours wore on.

In desperation, the county issued the injunction the police could enforce. The die was cast. Tensions mounted on both sides as attorneys for the frantic promoters filed appeals and crowds poured in every hour. Angry shopkeepers in Marlin mobbed the Sheriff's Office with complaints of their businesses being overrun by unruly crowds.

† † †

A POLICE MATRON knocked on Captain Delstra's door and handed him a teletype. "The Grant County Sheriff's Office is pleading for help from Western Washington police agencies," she said.

Delstra stroked his mustache as he read the teletype, then called Sergeant Breen into his office. "Read this, Jack."

Breen read the teletype, then looked inquiringly at Delstra. "Okay?"

"Have you heard about this?"

"I have. My oldest is a sophomore at Central Washington. She told me Junior Cadillac and another group called Dan Hicks and The Hotlicks will be there. Junior Cadillac by itself can draw crowds of four figures."

"Dan Hicks and The Hotlicks?" Delstra snorted good-humoredly. "Now I know I'm getting old!"

"They'll tear up those little farming towns, Erik, to say nothing of the violence biker gangs like the Bandidos or the Gypsy Jokers will bring when they show up to provide security."

"Yeah, I get that," Delstra mused.

"A rock festival spiraled out of control in Pierce County last year. Even with help from Tacoma PD, county deputies the fights, assaults on officers, rapes, felony-level drugs, and property damage went unchecked for days."

"I saw it on the news," Delstra said. "Out in the sticks somewhere, as I recall."

"This'll be worse because the Grant County Sheriff lacks the manpower to handle even a third of the crowds headed their way. Question is, can we legally help them?"

"It so happens we can," Delstra affirmed. "Two years ago, the state passed an inter-governmental cooperation act, which permits counties and cities to contract services to assist each other in emergencies where more manpower is needed."

"Well? Are we, I mean, are you...?" Breen asked.

"I want the same four officers you sent to restore order at the Trunk Lid last fall," Delstra said. "Pick four more men from our tactical squad. Tell Bill Harris to pick two men from Traffic. Tell them to pack for a five-day trip and meet me here at eight sharp tomorrow morning. Make ready enough jumpsuits, long batons, tear gas, mace and helmets for everybody, including you and me. There will be twelve of us."

† † †

AS THE TELETYPE from Bellevue PD arrived on Grant County Sheriff Ralph Hall's desk pledging support, Hitchcock snuck over to the Pancake Corral after shift briefing. Allie was busy with the usual noontime crowd. She was surprised to see him. He took her aside and explained the details.

"*You* want to go, or you wouldn't be here, honey."

"Stanford is still out and about."

"It's a huge honor to be hand-picked–you're not on the tactical squad, yet you've been chosen. It means you're one of the few. It'll be a feather in your cap the rest of your career."

"But–"

She cast a nervous glance at her customers as she put her hands on her hips "Who bought me a gun and taught me to shoot? I'm looking at him! Go! Trevor and I'll stay at my mom's. We'll be fine–we have Jamie with us, and my brothers live nearby. The guys will patrol the house while we're away."

He hesitated.

"Tell Jack Breen you're going," she said as she went back to her customers.

He smiled as he made his way back to his cruiser.

# CHAPTER TWENTY-THREE
## The Grant County Expedition

EAGER FOR ACTION and glad to escape the confines of the city on a rare out-of-town mission, an odd silence prevailed as ten hand-picked officers took their seats, four to a car, like strangers waiting to be introduced.

The threat of rain hung low in the early morning air as the caravan of three unmarked cars led by Captain Delstra headed east on Highway 10, recently renamed Interstate 90. The temperature continued cooling as they passed the towns of Issaquah and North Bend and ascended the heavily forested foothills, leaving the city stifle behind.

Otis and Hitchcock rode quietly in the back seat as the morning sun broke through the clouds when the caravan crossed the summit of Snoqualmie Pass into the semi-arid regions of Eastern Washington.

While the traffic officers in the front seat chatted quietly, Otis relived summers spent roaming the vast ranges of the Eastern Cascades with his cousin Eric. The living off the land they did, fishing, foraging and hunting for food prepared them for future missions with Special Forces units in Southeast Asia. He thought about the notes he made then, about encounters with wild animals and chance meetings with hermits, mountain men, sheepherders and prospectors, seeking shelter from a storm in a snow hole, and being charged by a bear with her cubs would one day become a book.

Hitchcock's mind dwelt upon Allie and Trevor until they passed the forests where he hunted with his father. Memories of himself and his father came rushing back, of hammering tent stakes into the ground, campfire meals, shivering beneath wool blankets, cold breakfasts followed by stalking the woods at break of dawn, rifles in hand, dressing and packing out a quartered elk or an antlered buck back to camp.

† † †

AS THE SCENERY changed from forest to desert, Boothe Stapp removed his shades and turned around in the front passenger seat to face Hitchcock.

Stapp, in his early thirties, had been "released" from two other police departments before coming to Bellevue. His blond hair, stocky build and striking similarity to the movie actor Robert Redford enabled him to seduce uncountable numbers of women, married or single, young or old. He cut a dashing appearance in his motorcycle uniform with bloused riding pants, gleaming black riding boots, and dark aviator shades.

Married three times, a womanizer without boundaries, Stapp fed his ego by seducing married women. He wasn't joking when he warned officers who had beautiful wives, *"Don't trust me with your wife."*

Rumors flew in the Department that he had affairs with women while on duty. His only credit as an officer was his skill as baton instructor for new officers and members of Captain Delstra's tactical squad.

"So, you missed the riot when they tried to shut down the Federal Courthouse in Seattle, Hitchcock," he sneered.

Hitchcock knew nothing about Stapp's reputation and had no prior dealings with him. "Wish I had been. I was in the academy," he said innocently. "What was it like?"

"They had us waiting in the courthouse lobby, on the ground floor-with teams from other departments," Stapp said as if to a child.

"We had orders to repel the demonstrators if they broke through SPD's lines. Through the windows we watched the mob come at SPD with rocks, bottles, chains, clubs, everything but the kitchen sink. SPD met them head-on, cracked heads and made a lot of arrests. The mob outnumbered the Seattle bulls. We knew that if it got past the Seattle bulls, we might die, but they didn't."

"I read about it. The *Seattle Star* seemed fairly objective, but the *Post Intelligencer* sided with the rioters, claiming SPD used excessive force," Hitchcock recalled, oblivious to Stapp's condescending attitude.

"You're the only one of us on this mission who's wet behind the ears, Hitchcock," Stapp sneered.

Hitchcock said nothing.

"The rest of us are veterans. I don't see why you're with us when you haven't had training. I hear you're quite the hot dog in Patrol, but I'm concerned you won't—"

"Shut up, Stapp," Otis interrupted with menace in his voice. "One more word from you and we pull over and I'll time how long you last against Roger. Five to ten seconds, maybe. In the short time he's been here, he's made more arrests and seized more dope than any four officers combined. Worry about yourself like the rest of us do. Let's see, how many citizen complaints are in your file? How many times have you been on the carpet in the Chief's office? And how many departments before ours gladly let you go? Three? Four? One more word, playboy, we stop and go no further until you fight Roger—or me."

Stapp's face reddened. Hitchcock was silent, taken aback by Stapp's animosity toward him and his dread of Otis.

"Scared?" Otis said. "You should be. Keep your mouth shut, face the windshield, or we pull over now, and see who's who. It won't make us late, either."

Like a spanked puppy, Stapp turned around, put on his dark aviator sunglasses to hide behind and sulked without another word for the rest of the trip.

† † †

THE THREE-CAR CARAVAN passed hippies packed into beater cars and hand-painted VW vans as they drove into the small farming town of Ephrata. Detachments from fifteen counties and fourteen cities, including thirty-eight state troopers in tactical gear arrived at the Sheriff's Office, bringing the total number of outside lawmen to two hundred sixty.

Sheriff Ralph Hall deputized all sworn personnel and gave commission cards and portable radios.

"Thank you all for coming" he said. "These crowds from the Coast already have us heavily outnumbered. Our citizens are being threatened. Trespassing and property damage is out of control and getting worse. They've taken over our parks, refused to leave, and more are arriving even though we put the word out that the festival is cancelled. So, do whatever it takes to protect our people and their property."

The sheriff hesitated, then continued. "Just so you understand the caliber of people we're dealing with: The Caterpillar D-8 bulldozer they used to clear the grounds was stolen from Oregon. We arrested the two men involved. Both had felony warrants out for them in

Oregon. The D-8 is being held for the owner. So, you better believe there's no way in hell we're gonna allow a rock festival here."

THE GYMNASIUM AT Wilson Creek Elementary served as barracks and command center for the visiting troops. Grateful members of the community set up sleeping cots and kept long tables of food and refreshments fully stocked.

† † †

CROWDS OF UNKEMPT flower children kept pouring into town in VW buses and cars marked with hand-painted peace symbols and slogans like MAKE LOVE NOT WAR and CHE, after the murderous Cuban Revolutionary Che Guevarra.

It didn't matter to them that the permit to hold the festival had been denied and the promoters announced the festival was canceled. Festivalgoers removed the barricades and quickly turned the site into an outdoor toilet and garbage pit. Determined to have a rock festival, they cranked up the volume on transistor or car radios and set to drinking and smoking pot.

† † †

ARRIVING ON SPUTTERING, snarling Harleys was the intended security team hired by the promoters, the Bandidos, a feared motorcycle gang, rivals of the Hells Angels.

Modern-day barbarians, bearded, long-haired, unwashed, muscular, armed and patriotic, unlike their hippie counterparts, they meant business. Many of them bore the hard stamp of prison time on their faces.

Three factions collided in an environment free of social restraints. Faction one, over a thousand sheep-like, soft, spoiled, self-centered kids, guarded by faction two, packs of human wolves—hardened, predatory outlaw bikers, tattooed, armed and violent. Faction three was society's attack animals in blue—most of whom had wartime military experience and little tolerance for either the sheltered, selfish babies in adult bodies or hardcore outlaws. They too were free from the usual societal restraints. The volatile chemistry between the three groups represented the growing fissures in American society.

The "make love not war" crowd taunted the men in blue and tried to befriend the wolves the promoters hired to protect them. The males among them whined or stood helplessly by when the bikers helped themselves to their women, dope and beer and thumped on them if they objected or wore the American flag on the seat of their pants.

The veteran-cops, fewer in number, were trained, experienced, disciplined, and ready for war. Let loose in a surreal no-man's-land, they waded boldly into hostile crowds, fueled by memories of being taunted with flag desecration, verbal insults, spit, and injuries from having rocks and bottles thrown at them.

† † †

THE EIGHTEEN-HUNDRED-ACRE festival site was just outside the town of Marlin, population less than fifty souls, about thirty miles east of Ephrata. Except for a low swale of green in the middle, where the rock bands would play, and a few clumps of sagebrush, the site was a dry, red-rock Martian-scape where reddish dust devils arose with the slightest puff of wind.

Delstra and his men struggled against the effects of dehydration under their jeans and T-shirts overlaid with dark blue full-body jumpsuits and riot helmets with visors and no air conditioning during twelve-hour shifts.

Early on, over a hundred youths penetrated the planned festival site in cars and vans. Many openly drank wine and beer and smoked marijuana when Grant County deputies cordoned the area off and blocked the road going in.

Besides the fecal stench made worse in the heat, swarms of flies pestered the troops as they made seizures of drugs in various forms, and alcohol, mainly beer. Deputies arrested nine young men in the first hour for drug possession, disorderly conduct and drunk in public.

Because of limited jail space, sheriff's deputies cited and released festivalgoers as much as possible. While the deputies were busy, dozens of other festivalgoers snuck past the Sheriff's roadblock, entering the site via the roadless desert. As they came, more out-of-town detachments of officers arrived. Already the Grant County Jail was overcrowded.

† † †

AT THE END of their first twelve-hour shift, the Bellevue detachment returned to barracks, tired from hours of standing guard in the heat, the tension of almost continuous crowd control and enforcing eviction orders without letup, and the stench and the dust.

After a few hours' rest, the men had time on their hands before their next shift. They had a town to explore, one they would probably never visit again. With a few bucks burning holes in their jeans, some went prospecting for strange women and adventure, while others poked around town or stayed put.

By the second day the festival site was clear of people, but not restored. The trash and the piles of human feces would be removed later. Instead of going home, the crowds of festivalgoers and outlaw bikers spread out in every direction, determined to party somewhere else. Citizen calls for help continued to pour in. Alcohol, drugs and drug paraphernalia were seized in massive amounts as the crowds spread out to farms, city parks and private property. More arrests were made for assaulting officers.

† † †

THAT NIGHT, HITCHCOCK, with Captain Delstra and seven other Bellevue officers manned a roadblock in Odessa, a town near Marlin on the second night. For the first three hours vehicles approaching the roadblock obeyed the orders to turn back without incident, verbal taunts were sometimes shouted as they left.

About midnight, four young men in a beat-up VW van pulled up.

Delstra approached the driver. "Restricted area. Turn around and go back," he commanded.

The driver, a young white male with shoulder length dark hair, wearing a tank top with a peace symbol hanging from a leather thong around his neck, cursed and flipped his middle finger at Delstra as he rolled forward at idle speed. The three others with him were males.

"Stop, I said!" Delstra shouted.

Those in the van shouted obscenities at Delstra as the van rolled forward, its front bumper pushing the wood barricade aside. Delstra sprayed the driver and everyone inside with mace until the canister was empty.

The van rolled to a stop. Hitchcock took a deep breath and held it. His eyes watered as he ripped open the passenger door, seized the closest passenger by the collar and yanked him onto the ground. He grabbed the next passenger in the same way.

Needing to step back for a breath, Otis ordered the

remaining passenger out. He complied, wheezing and rubbing his eyes. The others were on the ground, coughing, cursing, gasping, rubbing their eyes. Delstra arrested the driver for failure to obey a lawful order, the others in the van were charged with minors in possession of alcohol. The van was impounded.

An hour later a muscular loud-mouthed youth, long-haired, barefoot and bare-chested, got out of his car and stood nose-to-nose with Delstra. "You pigs can't stop us or kick us out. We've got rights!" Hitchcock positioned himself behind Delstra, holding his long riot baton at port arms.

The youth's bravado melted when Delstra, holding his thirty-six-inch baton in black-gloved hands, took a half-step forward and head-butted him with his helmet visor. "Your rights, sonny? What are you gonna do with 'em?"

The youth stepped back. He checked his forehead for blood. Delstra kept advancing, with Hitchcock two steps behind.

"Hey pig–uhh–you can't–"

*Whack!* Delstra head-butted him again. The kid touched his hand to his forehead again and saw blood on his fingertips. He clenched his fist, but seeing Delstra's chiseled anger in the refracted lights which said *take your best shot* without words, baton at the ready produced an instant change of mind. He backed away. Delstra followed, stepping on the offender's bare feet.

Hitchcock turned his head when he heard car doors open. Two of the youth's friends were about to intervene. Otis, helmet visor down, baton held at port arms, hard eyes drawing mental Xs on their torsos—marking where he would strike, never said a word. He didn't need to. Besides his helmet, visor and jumpsuit, Otis wore black leather gauntlet gloves with powdered lead sewn into the knuckles that gripped a thirty-six-inch riot baton.

The two stopped and stared at Otis before they exited the car. Otis took a half-step closer. With a solemn shake of his head that said "don't," they stayed in the car without a word.

Another carload of loud young men pulled up to intervene and were met by the rest of Delstra's men. Upon seeing helmeted officers and the dance in the dust between Delstra and a hippie male walking backwards with a bleeding forehead, they left.

THROUGHOUT TWO DAYS and nights, Hitchcock either made arrests himself or backed up his brother officers as they stopped and scuffled with carloads of festivalgoers on the roads and at roadblocks, seizing alcohol, drugs, and drug paraphernalia and arrested occupants for warrants.

Returning to the barracks, he called Allie collect from a pay phone to reassure himself that she and Trevor and Jamie were alright. Hearing her voice for just a minute refreshed him.

Before sleep overtook him, he wondered how Randy was holding up, if Mike Smith had come around, and if the prowler who escaped from him last fall was back on the prowl for new victims...

# CHAPTER TWENTY-FOUR
## The Shift to Chelan County

CAPTAIN DELSTRA BURST into the barracks at sunrise, shouting "We're being called to Chelan County! Everybody up!"

Hitchcock struggled to open his eyes. He looked around the room, thinking for a moment he was back in Army boot camp.

They ate and packed quickly. A caravan of marked and unmarked police cars and vans headed north through the desert on State Highway 28 to Chelan County in the north central Cascade Mountains.

The sunbathed orchards, desert dunes, scattered pines and the Columbia River sparkled as they crossed the bridge into Wenatchee, the self-proclaimed Apple Capitol of the World, and the county seat.

Sheriff Dick Nickell issued commission cards and assigned portable radios with special call signs as he told them to police the county's parks and shut down the rock festival wherever it may be happening.

Fearing arrest for outstanding warrants and seizure

of motorcycles made up of stolen parts, outlaw bikers hired to be security personnel, rode across trackless desert to Chelan County, heeding the rumor that the State Patrol had up a checkpoint on Highway 28, the route from Ephrata to Wenatchee.

† † †

IT WAS SUNNY and hot, and large crowds had already overrun the resort at Deep Lake by the time Delstra and his men arrived. The action got started right away when some young men Hitchcock recognized from Grant County began throwing rocks and bottles at them along with the usual obscenities from the top of a hill.

Delstra formed a V-wedge with himself at the tip, and led the charge at a run straight up the hill, head-on into a barrage of rocks, bottles. Police batons were swung with telling effect.

From the top of the hill, Delstra looked down at the bottom of the other side where another crowd of thirty or more hippie-types were camped unlawfully. On a bullhorn he ordered them out of the park. They cursed and flipped him off. He lobbed a tear gas grenade. It rolled into a tent, dispersing the occupants as a detachment from Tacoma PD moved in.

All day police commanders coordinated to set up new roadblocks and checkpoints on the run. Roving patrol cars initiated stops and made arrests as they did in Grant County.

† † †

HAVING GONE WITHOUT showers in the heat for four days, body odor preceded the festivalgoers and bikers by four feet.

As their funds ran out, many resorted to shoplifting food from grocery stores, or skipping out on their bill at restaurants. To keep partying and make it back home, others refueled at gas stations and drove off without paying.

More cops in riot gear arrived from Grant County. Unaccustomed to being outnumbered, outlaw bikers grumbled but left as ordered, but not without provocation. Tacoma officers jammed their batons into the spokes of their Harleys as they left as a taunt and a dare to fight, which none accepted.

After two almost round-the-clock days of nonstop crowd-chasing, Sunrise 71 was over.

On their way back, Delstra led the troops through the forest to the historic lumber and coal mining town of Roslyn, where he treated all the men to beer and burgers at The Brick Saloon, the oldest tavern in the state, established in 1889. All that is, except for Stapp, whom he posted to guard their cars. He was given a cold hamburger and a paper cup of water when the men left The Brick.

# CHAPTER TWENTY-FIVE
## Winding Down

THE SPOILED, HOSTILE crowds of his own generation troubled Hitchcock on his way home. He understood the mutual dislike between policemen and outlaw bikers, which he viewed as an ancient traditional soldier versus barbarian rivalry.

The hippies represented accelerating breakdown of societal mores and morals that would end America if it continued. Policing in super-clean Bellevue gave only glimpses of the spreading decline. Though most of his generation lived as peacefully and productively as any earlier generation, the size and lawlessness of these crowds couldn't be ignored.

Officers had been vaguely aware of reporters and news cameramen watching them in the distance. Before the dust settled, newspapers across the state released photographs and stories of the many confrontations between lawmen and crowds of festivalgoers with headlines like COMBINED FORCE OF LAWMEN CHOKING OFF FESTIVAL, and FACING THE MUSIC:

CALL IT A LAWMAN'S CONVENTION.

When the police pushed the crowds out of Grant County, and hundreds migrated to Chelan County, the headlines read: DEPUTIES CLOSE OFF PARK TO "ROLLING" ROCK FESTIVAL. When the conflicts ended, one headline summed it up : SUNRISE 71 SINKS IN THE EAST.

The Seattle papers ignored incidents involving the Bandidos, the outlaw biker gang the promoters hired to provide security. The gang's sexual assaults on women and beating up and stealing from their hippie boyfriends were ignored. Those who were arrested on warrants, or the stolen Caterpillar DC-8 grader they used to prepare the festival grounds were never mentioned. The focus of the Seattle papers was to smear the police. In the mind of the public.

What mattered to the cops and the communities they rescued was that they had restored order. Within police circles, *Sunrise 71* was dubbed *Sunset 71*.

THE MEN IN the car with Hitchcock grew quiet when the steep descent from the Snoqualmie Pass summit into Western Washington began. The scenery went from sun-washed mountains dotted with pine trees to sheet metal skies above thick forests of Douglas Firs draped over the steep slopes like a shaggy green shawl.

The hit song *I am Woman* sung by Helen Reddy came on the radio.

Wooten turned the dial before the song finished. He smiled when he heard Tammy Wynette singing *Stand By Your Man.*

"That's better," Otis said.

"We're better prepared now to handle anti-war protests because of this experience," Wooten said when the song finished.

"They'll be over next year," Otis predicted.

"What makes you say that? Will the war be over?"

"Nixon will end the draft. When he does, the protests will stop, but the war will drag on."

"So, you're saying the anti-war movement is really just an anti-draft movement?"

Otis nodded. "You'll see."

† † †

THE OUT-OF-TOWN MISSION had been a moral holiday for some of the married men. The unwritten code of loyalty precluded mention of the peccadilloes they had with local women.

Hitchcock didn't judge his brother officers, but their expectation of him to guard their secret exploits made him feel compromised. He appreciated that Otis and Sherman were true to their wives. They joined him in working out in the school gym, hitting the taverns and diners and turning in early. Walker was single.

# CHAPTER TWENTY-SIX
## Homecomings

LOVING ARMS SEEMED to open to Hitchcock when he pulled into the driveway. He smiled as he stepped into the aromas of dinner on the stove and bread in the oven. Trevor ran to him gleefully yelling "Daddy's home!" Jamie woofed and wagged his tail in welcome, and Allie slipped her arms around him.

"I've got four days off, courtesy of the City," he told Allie between kisses.

"Good. Dinner is ready. Can you guess what we're having?"

He closed his eyes and sniffed. "Beef stew?"

"Thy wife be Irish, sir. She makes only Mulligan stew," Allie said in her best Irish brogue.

"Yah, your Viking lover will eat anything you put in front of him."

"Thy feast be ready, m'lord," Allie said as she led him to the prepared table. "How was your trip?" she asked as he sat down.

"Like looking into the jaws of a poisonous snake."

"Oh?"

He tasted the stew, then nodded his pleasure. "I hate to tell you, but my pipe dreams about becoming a hippie carpenter living in a tree house after I retire are gone."

"I can't see you with long hair and a beard," she laughed.

"I just might surprise you one of these years," he smiled.

"The customers and the crew at the Corral followed the news accounts in the *P.I.* and the *Times* and updated me about it every day."

"It might seem heroic to some, but in reality, this was just crowd control on the run with a few scuffles, no real battles."

"Oh?"

"They didn't come to protest anything or do battle with us. They were just pampered kids out of town, away from mommy and daddy. They were free to act like preschoolers on a playground. They got drunk, got high and got laid while their parents were home, paying their bills.

"It didn't compare with the shutdown of the federal courthouse and the freeway last year. They came armed with shields, clubs, chains, rocks and bottles, intent on doing battle with the police, which is exactly what they did. Big difference."

"Were you involved in either of those?"

He shook his head as he reached across the table for a slice of homemade bread and buttered it.

"I was in the academy both times. Even so, seeing the size and the defiance of the crowds made me aware of the social decay that's setting in."

"This doesn't sound good," Allie said, frowning.

"What worries me is where this breaking down will take us as a country," he went on, "and I also wonder why the news media favors rioters and protestors and smear and villainize us like its policy. Because of their influence even law-abiding people curse and spit on those who protect them now."

"Did anyone spit on you?"

He shook his head. "Not this time, but a hippie punk spit on my uniform in the San Francisco airport when I was on my way home to be discharged."

"What did you do?"

"Left him laying where he fell," he shrugged.

She grinned. "My dad taught us a four-word saying which applies to every phase in life on this earth."

"Tell me."

"'This too will pass.'"

"Hmm," he nodded. "I like it. It's got universal application," he said. "With four days off right before my regular weekend, I'll have six days for us to take a day trip somewhere and catch up on a few things around the house and the garden. Since you're working tomorrow, I'm going to rest."

"Yes, honey. Rest, because I volunteered your services to help a neighbor for about three hours, day after tomorrow. Once you learn why, you'll want to go."

"Tell me in the morning."

"Don't you want me to tell you now?"

He smiled as he slipped his arm around her waist. "*You* are all I want tonight."

EVERY MEMBER OF the twelve-man team was welcomed back but one. Boothe Stapp found his tiny starter home dark and empty. A shut-off notice from the power company was taped to the front door. His wife left only the bed and the kitchen table, on which was an unstamped envelope from a Seattle law firm. It meant the end of his third time at bat.

Stapp took a bottle of Chivas Regal from the cupboard above the fridge, sat on the bed and poured a glass of the fiery amber liquid.

Thoughts of being humiliated by Otis in front of Hitchcock and another traffic officer dominated his embittered thinking by the time he finished his second glass. He poured a third. Otis exposed him as a coward, and twice Delstra caught him backing down in the face of confrontation. Delstra and Otis he dreaded, but his hatred for Hitchcock burned as pure as a flame.

As he began his fourth glass of scotch, his rage, his anguish boiled over to primal screams which shook the windows of his little house. As he drank, he brooded darkly and swore to get revenge on Hitchcock. He finally passed out as the first light of dawn seeped through the windows.

Unlike the other officers who went on the expedition, Stapp didn't take the next day off. He went to work, wearing his dark blue uniform with silver trim, and gleaming knee-high black motorcycle boots, dark Ray-Ban shades. He radioed himself in service and headed for a rambler house in lower Eastgate. As he hoped, the man's Ford F-250 pickup was gone. He parked his Harley Road King in the carport next to the wife's red Plymouth Satellite in the carport.

The young brunette woman smiled when she opened the door for him. She wore only a nightgown and he smiled back. "Welcome home, mighty hero. You must be tired after crushing all those hippies and their bikers."

"Never too tired to see you," he said. "Is he—?"

She opened the door wider. "Darrell is on a short workday. He just left. We only have an hour."

He snickered as he passed her husband on the street.

HEADING DOWNTOWN TO catch up on his quota of tickets before the month ended, Stapp set up on the busy corner of NE Street and 104th Avenue. He spotted a beautiful blonde woman driving by with kids in a late model gray Jeep Wagoneer, and followed her to her house on 98th Street. He stopped down the block and watched Allie Hitchcock take her kids into the house and return to unload her groceries.

When she went inside her house, Stapp cruised past the house and copied the license plate number.

# CHAPTER TWENTY-SEVEN
## Behind Closed Doors

THE SECRET MEETING at City Hall the next morning was grim. "The direction this police department is headed in must be stopped," the chief assistant to the city manager announced.

Her face was a picture of frustration as she looked around the room, seeing only somber faces. "The tactical squad Captain Delstra formed in violation of our orders to the Chief participated in riot control twice in Seattle. Then, the line officers formed a bargaining unit, a guild, they call it, which was approved by the IRS, so now we must recognize and negotiate with their guild. And we'll have to pay overtime at time and a half, and a fair wage," she said.

"Ouch," one member said.

The others in attendance sat in sullen silence.

"Worse yet," the chief assistant went on, "*Captain* Delstra has gone rogue, raising the public profile with his macho adventuring in Eastern Washington. Since the *current* chief is no help to us and we can't fire him, I'm open to suggestions."

An intern from the University raised his hand.

"Let's hear it," the chief assistant said.

"According to the *Seattle PI,* for years, district cars each had an 'eat spot' where they received free meals and coffee. Same for the walking beats. For the restaurants, cops dropping by at any time ensured they had an effective deterrence against robberies. Over time, the cops' appetite went beyond free food. A couple times they didn't have time to eat, so they collected the price of a meal instead. That led to payoffs."

"What does it have to do with Bellevue?" a senior aide asked.

"We can use that history here. Our downstairs source says a paternal relationship exists between the Seattle and Bellevue departments. It would destroy your department's credibility," the intern replied, grinning.

A senior assistant shook her head. "In the ten years I've lived here, no Bellevue officer has ever been seen or accused of doing any of those things. What you propose would make us false witnesses."

"So what?" the intern scoffed. "They're called pigs for a reason. Let's ride the coattails of what's going on in Seattle. My girlfriend is a waitress at a new diner downtown called Rusty's. She tells the cooks when an order is for a cop so they can spit or blow their noses into the food."

Some at the table made faces at each other, chuckled

and shook their heads, but no one said anything.

The intern continued. "My girlfriend'll tell the pigs the bill is on the house. Since some of them flirt with her when they come in, they should take the bait. Once they do, we can call the news people to go undercover and expose them to the public."

"What you're talking about is unethical and illegal. The legal term is entrapment," the senior aide said. "The CM dislikes police, but he won't allow anything illegal or deliberate character assassination. The CM knows, as I do, their new guild president would not only blow the whistle on us to the press, but they would also sue us in court–which would be the undoing of everyone here. We want *legal* ideas to stop the path this Department is taking. Come up with something by the end of July."

# CHAPTER TWENTY-EIGHT
## Taking Care of Business

THE AFTERNOON WAS hot at Lake Hills Park a week after the demise of *Sunrise 71* when a gathering of young families with their little ones came to picnic and socialize. Toddlers pushed their trikes to the top of a grassy mound and squealed happily as they rode to the bottom.

Four shirtless young males, smoking cigarettes, two of them carrying large brown paper bags, strolled into the park. They sat on the grass next to the swing set where grandparents were playing with the two and three-year-olds. They cracked open brown bottles of beer and flipped the caps at the kids.

"No drinking in a public park," scolded one grandfather.

"Shove it, old man!" they scoffed as they hoisted their beers to him in a mocking manner. They leered at each other and laughed as nervous parents removed their kids from the swing set.

Tension continued to mount when four more

teenage males of similar description arrived, bringing more beer. They began smoking pot, pointing and laughing at the clumsy efforts of an infant stumbling as he tried to walk. The two fathers glared at the troublemakers but said nothing as their families withdrew to the picnic tables. The long-haired group became louder in their laughter, sprinkled with shouted four-letter obscenities.

The dads confronted the drinkers about their language in the presence of women and children. Insults led to shoving and shouting. One of the grandfathers walked to the nearest house and asked that the police be called.

Lee Wooten and Ray Packard, veterans of Sunrise 71, were dispatched.

A rock bounced off Wooten's cruiser when he arrived. The families gathered their little ones and hustled out of the park. The rock-and-bottle throwers took the top of the small hill and called down taunts and obscene insults at the officers. Marked cars from Districts Five and Six arrived. Wooten got his riot helmet and a handful of plastic ties as extra handcuffs from the trunk of his patrol car.

"We'll form a flying wedge," Wooten said, "with me at the tip, two of you behind on either side of me, Ray covering our backs. We'll arrest 'em all if we can; figure out the charges later."

Obscenities and taunts were shouted from the hill as

the four helmeted officers ran head-on into a barrage of rocks and beer bottles. Two fled at the sight of an organized charge of baton-wielding uniforms. Six were fought, arrested and taken to the ER in handcuffs.

Two hours later, Captain Delstra watched from his window as two patrol cars backed into the prisoner loading bays and six cursing, bandaged, handcuffed young men were pulled from the back seats and marched up the steps and down the hall.

Sergeant Breen appeared in Delstra's office door, papers in hand. "Looks like our adventure in Eastern Washington is paying dividends already, Jack."

"Their takeover of a park was short-lived," Breen said. "The only injuries are theirs. Front desk is getting phone calls of thanks from citizens who were there."

"Music to my ears," Delstra smiled.

# CHAPTER TWENTY-NINE
## Master and Commander

THE LAST SECOND shift cruiser came in and parked at the station. The officer scowled as he got out and grabbed his briefcase.

"What's up?" Otis inquired.

"Dead as a doornail all day. Hope it improves for you guys," he replied as he trudged away.

The squad radioed themselves in service.

Dispatch came on the air: *"Three Zero Seven and Three Zero Four, respond Code Two to Herfy's in Crossroads—a crowd of thirty juveniles trespassing, blocking and creating altercations with customers."*

Thirty or more rowdy teenage males were loitering around the new Herfy's burger franchise, yelling, smoking, throwing opened cans of pop across the parking lot at each other, blocking customer access to other adjacent fast-food joints.

Otis shouldered his way through the crowd. He contacted the Herfy's manager, a short, thin man in his thirties with glasses and thinning hair. "Under the law, you must tell trespassers to leave before anyone can be arrested, and they have to refuse. Did you tell them that?"

"I was afraid to," the manager replied.

Otis led the manager by the arm to the unruly crowd. "You are blocking customers!" He said in a tremulous voice as he stood next to Otis. "If you're not a paying customer, you are trespassing, so leave!!" He nervously looked at the crowd milling on all sides, snickering and scoffing. He took a deep breath and said, "I order all of you to leave at once or I'll charge you with trespassing!" The crowd, emboldened by the manager's shaking, stared at the manager, who glanced fearfully at Otis and went back inside.

Otis seized the nearest three youths. "You three are under arrest for trespassing."

A husky youth tried to shrug Otis off and collapsed when Otis pinched a nerve at the base of his neck. The crowd booed and jeered as Sherman pushed his way in to back up Otis. A tall kid, older than the others, twice tried to block Sherman as he helped Otis shove the three prisoners through the crowd and cram them into the back seat of Otis's cruiser.

Sherman waded back into the crowd and seized the kid who interfered. Otis called for more aid as Sherman placed two more loud-mouthed youths in his cruiser.

Walker responded and arrested a juvenile male for alcohol possession and trespassing as Otis and Sherman headed for the station with their prisoners.

Walker came on the air: "Three Zero Eight, Radio, assistance needed. A crowd of juveniles slashed my tires and removed my prisoners from the back of my car."

Hitchcock responded Code Three.

† † †

FIGURING THEY WOULD be called there the next night, Hitchcock and Walker went to Herfy's right after shift briefing. Otis and Sherman were dispatched there again for crowd control. The four met at the far edge of the parking lot, in full view of the crowd. They opened the trunks of their cruisers and put on their helmets and gloves and took up their thirty-six-inch batons.

They started toward the crowd side-by-side. Suddenly Sergeant Breen pulled up in a marked supervisor's cruiser. Captain Delstra, in short-sleeve uniform shirt, gold braid on his hat, got out and waded right into crowd.

Astonished, Hitchcock and the others with him closed in to defend the captain.

"Go home, kiddies or spend the night in the jail if you're old enough, or the Youth Center if you're not," Delstra ordered.

The crowd melted back in silence. Two of the older and bigger youths held their ground, staring at Delstra.

One scoffed at Delstra. "We have a right to—"

The heel of Delstra's palm slammed into his chest,

knocking him back, the one next to him got the same.

"Go home, sonny, or go to jail. I'm not asking."

The first kid Delstra pushed broke into tears. The crowd began leaving quietly as the second kid Delstra pushed apologized and left. In less than a minute the rest of the crowd was gone.

Hitchcock glanced through his helmet visor at Otis. "How come we can't do that?"

"We're not Erik Delstra," Otis said.

After Delstra's appearance, the loitering at Crossroads ended, and Hitchcock and the rest of the squad plunged into working their beats.

# CHAPTER THIRTY
## 200 Grain Pumpkins

IN SPIRIT, THE post-shift After-Hours Fellowship gatherings were akin to ancient tribal rituals in which the men of the tribe, young and old, squatted on the ground before the fire. Free from the restraints of their women, they ate, drank, bragged, joked and told stories far into the night.

The story the Fellowship talked about most when the booze flowed was of Hitchcock and Sherman shooting it out toe-to-toe with a drug-dealing pimp and his hench-woman who ambushed them from a stolen car. The Department supported Hitchcock and Sherman so well the line officers had nothing left to gripe about. It was like taking a bone from a dog.

It wasn't long before they found a new gripe.

"Did you guys hear about the SPD officer who was shot at by the driver of a carload of bad guys on Capitol Hill?" LaPerle asked as he took his first sip of whiskey.

The men shook their heads as they stared at LaPerle, drinks in hand, eager for a new secondhand adventure.

"The bad guys were stopped at a stoplight next to the patrol car. The driver opened fire on the patrol car for no reason. The officer, name of McDowell, piled out of his cruiser, jumped on the hood of the bad guy's car and emptied his revolver right through the windshield, killing the shooter. The others in the car gave up at once. If the same situation happened here, the officer would be dead," LaPerle said between sips of scotch.

"What do you mean?" Hitchcock asked, still sober, having decided to limit himself to one drink.

Frenchie LaPerle was the Fellowship's ballistics expert. He loaded practice ammunition for other officers and members of the Brass, Captain Delstra included. When Frenchie talked guns and ammo, they listened.

"Our duty ammo can't penetrate windshield glass," Frenchie said. "The loads are weak; the bullets are too heavy. SPD issues Super Vel ammo—one-hundred-grain hollow points which move at twelve hundred feet per second; very hot for .38 Special."

"Super Vels are what we got to shoot when we were in Seattle's academy. They went through windshield glass no problem," Hitchcock recalled.

"But what does our City make *us* use?" LaPerle stated. "Two-hundred-grain, round nose pumpkins, and I mean 'pumpkins' because they're twice the weight of Super Vels and move at half the velocity, or less. I evaluated our stuff and theirs on my chronograph."

Jason Allard was an Army explosive ordnance

specialist with a life-changing one-year tour in 'Nam under his belt, which he spent setting explosives for the enemy and disarming their bombs. Allard loved ballistics, bombs, booby traps, anything that goes bang. Like LaPerle, he freely gave his opinions with authority when he drank, asked for or not.

"Frenchie's right," Allard pontificated. "The loads we're stuck with might as well be renamed *widowmakers*. I carry Super Vels when I'm on duty. To hell with the pumpkins."

"The pumpkins did all right for Hitchcock and Sherman last fall, didn't they?" Walker said.

"They weren't firing *through* anything. The rear window was already blown out by Guyon's shotgun. Hitchcock's speed and accuracy—three shots to the head–1-2-3–put an end to him," LaPerle said.

"Only one result is possible, no matter the caliber, with *that* kind of shooting. And Tom drilled Guyon's whore in the driver seat right through the spine as she shot at Roger, saving Roger's life," Frenchie proclaimed, woozily beaming with pride.

"Would to Man Above that we're all able to shoot as well in an attack," Clive Brooks slurred, an admiring grin on his red face.

"Tom's rounds killed the other shooter after passing through the back seat," Hitchcock said.

"Even so, they're weak, slow loads. Why are we issued them? What's the logic?" Allard asked.

"LAPD issues slow-moving 158-grain ammo on the theory if an officer is disarmed, he will be less injured if he's shot with his own gun," LaPerle added.

"What a negative statement about the ammo you expect others to use," Otis said in a rueful manner.

"I know why we use pumpkin bullets," Brooks, the son of British immigrants, offered.

"Tell us," Walker said.

"Delstra told me that he and the Chief read about the British Army using that bullet weight successfully in their .38 Webley's in World War One. The longer, slower slug tumbled at lower velocities, making them equal to larger caliber slugs in stopping power but with low recoil. Supposedly that made them effective for close range fighting in the trenches. They continued to issue it during World War Two."

"They *would* be deadly if they really did tumble, but we're not soldiers fighting soldiers in trenches," LaPerle said. "We're cops, we need ammo that can penetrate car glass, wood, metal, sheetrock walls and still hit the bad guy. I propose we field test our load against the Super Vel."

Walker, well-oiled up by his third glass of scotch, liked the idea. "Yeah! And I know just the spot! I found an abandoned car deep in the woods on a dirt road below Somerset Hill. It's not a stolen. Our gunfights often involve vehicles, so let's field test the two loads on the junker—like now!"

Walker turned to Hitchcock as the others stood to leave. "Sorry, Roger. I was going to save this for us to shoot, as everybody in Dispatch knows we practice on slow nights at the city dump, but we should share the fun."

Six officers, their uniforms under civilian jackets, piled into three cars. Hitchcock led the way while Walker gave directions to the site through early rush hour traffic to the steep uphill grade of Somerset Drive for a quarter mile, then turned right on a narrow but level dirt road through a thick forest.

Almost a hundred yards along a dirt road from the paved street they came upon an early '60s light brown Rambler American, sans engine, wheels and rear axles. Everyone except Hitchcock, Otis and Sherman carried Super Vel ammo in their guns. LaPerle handed out cotton wads and empty .38 shell cases for ear protection.

They all faced the front to avoid ricocheting bullets as they took turns shooting at the windshield. Every round of issue ammo only smeared the glass.

"This is all the proof we need," Allard said, "our load can't even crack a curved windshield or penetrate flat door windows. God help us all."

Otis fired another round of department-issue ammo through the hole in the rear window into the back of the front seat. The bullet passed through the seat, making a round hole in the dash. It didn't tumble as the Brass claimed it would.

As expected, the Super Vel loads penetrated the windshield, door windows, doors and interior upholstery. The lighter, faster 110-grain hollow-point slugs expanded almost to the diameter of a dime when going through windshield glass and fragmented when going through car door metal without fail.

"Somebody grab that big piece of cardboard inside the car," Hitchcock said. "I want to try something."

From seven paces Hitchcock faced the sheet of cardboard and pulled out his double-barrel Derringer from his waistband holster. "This is loaded with our duty ammo, but the barrels are short," he told those standing behind him. "Let's see if the bullet tumbles."

He cocked the hammer and fired. Instead of a round hole in the cardboard the bullet left a gaping hole an inch in length. Surprised, Hitchcock turned to the others. "How about that! I'll shoot again to make sure."

The second round had the same effect.

"Now it makes sense," LaPerle said. "The four-inch barrels of our guns burn more powder, which builds velocity, so the bullet doesn't tumble. Also, our ammo is hotter than the British load which used a shorter case and a lighter powder charge, Thirty-Eight Revolver, I think it was called. So, a longer, heavier slug moving at less velocity *would* be more likely to tumble."

Walker checked his watch. "Hey! We've got time for another round at my place if we go now."

"Let's split," Brooks said. "With all the shooting

we've done, the houses around here will be calling in."

As the three-car caravan headed back to Walker's lair, they waved at the two black-and-white units heading Code Two toward the Somerset woods. Hitchcock turned to Walker as he drove. "It's a mistake for those guys to carry unauthorized ammo,' he said.

"Why?" Walker asked.

"The City will use it as an excuse to throw them to the wolves in a lawsuit."

Walker's eyes widened. "I never thought about that. But it's our butts on the line. What do we do, then?"

"Carry a backup gun, but loaded with pumpkins."

† † †

CAPTAIN DELSTRA STROKED his mustache and smiled a knowing smile when he read the request forms the civilian in charge of the armory brought him. All third shift officers were requesting replacement issue ammo on the same day.

"Shouldn't this request be looked into? A lot of calls came in about gun fire in the forest south of Somerset yesterday. Now all these guys on nights are suddenly out of ammo," the station officer asked.

"Nah," Delstra smirked as he handed back the request form with his signature. "Since we haven't had a range going on four years, the boys are doing what they can to stay alive, as they should. It's a different world out there, now."

# CHAPTER THIRTY-ONE
## There Ain't No Cure
## for the Summertime Blues

*Shift Briefing*
*7:45 P.M.*

HITCHCOCK AND THE rest of the squad watched Jack Breen at the podium, scowling and scratching his blond crew cut as his nicotine-stained fingers flipped through the latest bulletins, waiting for his raspy pack-and-a-half-a-day voice to tell them what was so bad.

"According to the latest Crime Analysis reports," Breen finally said, "commercial burglars are kicking our butts at night while we're chasing calls. The downtown is the hardest hit, but Districts Four and Seven are also getting hammered."

The officers were silent as Breen continued.

"The new M.O. is to listen to call in false emergencies at distant locations from where they plan to hit. They listen on their police scanners for responding units to arrive at the fake call, then hit their target and get out before we clear the scene."

"That explains why we had an unusual number of fake calls on the West Side last month," Brooks said.

"These aren't bored kids breaking into the house next door for booze and money," Breen said. "These are adult pros in cars. They have tools, walkie-talkies and police monitors. Crime Analysis says the patterns show the teams have staked out certain zones for themselves. One gang runs in the downtown core. Others target the industrial shops and shopping centers of District Four, and another group is apparently hitting apartment and store parking lots in Crossroads."

"It's time we re-think the kids with police scanners who keep showing up at our calls," Hitchcock said, "it's very possible some of 'em are lookouts for the adults."

"They drive around all night, chasing our calls and alarms," LaPerle said. "They often arrive at calls ahead of us. If contacted by an officer, they present themselves as wannabe cops, police buffs, and we dismiss them as harmless goof-balls."

"The crooks have portable radios, but we don't," Sherman grumbled. "What's the City done about it? Nothing, like they did about our range?"

"Speaking of portable radios," Breen said, holding up a sheet of paper, "the downtown foot patrols are being restarted for the summer. If you want overtime and a change of pace, be the first to sign up."

"Well, Roger, what about it?" Walker asked. "Guys from all divisions are gonna volunteer. What about us?"

Hitchcock shook his head. "I got a nagging feeling I better tend to business in Eastgate."

"I'm going for it," Walker said, "need the overtime."

† † †

THE LUSTY PACE of the action in the bars of blue-collar Eastgate matched the humid summer heat. On his patrol car radio Hitchcock listened to parking lot fights being broken up and arrests being made for burglary and car prowling by the foot patrols as he focused on Eastgate, the goings-on at The Great Wall especially.

At Charlie's Place, single, underemployed, or unemployed moms, if their faces, figures and ambiance were at least somewhere on the sensuality meter, moonlighted in the world's oldest profession on weekends for supplemental income.

One of these was an especially attractive blonde, despite the fact she was west of forty. A regular at Charlie's on weekends, she restricted her clientele to the same small group of truckers. Except for her, Wally Evans, the owner of Charlie's, screened the ladies' potential customers with either a shake or a nod of his head. "Business" was conducted across the driveway at Kane's or the Eastgate Motel. When the motel rooms were full, local ladies of the night conducted business in the parking lot, which Hitchcock and Walker cracked down on.

They were clearing a disturbance call at the Eastgate

Mobile Manor, a low-income trailer park of vintage single-wide trailers on blocks, when they heard a man's voice in the trailer next door to the call, and a woman's loud laughter as she said in a strong British accent: "Come now Luv! It'll be two hours *at least* before he's home!"

Walker chuckled as he got in his cruiser. Imitating a British accent, he said, "Sounds like there'll be a *bloody* good show later on, ay wat!"

"Aye, that it does, old chap. We should make ourselves available. I like a good show," Hitchcock returned.

# CHAPTER THIRTY-TWO
## A Red-Letter Night

THE NIGHT WAS moonless, cool and dry when the calls came pouring in at the stroke of 8 p.m.: *"Three Zero Six and Three Zero Five, multiple adult males involved in a fight-in-progress, at Charlie's Place, injuries reported. Code Three."* Hitchcock sped from the station, followed by Ray Packard.

Threading along the dark, winding curves of tree-lined Richards Road, Hitchcock heard another call come in: *"Three Zero Seven and Three Zero Eight, fighting and juveniles drinking outside the Lake Hills Roller Rink, Code Two."* Otis and Walker responded.

A crowd of eight men and women in checkered flannel shirts and boots were gathered in Charlie's parking lot, talking excitedly about the fight inside. As Hitchcock was about to report his arrival, Otis came on the air with young voices shouting in the background: *"Three Zero Seven and Three Zero Eight headed to the station with five in custody."*

Hitchcock and Ray Packard burst through the back

door of Charlie's, batons at the ready. The fight was over. Two young construction types, both bleeding facially, were leaning on the edge of a pool table, being attended to by their girlfriends. Wally Evans the owner, was behind the bar. Hitchcock looked at him and shrugged.

"The other two guys split when they heard you guys were coming," Wally said.

"What happened here, you guys?" Hitchcock asked.

The older of the two, his girlfriend holding a napkin to stop his nose bleeding, shook his head. "We were talking when we shoulda been listening, officer."

The phone behind the bar rang as Hitchcock asked, "Who were they?"

"Don't know 'em," the other fighter said through bleeding lips.

"Call's for you, Roger," Wally said, reaching over the bar to hand him the phone.

Hitchcock took the phone, listened, then said, "We're on our way" then hung up. He turned to the two fighters: "You boys don't know the other guys and you wouldn't press charges if you did, so we're oughta here. We got another call to go to."

"Where we goin?" Packard as they trotted to their cruisers.

"Bowling alley—women duking it out."

"Hot-damn! A cat-fight!" Packard grinned as he piled into his cruiser.

As Hitchcock started his engine, the radio crackled:
*"Three Zero Four and Three Zero Two, crowd disturbance at the Trunk Lid, no further details at this time. Code Two."* Sherman and Forbes responded.

The sounds of women shouting curses and screaming drew Hitchcock and Packard past crowded bowling lanes to the lounge. A heavy glass ashtray sailed past Packard's head, missing by an inch when he walked in. He arrested the woman who threw it.

In less than an hour the booking room and the holding cells were packed with prisoners, and more calls were coming in.

Hitchcock and Brooks were the only units available when a kidnapping-in-progress call came in.

They arrived at the Bellevue Motel, a roadside collection of early '40s era one-room cottages on the northern outskirts of the downtown. The nervous manager pointed a shaky finger at Cottage 3.

The door was open.

Hitchcock and Brooks entered the musty-smelling room with guns drawn.

Against the wall was an Elvis Presley impersonator, a dapper white male in his thirties, hair combed straight back, long sideburns, a white, high-collar, rhinestone-studded costume hung in the closet. Sweat glistened on his face. His body trembled.

"Save me, Officers!" he begged, almost in tears. "These men are trying to force me to go with them against my will!"

The two huge goons looked as though they could have been professional linebackers in their youth. The bigger of the two calmly handed Brooks his Nevada driver's license, his bail bond recovery agent license, and court papers authorizing recovery of Claude Tompkins to be brought to the Clark County Superior Court in Las Vegas for revocation of bail.

"Are you Claude Tompkins?" Brooks asked.

"Y-yes, Officer! I don't want to go with these men!" he said, starting to cry.

"You're a bail jumper, Tompkins," Brooks said. "If you're real polite and cooperative, maybe these guys will loan you a crying towel. Adios."

Brooks chuckled as he stepped out of the cottage. "Wish all our calls tonight would be so quick and easy."

"Not tonight," Hitchcock said. "Something tells me I better get back to Eastgate."

Dispatch had another call as soon as Hitchcock cleared: *"Fight in Progress in the Mustard Seed Too. Several male subjects involved. Injuries reported. Code Three."*

Hitchcock and Walker arrived at the same time. They heard shouting and fighting inside the tavern as they got out of their cruisers.

A woman in the car parked next to Hitchcock screamed "Stop! You're hurting me! Aaaahhh! Don't! Please Don't! Get off me!"

Hitchcock shined his flashlight through the driver

door window. The man in the driver seat was almost on top of the woman next to him. She was hitting him with her fists, her head twisting side-to-side, her face contorted with pain, her feet thrashing, her fists beating his head, crying and begging him to stop.

The door was locked.

Hitchcock shattered the driver door window with his eight-cell Kel-lite flashlight. The shower of broken glass had no effect on the man or screaming woman.

"Police officers! You're under arrest!" he shouted. The man tried wrestle Hitchcock when he grabbed him by his collar and flung him face-first onto the pavement.

What Hitchcock saw next stopped him cold. The woman bound across the front seat and out the driver door. Her blouse was torn completely open. Her right breast was bleeding from the nipple, which was dangling by a piece of skin, almost completely bitten off.

The suspect scrambled to his feet and pummeled Walker with his fists. Hitchcock turned to help Walker when a pair of hands grabbed his face from behind, fingers groping for his eye sockets. He shook the new attacker off and turned around—it was the victim, her bare chest and abdomen smeared with blood.

"Leave him alone!" She shrieked, her hands rapidly slapping Hitchcock's face and chest, her nipple dangling and dripping blood.

The ruckus inside the tavern was still going on as he shook the woman off and helped Walker get the man in handcuffs.

The woman broke down sobbing as Hitchcock handcuffed and placed her in the back of his cruiser, away from the eyes of the crowd of mostly men that had gathered.

He keyed his mic: "Three Zero Six, Radio, we encountered an assault in progress in the parking lot when we arrived. We have two in custody. We need an ambulance for the victim and two more units to handle the barfight."

† † †

CALLS STOPPED COMING in at 1:10 a.m. Like the calm before the storm, anticipation filled the air. No one had gone to eat so far. Only Denny's and Sambo's were open. No one asked to go.

The tense quiet dragged on, making everyone uneasy. By 2:00 a.m. Dispatch asked for a radio check of all units.

At 2:11 a.m. the emergency lines in the dispatch center lit up again like a surprise house party. Hitchcock and Walker rolled on a domestic disturbance at the Eastgate Mobile Manor. Hitchcock arrived. Neighbors gathered outside unit 25, listening to the noises of breaking furniture, men cursing and a woman with a strong British accent screaming, pleading and laughing.

Hitchcock keyed his mic. "Ira, get here quick. Got a crowd outside and the fight inside's in full swing."

*"Right behind you."*

The door was locked and opened to the outside, so it couldn't be kicked in. The sounds of fighting inside raged on. Hitchcock pounded on the door.

"Police! Open up!"

No letup.

Walker nudged Hitchcock aside.

The doorknob disappeared into the former wrestler's oversize hands. He twisted counterclockwise. The lock broke with a snap.

Two clean-cut, well-built men in their late twenties, their white business shirts covered with blood, winded, gripped each other by the front of the shirt with one hand and bludgeoned the other with his fist.

Across the room stood a woman so startlingly beautiful that Hitchcock and Walker stopped at the sight of her. Long raven-black hair, ivory skin with a rose tint, large, luminous violet eyes and a voluptuous figure, she stood, entranced by the combat.

Hitchcock and Walker shook themselves and picked their way through broken and overturned furniture to the grappling fighters.

"Break it up! You're both under arrest!" Hitchcock ordered. He grabbed the closest fighter by the back of his belt. Hitchcock covered his gun with his strong hand and twisted violently toward his right to protect it as the fighter wrestled him to the floor. Walker picked him off Hitchcock like a wet towel and flung him into the pile of broken furniture.

Though the other fighter was bloody and gasping, he squared off with Walker in a boxer's stance. Walker moved straight in with a knowing smile on his face. He didn't even bother to block the fighter's punch to his face. He kept smiling as he took him to the floor in a wrestling lock and handcuffed him. The man who attacked Hitchcock was on the floor, face and hands bleeding, too out of breath to resist being handcuffed.

Hitchcock got to his feet. He wasn't upset. To him, a fight was a fight, and it was over. He faced the two fighters on the floor, in handcuffs.

"You guys are under arrest for assault, assaulting a police officer, and resisting arrest. We'll think up some more charges at the station. Stay down until you catch your breath and agree not to fight anymore," he said.

Turning to the woman, Hitchcock asked, "Who are you, and what happened here tonight, miss?"

"I am Cindy Rockingham," she said in a crisp upper-class British accent. With her hands on her hips, she smiled lustfully as she inspected Hitchcock up and down.

"This is my place, and these are my men. They live with me and got to fighting over me. Bloody *awful* thing, you know!" she said, delight written over her strikingly beautiful face.

"My boys will stay here with me," she commanded.

"They're going downtown," Hitchcock countered.

"I won't press charges," she said, pouting as Walker

stood the two fighters up.

"*We're* pressing charges," Hitchcock said.

"I won't let you take them," she insisted, her arms crossed.

"Keep talking and we'll book you for aiding and abetting disorderly conduct and injury to property. I'm sure the female inmates in the women's jail will give *you* a *warm* welcome," Hitchcock replied.

She scowled and looked away.

Her lovers kicked and head-butted each other as soon as Hitchcock and Walker stood them up.

As they fought the handcuffed combatants into their cruisers, Hitchcock heard Dispatch come on the air again: "*Radio to Three Zero Three, respond to reports of a possible 220 adult white female adult in a dress dancing down the middle of 104th Avenue at SE 16th Street. Code Two.*"

LAPERLE SPED SOUTH from the downtown. A mile later, in front of the closed Pancake Corral, he saw cars swerving, braking, almost colliding with each other — and a woman dancing in the middle of the street.

A slender woman with long dark hair, dressed in a filmy dress that fluttered and flew with her gyrations, danced in the two center lanes, singing and snapping her fingers over her head as if they were castanets and tossing her head to imaginary drumbeats. She bowed as if she was onstage before an excited audience, causing passing cars to honk and swerve.

LaPerle keyed his mic and said, "Radio, arriving at-hey! What the–"

The woman hopped into the back seat of his cruiser and shut the door. She pushed red grapes to him through the wire mesh screen separating the front and back seats.

"Peace, man in blue!"

"What's the situation, lady?" LaPerle asked.

"The moon is in the Seventh House and Jupiter aligns with Mars!"

He shook his head forcefully as if to empty her words out of his ears. "What?!"

"Peace will guide the planets and *love* will steer the stars," she announced in a low, seductive voice.

"What?! What are you talking about?"

"Don't you...haven't you, man in blue, heard this is the Age of Aquarius!"

"Uh, well, maybe. but you're *not* supposed to be back there unless you've been checked for weapons! You can't just go around jumping into police cars!"

She leaned back against the seat and flopped her arms outward. "Come check me out, brother. You can have all Renfro's got–love, love, love, you he-man in blue, you," she cooed.

LaPerle grabbed his radio mic: "Have someone waiting outside to meet me at the station. I am en route with an unidentified white female adult 220 from the sixteen hundred block of one-hundred-fourth avenue southeast, starting mileage –"

"This is the dawning of the Age of Aquarius, *Aquaaar-eeee-uuus!*" Renfro squealed in the background.

*"Received. A supervisor will meet you at the station to assist."*

THREE BEEPS FROM Dispatch: *"Emergency traffic only. Three Zero Five, respond to a completed suicide just discovered, at one twenty-eight-sixteen, Southeast Eighteenth Street. The victim's family will meet you at the scene. We are calling the coroner's investigator and a detective supervisor now."*

Ray Packard replied, *"En route, ETA five."*

THREE BEEPS FROM Dispatch: *"Emergency traffic only. Emergency traffic only. Three Zero Two and Three Zero One, respond to a sexual assault just occurred at nine six nine eight, Northeast Twenty-Third Street, victim on the line describes the suspect as an adult white male wearing blue-hooded sweatshirt, armed with a knife."*

Clive Brooks radioed his arrival at the scene.

Mark Forbes caught movement in his peripheral vision as he rolled into the neighborhood seconds later. He switched on his overhead spotlight in time to see a tall male figure about three car-lengths ahead, wearing a dark blue-hooded-sweatshirt and jeans, running eastward across the street.

As Forbes bailed out of his cruiser and gave chase, Dispatch beeped three times. *"Emergency traffic only. Emergency traffic only. Three Zero Seven, arson in progress. Chevron station at the corner of One-Forty-Eighth Avenue Northeast and Northeast Twentieth Street. Code Two. Fire Department is on the way."*

Otis replied that he was en route.

Forbes dashed between the two houses where the suspect went seconds ago. A frenzy of barking dogs drew him to the east, sprinting through backyards and over fences.

From the top of a fence Forbes saw the suspect going over a fence ahead of him. Forbes pumped his legs harder, crossing the yard to the next fence, just ahead of a snarling medium-size dog. He spotted the suspect again, passing through the gate of another backyard, apparently unaware that he was being pursued.

It was dark and the suspect was too far ahead to shout a command.

*Gotta get closer!*

His legs shook when he reached the street. He saw the suspect less than a block ahead, running toward a dark-colored sedan.

The interior light went on as the driver door opened. Forbes's legs wobbled like rubber. His lungs burned; his heart pounded as if it would pop out of his chest.

He stopped in the middle of a street lined on both sides by sleeping houses, about to collapse. Gasping, he

218

drew his service revolver and took aim at the suspect, about thirty yards away. His heaving lungs made steady aim or seeing his sights impossible.

"Police officer! You're under arrest! Stop or I'll shoot!" he shouted between gasps.

The suspect turned toward him for a moment, but the suspect's face was obscured by the hood and low light.

The interior light went out when the suspect closed the door. The engine started and the brake lights came on. Forbes took aim a second time. His heavy breathing made a steady aim impossible. Desperate, he began to squeeze the trigger—then stopped.

*I'm in a neighborhood. Can't risk a shot.* He holstered his gun and forced his legs into a wobbly race to get close enough to read the license number before the car left. The rear license plate light didn't come on. He didn't get close enough to read even one number.

Forbes fell to his knees in the middle of the street. Putting his palms on the pavement, he threw up until his stomach was empty, leaving only dry heaves. He staggered back to his cruiser, gasping, heart pounding frightfully hard, wiping puke from his mouth with the back of his hand.

He staggered back to his cruiser.

Dispatch was trying to reach him when he opened the door and radioed in.

Brooks let him into the victim's house.

A catatonic gray-haired woman with facial injuries looked up at Forbes, his uniform soiled and in tatters. Her expression was blank. She said nothing.

"What happened?" Brooks asked.

"I saw the suspect running from here as soon as I arrived. I chased him for blocks, but he got away."

"Mark," Brooks said, "this is Mrs. Abernathy. A man attacked and assaulted her tonight. Per Sergeant Jurgens, take her to the ER for a medical examination. Remain with her until a detective relieves you. I'm to keep the scene secure until another detective relieves me."

Forbes gently approached the victim. Brooks had bandaged her face. He extended his hand to her. "Mrs. Abernathy, I'm Mark Forbes. I'm terribly sorry about what happened to you. Would you give me your hand so I can take you to my car and we can go to the hospital?"

The vacant stare in her eyes penetrated Forbes's soul as she trustfully placed her hand in his and he led her to his cruiser.

FIREMEN WERE DRENCHING the last of the flames when Otis arrived at the Chevron station. The floor-to-ceiling window had been smashed out. Inside, a large rock was among shards of glass on the floor. The scorched interior walls were dripping wet from the fire hoses. Acrid smoke lingered in the air.

"Somebody smashed out the window, forced the

office door open, tried to pry open the floor safe, then set the place on fire," the battalion chief summarized as Otis scanned the scene with his flashlight.

Tool chests on the benches in the two-stall service bay were open. An empty one-gallon metal gas can lay on its side on the floor. The door to the manager's office had been pried open. Two pry bars and a short-handled sledgehammer laid next to the floor safe, its dial was mangled.

Sergeant Breen arrived.

"They threw the rock through the window then kicked out enough glass to get in," Otis said. "They used pry bars and a sledge from the mechanics' bench to pry open the manager's office. When they couldn't open the floor safe, they doused the place with gas, tossed a match and split."

Breen looked the scene over, saying nothing.

"The fire is a diversion, Jack" Otis went on. "There's only a fire alarm here. The crooks are making sure we're here so they can hit someplace else."

Breen nodded, returned to his cruiser and closed the door. He was on the radio for several minutes.

"The owners will be here in a few minutes," Breen said.

"The dicks'll have to process the scene," Otis said.

"Right," Breen agreed. "Before the owners get here, canvas the area for other burglaries, check the 7-11 on the corner and any other open businesses. Ask if anyone came in tonight smelling like gasoline. I'll hold down the fort until you return."

Otis's canvas of the area turned up nothing. The gas station manager was talking with a detective while another dusted inside for latent prints when he returned. Frank Kilmer's high intensity lamps bathed the scene with light as his flash gun went poof and his camera shutter snapped repeatedly.

Sergeant Breen keyed his radio mic. "All units: stolen vehicle information as follows: stolen tonight from the Chevron at 148th Avenue and Northeast 20th Street: a tan sixty-eight, full-size Pontiac four-door sedan, Washington license Ocean-George-Paul-Five-Six-Zero. Vehicle was stolen within the last hour."

THREE BEEPS FROM Dispatch: *"Emergency Traffic only. Four-Twenty and Three Zero Seven, domestic violence in-progress—knife involved, one person seriously injured from stab wounds, at two-six-five-seven-eight, One-Sixty-Fifth Place Northeast. Ambulance on the way."*

"That's the Harmons again," Otis said. "Third DV call this month."

"I'm your back-up. What a night this is," Breen said, shaking his head in dismay.

"Follow me," Otis yelled as he ran to his cruiser.

IN THE BOOKING room, one of the assault suspects from the trailer park sucker-punched Hitchcock during fingerprinting and sprinted down the hall for the door.

The suspect had reached the darkened library parking lot when Hitchcock tackled him. The suspect leaped to his feet and swung a roundhouse punch. Hitchcock ducked under it and knocked him into the rockery with a right cross to the jaw. He seized the dazed suspect by the front of his shirt and half-dragged him back into the station, mouth bleeding.

"I need a doctor," the suspect mumbled as blood dripped from his mouth between his fingers.

"Forget it," Hitchcock snarled. "They've got docs at the county jail. I'm gonna finish your fingerprints, then I'm adding Escape from Custody to your charges. You try anything else, I'll hurt you worse."

SUSPECTING THE FIRE at the gas station was set as a diversion, and that the suspects were able to monitor police radio traffic, Sherman, the last available unit, stayed off the air and headed to Crossroads.

Right away he spotted a station wagon, not a sedan, that otherwise matched the description of the stolen car came out of the closed shopping center parking lot.

Instead of entering the street ahead of Sherman, the driver waited until he passed, then dropped in behind him.

Sherman pulled off to the right and stopped.

The driver and the passenger in the front seat turned their heads, staring intensely at Sherman as they passed.

Sherman keyed his mic: "Three Zero Four, Radio—confirming the car stolen from the Chevron is a sedan?"

Dispatch: *"Correction. The stolen vehicle is a station wagon, not a sedan."*

Sherman: "Stand by, I think it's right in front of me."

The station wagon turned right at the signal.

A former professional race car driver, Sherman hung a right at the signal, then accelerated to close the gap.

Sherman: "Following the stolen vehicle westbound on Northeast Eighth from One Fifty Sixth Avenue, tan Pontiac station wagon, bearing Washington plate Ocean George Paul Five-Six-Zero."

He caught up to the station wagon and activated his red overhead emergency light. "Suspect vehicle turned right, northbound One Forty-Eighth Avenue. They're not stopping. Two male subjects on board. I need back-up."

Dispatch: *"Be advised, Three Zero Four, no backup units available until—"*

Sherman was gaining fast on the stolen wagon. He cut in, shouting over the wails of his siren: "Pursuit continuing north on One Forty-Eighth. Approaching Bel-Red Road—we're doing eighty-five and climbing."

The traffic signal ahead was red. A couple cars passed through on the green light. The stolen station wagon kept accelerating. Fearing a crash, Sherman eased back and activated his siren to alert any vehicles approaching the intersection. The signal turned to green as the Pontiac wagon went slightly airborne. Sparks flew as it bounced, scraping the undercarriage on the asphalt. Sherman slowed through the intersection, then slammed the gas pedal. The suspect vehicle was twenty or thirty car-lengths ahead

At the Chevron Station, a detective ran to his car radio and keyed the mic as the stolen wagon blasted past, with Sherman in pursuit.

*"We cannot assist, Tom. We have no lights or emergency equipment."*

Sherman: "Pursuit now headed north on One Forty-Eighth, at ninety! Ask Kirkland PD if they can spare a unit to assist!"

Dispatch seconds later: *"Kirkland PD advises no units available."*

Sherman: "Call County!"

Dispatch, seconds later: *"Negative on King County. No units in the area."*

The fleeing wagon's brake lights came on as it turned left and headed downhill on a two-lane country road, whizzing past small farms where Sherman and other officers often caught loose horses and other livestock on morning shift.

Sherman: "Fleeing vehicle turned left. Headed west on Northeast Thirty-Fifth and accelerating!"

Dispatch: *"Be advised, we have no back-up or assistance available. State Patrol on the line; they say they have no one available."*

At the speed he was doing on a dark country road, Sherman dared to key his mic only once: "I'm taking these guys off the road!"

Crossing into the oncoming lane, Sherman sped up until he was alongside, whipped his steering wheel to the right, clipping the left rear quarter panel of the wagon. It veered to the right, leaped the ditch, plowed through a barbed-wire fence with a loud screech, jerking a fence post out of the ground as it careened and bounced across open pasture, until it came to a stop, trapped in soft dirt and tall grass.

Sherman skidded to a stop and backed up. He put his spotlight on the station wagon, fifteen yards from the road.

Interior lights came on as both front doors of the station wagon burst open. The driver stepped into the spotlight and looked back at Sherman, who chuckled as he said, "Devon Caldwell, as I live and breathe."

Caldwell and his passenger ran headlong into the darkness. Unfazed, Sherman keyed his mic: "Pursuit has ended in an open field at the one-forty-two-hundred block of NE Thirty Fifth Street. Two male suspects, one I recognize, fled on foot. I'll be away from my unit to check the stolen car."

He chuckled as he shone his flashlight into the front passenger side window of the station-wagon. Its engine was dead, the radiator was steaming and hissing, headlights beamed into the night, and classical music played on the radio.

Something dark filled the entire back area. Not knowing what to expect, he opened the right rear door with one hand on his gun. Mink furs—mink—full-length coats, hats and wraps, each one having a label, filled the station wagon from the back of the front seat to the back window.

"But of course! What else fits with classical music?" Sherman chuckled to himself.

Sergeant Breen approached, stoic as always. "Great work once again, Tom," he said, shining his flashlight on the heaps of furs. "Kilmer'll be here in a few."

"What happened at the Harmons's place?"

"Won't be hard to figure out where the furs came from. Each one has a label," Breen said as if Sherman hadn't spoken. He radioed Forbes who had just cleared the hospital and was the only unit available.

"Head up to Crossroads Mall. Check the fur store at the back and get back to me."

Sherman waited in silence.

"The Harmon's situation finally went over the line tonight, Tom," Breen replied. "Chester and Natalie got to drinkin' again, then they got to fightin' again. Who knows what it was about? Chester whacked her, she fought back. He beat her so bad she stabbed him with a steak knife to save herself."

"I'm not surprised," Sherman said sadly.

"Fortunately, Otis, with his history of being an Army medic in 'Nam, saved his life, but he lost a helluva lotta blood," Breen said.

"What about Natalie?"

"Joel arrested her after the ambulance left with Chester. He took her to the ER to be stitched up too."

Sherman shook his head. "I like Chester when he isn't drinking."

"Chester might be past tense before sunrise."

The radio crackled. Forbes came on the air: *"I'm at Eva's Fine Furs. Picture window's been busted out. Someone chucked a big rock through the wind and kicked in the rest of the glass. The store's been completely cleaned out."*

"Same M.O. as the gas station," Sherman muttered.

"Secure the scene. I'm on my way," Breen replied. "Radio, send a tow truck to 14200 block of Northeast 35th Street, the vehicle is to be taken to the station for processing. Call the owner of Eva's Fine Furs, get him or her to contact us at their store. Then call Sergeant Jurgens. Tell him we need another detective for crime scene processing."

Breen asked Sherman. "What's with the music?"

Sherman smiled. "I was wondering when you'd notice. That's what was playing when the chase ended."

"Go on!" Breen said incredulously. "Burglars and car thieves playing classical music as they plunder the town? That's too much! Do you recognize the music playing in the car when I got here?"

"I think I do, but you tell me, Sarge."

"Mozart. 'A Little Night Music.'"

"We got PC to arrest Devon Caldwell. I recognized him as he bailed out. He was the driver, and I think the passenger with him was his brother," Sherman said.

"I'll tell the dicks. When they arrest him and his partner, ask why they had Mozart on the radio."

"For sure," Sherman said, still amused. "Maybe they were listening to Beethoven before. 'Burgling with Beethoven' sounds kinda catchy."

"Definitely has a ring to it," Breen said, grinning.

Breen left. Sherman strolled around in the grass to stretch his legs as he waited for the tow truck. The cool breeze and the scent of uncut grass refreshed him. An exhausted-looking Frank Kilmer as he arrived, camera and flashgun attached, and a canvas bag of film, lenses and accessories slung over his shoulder. "Helluva night, Tom. Never seen a weekday night like this. I'm almost out of film!"

# CHAPTER THIRTY-THREE
## A Sunrise Ending

*The Station*
*3:55 A.M.*

FIRST SHIFT OFFICERS heading for their cruisers stopped to gawk at the tow truck bringing in a battered station wagon, followed by Sherman's banged-up cruiser. Sherman smiled as he answered their questions while logging and tagging each fur piece which Frank Kilmer photographed.

After the store owners left with their recovered property, a sudden smile spread across Kilmer's face. "Hey Tom, let's do a shot of you with your damaged fender for Department history. Ham it up!"

Placing one foot on the damaged front bumper, showing the crushed right fender, Sherman curled and flexed his right bicep as he smiled into the camera.

The Caldwell brothers arrived in the back of a detective car. Devon Caldwell smiled sheepishly when Sherman entered the interview room.

"I advise you to find another line of work, Devon. Your getaway driving really sucks," Sherman said, grinning fondly at him like an uncle to a nephew.

Caldwell chuckled, shaking his head. "I guess I should, huh? What was that trick you did that knocked us off the road, Officer Sherman? That was something."

"It's a pursuit tactic called the 'pitman maneuver.' You know, something's got us puzzled, Devon: the car you took was playing classical music when you guys bailed out. What's the deal with that?"

"Oh yeah," Caldwell said, tilting his head back with a smile. "We was gonna change it to something else, but we didn't 'cause the music it was kinda soothing. So that's classical, huh?"

"Yep. And guess what? My sergeant knew the name of the tune and the composer's name."

"Yeah? Who's the dude who could write music like that?"

"A guy named Mozart. He lived about two hundred years ago in Europe. The tune is called 'A Little Night Music,'" Sherman replied.

Devon laughed an honest belly laugh and slapped his knee. "Hah! Takes a sergeant to know those things, I guess."

† † †

SERGEANT JURGENS MET Detective Meyn and Police Matron Char Norris as they brought battered, fragile Florence Abernathy to the station from the hospital.

"Use Bostwick's office to get her statement," Jurgens said. "It's as far removed from the racket down the hall as we have."

As Meyn, the police matron and the victim took seats in Bostwick's office, Sergeant Jurgens taped a sign on the door: VICTIM INTERVIEW IN PROGRESS – DO NOT DISTURB.

Jurgens met Sherman in the hallway. "A wild night. One for the books, Tom. Going home now?"

"Not just yet. I want to check on Natalie Harmon in the booking room. After breaking up so many fights between her and her husband, thought I'd say hello."

Jurgens nodded his approval.

"By the way, Stan," Sherman said, "in case you forgot, the Caldwell brothers smell like gasoline. You might want to take their clothes as evidence for lab testing before it evaporates."

Jurgens snapped his fingers. "Ah! Thanks, Tom! In getting a search warrant for their home, I forgot about their clothes. By the way, we found the car they drove to the Chevron station. They hid it at the Sears store across the street. They stole the station wagon from the gas station to hit the fur store."

"Aha. That makes us even," Sherman grinned. "I forgot about evidence from other burglaries they'd have at home, or how they got from home to the gas station in the first place. I guess we're both tired. See ya."

# CHAPTER THIRTY-FOUR
## The Morning After

THE STATION SOUNDED more like Saturday night in the Bronx than suburban Bellevue when the Brass began arriving at 8:00 a.m.

The hysterical shrieks of a woman in the booking room, grieving that she might have murdered her husband and the shouts of rowdy felons in the holding cells carried to every office. Third shift officers, whose shift ended four hours ago, were writing reports and fingerprinting prisoners. Officers and detectives waited in line to book evidence into the evidence room, station officers were handcuffing rowdy prisoners for transport to the county jail.

In the bull pen, sleepless detectives rubbed their eyes and gulped cold coffee to stay awake after working all night. The discordant sounds of phone calls and interviews, interrogations and clacking typewriters and the office percolator chugging fresh coffee was akin to orchestra members tuning their instruments before the concert began, and cigarette smoke hung in the air.

At the public window by the station door, indignant parents and outraged friends of prisoners in the booking room argued, scoffed and sneered at the duty sergeant as they posted bail.

† † †

INTO THIS CAULDRON of chaos Lieutenant Bostwick arrived. Bewildered at first, his face quickly became grave and dark when he realized his office was being used. He ripped the DO NOT DISTURB sign from his office door and threw it open, scaring the bandaged, disheveled elderly woman sitting in a chair, bruises and stitches on her swollen face, forearms and hands.

With a sneering glance at the woman, he grabbed Detective Meyn by the sleeve. "Step outside," he hissed.

Shocked, Meyn turned to the victim. "Excuse me for just a moment, Mrs. Abernathy," he said politely as he closed the door.

In the hallway by the station door, a scowling, red-faced Bostwick shook his finger in Meyn's face. "What is the *meaning* of this? You have *special rooms* for this!" he hissed.

Meyn lifted his hands in a pleading gesture. "Please understand, Lieutenant: Our interview rooms, the holding cells and the booking room are *still* full after last night. It's after eight, and all the night shift officers are still here. The woman in your office was raped and beaten in her home last night. She needs a private place to tell us what happened. Sergeant Jurgens set us up here so she would feel – "

Bostwick's eyes bulged, and his face contorted with disgust at the word 'rape.' "She was *raped*? he said, his upper lip sneering. "*Raped? I don't care. I'm* the lieutenant and *that-that woman* does *not* belong in my office. Find another place to talk to her. You will also clean the chair she's sit – "

A strong hand gripped Bostwick's arm above the elbow from behind. His heart almost stopped when he turned around. It was Captain Delstra's iron grip that was crushing Bostwick's arm. The lieutenant froze, open-mouthed.

"The victim is a *lady*. The *detective* is helping her, and he needs your office, *Lieutenant*," Delstra said tersely. "I *order* you to sit on this bench until they are done. Detective Meyn can and will take all the time he needs to help this lady; all day if he wants. He can write his report there if he wants, no matter what *your* schedule is. You are not to leave this bench until Detective Meyn says you may have your office back. *Never* again will you give Detective Meyn orders like you just did. If you disobey my orders by leaving this bench before Detective Meyn is finished, I will write you up for insubordination. Do you understand?"

Bostwick stood, frozen in place, speechless. Clerks, officers and civilians in the hall stared at him. The jelly-pack of fat under his chin shook with fear; his face and ears burned bright red.

Bottled rage darkened Delstra's face. "Do you understand, *Lieutenant*?"

Bostwick cast nervous glances right and left as if he was looking for an escape route. He forced a "Yes."

"Yes, what?"

"Yes, sir." Bostwick replied in a hoarse whisper.

Clerks and members of the public stared and snickered as Bostwick obediently took a seat on the long, battered wooden bench by the door that had seen lifetimes of trouble and tragedy.

The humiliated lieutenant added to its history, sitting there numb, staring straight ahead, ignoring the stares of the public, some curious, others mocking as they came in to post bail or make a report.

Against background noises of a woman's shrieks and sobs, men in the cells cursing and slamming things around, Delstra told Meyn, "No need to move the lady, Larry. Finish helping her. Take all the time you need, even if it takes all day and tomorrow."

† † †

IN THE BOOKING room, Natalie Harmon seemed to sense the coming of the Grim Reaper. "I'm *sorry*, Chester! I didn't want to stab you! You *know* I had to! I don't want you to die!" she sobbed, tears and snot mingling on her face. "Don't *die* on me, Chester, please! I love you baby, baby, baby!" she wailed. "Don't let him die, Lord!"

Otis sat next to Natalie at the booking desk, filling out the arrest forms.

Sherman secured his gun in the gun locker and sat next to her on the bench. "Natalie. I'm sorry for what happened too, all of us really like you and Chet," he gently told her.

Natalie wiped the snot running from her nose with her sleeve as she clutched Sherman's arm.

"Thank God you're here, Tom! You *know* I didn't want to hurt him. Not on purpose! But when he...then I—"

Sherman touched her shoulder. "Natalie, stop. Don't say another word. You need an attorney. I just came by to say hello and tell you how sorry we are. Is there anyone you want me to call for you?"

Ignoring the barrage of obscene chatter coming from male inmates in the holding cells around the corner, Natalie's head drooped as she sniffled. "Tom, if Chet dies, I want you to be the one to tell our daughter, Annie."

"She still lives in Kirkland?"

"If Annie's good lookin' we'll check on her for ya!" a man in a holding cell around the corner said, which got the other prisoners laughing.

Otis slammed his pen on the desk. "Excuse me for a second, Natalie," he said as he headed for the holding cells, keys in hand. Then came the sound of a cell door opening,

"It wasn't me, officer," young male voice said. "Me neither," said another.

There was the sound of a scuffle, a man cursing, more scuffling, then silence. Otis returned, nodded at Sherman as he softly closed the steel door to the cells, which were quiet.

Natalie nodded, her head and shoulders drooping, a broken woman. "Annie lives with her husband and her new b-baby, Tom."

"I hope it won't be necessary, but if needed, I'll go in person."

Wiping tears and snot on her sleeve again, Natalie blurted "God bless you, Tom Sherman!"

† † †

SHERMAN WAS HALFWAY down the hall when he met Hitchcock headed the other way. "Animal control problems in the Eastgate zoo, I presume?" he chuckled, nodding at the ripped left sleeve of Hitchcock's shirt.

"Yeah," Hitchcock chuckled. He gave Sherman the run-down on the love triangle call.

"Going home now?"

"Nah. Walker and I volunteered to take prisoners to the jail since there aren't enough first shift guys to spare and the station crew is busy upstairs with prisoners in court. Besides, I need the O.T."

"Owning two houses like you do, each with a mortgage, I can see you needing overtime."

"By the way, Tom, we listened to your chase on our way to the station. Even our prisoners were impressed by what they heard. Before the chase ended, Ira told them 'Nobody outruns Tom Sherman.'

At that moment, Stapp swaggered through the station, blond hair slicked back, dark aviator shades, bloused riding pants, black boots, pressed uniform shirt. He stopped and scowled at Hitchcock, then walked down the hall to the traffic office.

"I think he doesn't like you," Sherman snickered.

"If he ever does start liking me, it's a sign I'm doing something wrong."

† † †

DETECTIVE MEYN RELISHED watching the hated Bostwick stewing on the public bench, trying to cope with the odd stares when members of the public came in to post bail or turn in accident reports.

He took his time getting a detailed tape-recorded interview of the victim and a sketch of the rapist with the Identi-Kit. Instead of leaving after the victim left with another detective and a police matron, Meyn toyed with Bostwick by writing up his notes in long hand.

Suddenly his pen gave out.

He opened the center drawer of Bostwick's desk looking for another pen. In plain view was a business card for The Great Wall restaurant in Eastgate. On the back of the card was the name of the owner, Juju Kwan, and, he assumed, her home phone number and address.

On two three-by-five notecards were the names and phone numbers for certain members of the City Manager's staff. On another he recognized the names and phone numbers of reporters with the *Seattle Post Intelligencer*. known for writing articles slanted against law enforcement.

These he crammed into his notebook folder, unsure what he would do with them. He ignored Bostwick as he headed back to the Bull Pen.

He began typing his report as he listened to his taped interview of the victim. When he opened his file folder to find his notes, the written materials he took from Lieutenant Bostwick's desk fell to the floor.

He looked at the writing more closely. It seemed he had seen it before. After studying them for a couple more minutes, he took them to the copy machine.

† † †

HITCHCOCK FELT PUNCHY by the time he returned from taking prisoners to the King County Jail. It was almost noon when he hung up the keys to his cruiser and started out the door.

"Wait a minute, Roger," Detective Sergeant Jurgens said. "Captain Holland wants to see you before you go home."

His body sagged from exhaustion as he followed Jurgens down the corridor to the detective section. But the thought of the head of detectives wanting to see him made his mental wooziness dissipate with every step. As he came to the captain's closed door, he wondered *What could be so important that it couldn't wait?*

He found Captain Holland at his desk, looking neat and professional in his dark suit, white shirt with silver cufflinks and brown striped necktie tied in a Windsor knot.

"I realize you've pulled a long shift, Roger, but I want you to be the first to know."

At those words Hitchcock was wide awake.

"We got a call from SPD this morning," Captain Holland began. "Yesterday some mushroom hunters found a deteriorated body in the woods. The autopsy determined the cause of death was a single gunshot wound to the back of the head. The decedent's identity hasn't been released to the public yet, but the body is that of Andrew Stanford, the one who attacked your home."

Shocked, Hitchcock held his silence, knowing Holland had more.

"Weeks ago." Holland went on, "SPD found Stanford's car hidden in brush below the West Seattle Bridge. There was blood on the front passenger seat. The state lab determined it was animal blood. I remember you said you saw a knife lying on a piece of bloody newspaper on the passenger seat of Stanford's car."

Hitchcock nodded but said nothing.

"Maybe no one told you," Holland continued, "but

Meyn and Williams found bloody newspaper in the trash where Stanford was staying. If the lab matches the blood on the newspaper to the dog that was killed at your place, we have the evidence we need."

"I didn't know about the bloody newspaper or Stanford's car being found," Hitchcock replied. "What took SPD so long to tell us about Stanford's car?"

Holland shrugged as he said, "Few people at SPD knew we had an interest in Stanford."

"We gave them his car description when detectives went to arrest him." Hitchcock countered.

"True, but SPD is a thousand officers strong, not a hundred twenty like us. Their city is bigger and much busier than ours. Stanford just slipped through the cracks."

"Even with Stanford dead and the other guy hiding out in Taiwan, life won't return to normal for my wife and I. Whoever sent them knows we don't know who they are, and they are still here," Hitchcock reasoned.

"We think the people who snuffed Stanford also killed the hitman you arrested at Charlie's Place last year–Wilcox," Holland said.

"How do you figure?"

"Stanford's body was found in the same spot where Wilcox was."

Stunned a second time, Hitchcock nodded, "I get it," he said, staring at the floor, "this is deep."

"Surprised?"

"Not really, now that I think about it, Captain."

"How so?"

"Otis predicted this would happen to Stanford."

Holland's eyes widened. "Otis? How's that?"

"Vietnam."

"Otis and you were in Vietnam."

"Joel was a medic in the Rangers in the Golden Triangle before the war really got started, back when Eisenhower was President, then Kennedy," he replied. "While on patrols he came across the remains of people the VC executed because they collaborated with us. They staged the bodies the same way as Wilcox. Four years after Joel was there, I saw the same thing on our patrols which were in a different part of the country. I saw the manner of Wilcox execution and body staged in the same way."

Holland lounged back in his chair, looking at Hitchcock, so quiet and pensive. "So, based on your experience over there, it's not East Coast mafia?"

With a shake of his head, Hitchcock said, "Based on what I saw there, and now here, it's heroin from Vietnam that's killing people. Criminals are using it as a murder weapon. The roots are in Asia."

"So, the feds, and the agencies we work with, are wrong, and we need to refocus our efforts?"

"If we hope to stop the destruction before it's too late, yes," Hitchcock replied.

PATTY FROM RECORDS stopped him in the hall as he headed out the door. "I heard you were still in the building, Roger. I think you'd better see this," she said, handing him a teletype.

It was a registration check on the license on his Jeep Wagoneer. "It was made two days ago at 12:30 in the afternoon," he said. "Who requested it?"

"Playboy Stapp. He does this with every good-looking woman he sees. He's a stalker. Thought you'd want to know."

He looked at the teletype as he folded it and put it in his jacket pocket. "Thanks, Patty. I'll handle it."

# CHAPTER THIRTY-FIVE
## "You Can't Recall a Bullet."

*Shift Briefing*
*The Next Night*

"NICE OF YOU to join us, Cinderella," Otis said as Hitchcock seated himself next to him. It wasn't the setting for the usual banter. Officers shifted uneasily in their seats, glancing in the direction of the podium, muttering among themselves, adding to the tense atmosphere because Detective Sergeant Jurgens was at the podium with Sergeant Breen.

"We've got two sexual predators to catch before somebody dies," Jurgens said, his voice interrupting the chatter as he handed out a stack of bulletins with composite sketches.

"The latest victim is a middle-aged widow who lives alone on our side of Clyde Hill. The suspect pried the kitchen sliding door open while she slept. He bound her with a rope he had with him, beat and raped her. He wore a blue hooded sweatshirt and told her he would come back. This is the second attack by this suspect on this victim."

The room was silent as the copies were passed around.

Hitchcock studied the sketch. The prowler who escaped from him almost eight months ago was much older than this suspect.

"As in previous cases, the suspect struck at such a late hour the likelihood of witnesses is nil." Jurgens said. "Forbes chased the suspect from the scene, over fences and through back yards for blocks but the suspect made good his escape in a dark two-door sedan of General Motors make."

Silence held the squad room.

"This is the city's fifth attack on a sleeping woman in her home by a man wearing a dark blue hooded sweatshirt," Jurgens went on. "The first three occurred in the Lake Hills and Robinswood neighborhoods. He was armed with a knife and made the victims touch his private parts. The description of *that* suspect is of a tall, lean, physically fit white male between forty and fifty, described by one witness as resembling the TV actor Eddie Albert."

The memory of catching the original prowler last fall, fighting him into custody, and watching him escape came back to Hitchcock as he listened to Jurgens. He knew then the suspect would continue and escalate his attacks—he couldn't stop.

"The last two attacks happened on the west side," Jurgens continued. "The suspect in both cases was described as in his twenties. We think the publicity the first suspect received inspired the younger one to wear the same disguise. The younger suspect is already more aggressive and violent than the original. At the rate his violence is increasing, homicide is imminent unless we catch him. So far he has confined his attacks to the west side of town."

"Are these attacks happening anywhere else? Kirkland, or the county?" a Traffic lieutenant asked.

"We've been checking on that almost daily, but so far these attacks are unique to Bellevue."

"What specifically do you need from us in Patrol, Stan?" Sergeant Breen asked.

"Increased emphasis patrols in neighborhoods are our best shot at catching either suspect," Jurgens replied. "It's to our advantage that you guys work the same beats every day. Familiarity with who lives and works in your districts and what they drive increases the odds of spotting either of them."

He glanced at Otis on his left, Walker on his right. Both were scribbling in their field notebooks.

Sergeant Jurgens continued.

"In every instance, the victim was attacked in the privacy of her home, which means the offender selected the victim, knew where she lived, that she lived alone, and pre-planned the attack. To find out how the offenders select their victims, we've re-interviewed every victim. So far, no clues. It appears both offenders select their victims by prowling and stalking, which means increased patrolling is our best chance of catching him."

"What about door-to-door salesmen, city utility or power company employees?" Sherman suggested.

"We covered that angle—negative results," Jurgens replied. "Until we identify and arrest one or both suspects, intensified patrols of residential streets, including apartment parking lots, are needed.

"Second, we want the names of anyone you can think of who might be one of the men we're looking for. When you're not taking calls, be in your neighborhoods, investigate strangers. That's all. Any questions?"

No one said anything.

Hitchcock remained still, lost in thought as the squad room emptied out.

Sherman returned a moment later. "What's up?"

"I can't stop thinking about the women he victimized..." he said, his voice trailing off.

"The one you chased was the original, the older guy," Sherman said.

"The younger one was inspired by the one who got away from me, Tom. Because I failed, women are being raped and one of them will die."

"Move forward, Roger. It's all you can do. You can't recall a bullet."

# CHAPTER THIRTY-SIX
## "Nice Pinch!"

CALL-WISE, THE night had been slow. The weather was warm, muggy and windless, the kind of night where either nothing happens, or all hell breaks loose.

At 2:00 a.m. Walker came on the air. *"Roger, contact me on SE 10th below 156th. Come quick, but Code One,"* his voice sounded hushed and urgent.

He found Walker standing beside a decrepit white early '60s Pontiac Bonneville parked against the curb.

"What's up?"

"Keep your voice down!" Walker whispered. "This car wasn't here fifteen minutes ago. The hood's warm. It's registered to some guy in south Seattle. Records is checking him now."

Hitchcock looked around the neighborhood. Every house was dark. He shrugged as he whispered, "Maybe a visitor?"

"See any houses with lights on?" Walker asked. "One of the first blue-hooded victims lives a block from here. In case this is our guy, let's block his car in to keep him from getting away while we look for him."

A sudden eruption of dogs barking two houses away shattered the quiet as Walker snugged his cruiser up against the rear bumper of the Pontiac and Hitchcock backed his against the front.

Dispatch came on the air: *"Radio to Three Zero Eight, respond Code Two to prowler-in-progress at One-Five-Five-One-Zero, Southeast Tenth Street. Woman caller hears someone in her back yard."*

Walker keyed his mic. *"Already here with Three Zero Six. Advise the caller to turn on her front porch light and answer the door when I knock."*

They jogged side-by-side to the address, which was in the direction of the barking dogs, holding flashlights and batons in their belt rings with their left hands, right hands on their holstered guns.

"Take the back, I'll contact the lady," Walker whispered.

A light by the side of the front door of the small late fifties' rambler came on as Walker crossed the front lawn. The front window curtain parted momentarily when he knocked softly on the door.

"Who's there?" A woman's voice inside asked.

"Police officer."

The door opened a crack. A shriveled woman who appeared to be in her fifties with curlers in her gray hair peeked out with one eye. "My do-awg bahked when the neighbor's do-awg behind me, a Great Daayne, went crazy," she said in a strong Brooklyn accent. "I hoid some crashin' aray-yound, a man yelled, so I cawled."

"Did you call your neighbor, ma'am?" Walker asked.

"Did *I* call 'em? Why should I? Don't know 'em a-tall. I ain't the pleece, *you* are," she said as she slammed the door.

Hitchcock met Walker at the caller's backyard gate.

"The woman believes the noise came from the neighbor right behind her. A dog barked, a man yelled, then crashing noises."

"I checked the backyard," Hitchcock said. "The lights in the house behind this one are off, but we should check."

Walker rang the doorbell. A small dog inside began barking. Lights came on as a fortyish man in a white T-shirt and pajama pants opened the door. "Yes, Officers, is anything wrong?"

"Excuse us for bothering you, sir, but we're responding to a call from a neighbor who heard a dog barking, crashing noises and a man yelling. She thought the noise might have come from here. Has anyone here heard a disturbance outside?"

The man at the door shook his head and sighed. "Let me guess: the caller is the woman right behind us."

Walker hesitated. "Is that a problem?"

"Aha. So, Nellie called you," he said with a knowing nod. "My wife and I've had nothing but trouble with her since we moved in six months ago."

"Trouble?" Walker echoed.

"Our dog barks too much, our kids are unruly, she wants our side of the fence between us painted the same color as her house, our TV volume is too high, turn it down, my lawnmower is too noisy, anything. After seeing her, can you believe her claims she was a professional model in New York?"

Walker compressed his lips to keep from smiling. "So, the noise we came to investigate didn't come from here?"

"We went to bed about ten. Our dog didn't bark until you rang the doorbell."

A woman wearing a yellow bathrobe appeared next to the man. "My husband is right, officers. Nellie's a nut case. Every chance she gets, she says she was a stage actress and a model in New York, and danced as one of the Rockettes at Radio City Music Hall. She acts like the femme fatale no man can resist. She's delusional. My husband isn't the only married man in the neighborhood she calls—"

Walker held his hand up. "Folks, I hate to interrupt, but time is critical, and we need your help," he said. "There's a white Pontiac sedan on the street one block over. I patrol this neighborhood every day and I've never seen it here before. Do you know if it belongs to a neighbor or a frequent visitor?"

The man and his wife glanced at each other. "No,

we don't think so," he replied.

"Okay then," Walker said, "we'll be poking around outside for a bit, making sure everything is safe. Do us a favor and keep your dog inside. Call the station if anything else comes up. They'll know how to reach us."

Two houses down, a man suddenly appeared from between two houses where the lights were out. He entered the street at a hurried pace, head bent down. Hitchcock and Walker said nothing as they increased their walking speed to close the distance. The man turned, saw them and broke into a run.

"Stop! Police!" Walker shouted. They gave chase. The man turned right, dashed between two homes, flipped the latch of a wooden gate and disappeared into the backyard.

"Stop! Police! You're under arrest!" Walker yelled as he and Hitchcock ran through the gate after him.

The fleeing suspect looked over his shoulder at the two uniforms chasing him as he hoisted himself over the back fence and dropped into the adjacent backyard.

Two large dogs chased Hitchcock as he sprinted across the backyard. One of them nipped the cuff of his pantleg as he scaled the fence.

Another cacophony of barks and growls erupted as Hitchcock continued pursuit, vaulting over the top of the six-foot high fence just in time to spot the suspect desperately groping for the latch of the gate across the yard. Not finding it, he scrambled over the gate and disappeared.

Walker split off from Hitchcock, circled around the last house and ran up the street in time to see the suspect, out of breath, throw his hands in the air at the sight of two police cruisers blocking the Pontiac. He rushed the suspect from behind, slamming him against the driver door of his car so hard he crumpled to the ground.

"You're under arrest for prowling and investigation of attempted first-degree burglary," Walker said as he scooped the collapsed suspect up and flung him face-first, feet back, hands against the Pontiac in the classic search position.

Hitchcock peered at the suspect's face as Walker handcuffed him. He matched the description of the youngest blue-hooded sweatshirt rapist.

The suspect was winded. He acknowledged his Miranda rights. Walker checked his driver's license. "Do you still live at the address in Seattle that's on your driver's license and car registration, Terry Oldham?"

"Yes, sir," the suspect said, his tone surprisingly polite.

"You're a long way from Seattle. What are you doing here?"

The suspect shrugged, still trying to catch his breath. "Got lost, I guess."

Walker pushed his hat back on his head. "Come on," he said with a knowing grin," you can do better than that."

The suspect stared at the ground, saying nothing.

Walker turned to Hitchcock. "Partner, what do you think? We've heard some whoppers in our time, but this ain't one of 'em. This guy's lack of creativity is breathtaking. Oh wait! Do I smell beer on your breath?"

He leaned close and gave the suspect a dramatic sniff. "Ahh! So *that's* it. We'll blame everything on alcohol if you tell us where you did your drinking."

The suspect seemed genuinely embarrassed as he grinned and shrugged as he shifted his wrists within the handcuffs. "I can't remember the name of the place."

Walker opened the rear door of his cruiser. "Um-hm. Have a seat in my limo until we figure this out."

Dispatch came on the air for Walker: *"See the woman at One-Five-Five-Two-Nine, Southeast Ninth Street, possible burglary attempt just occurred. Suspect described as a white male, mid-twenties, tall, wearing a green shirt."*

Walker turned in his seat. "Hear that? You're wearing a green shirt. Is this the house you were running from?"

No reply.

"Now's the time to tell me what the woman will say."

Oldham shook his head and said nothing.

"Watch him until I get back," he told Hitchcock.

Minutes later Walker returned with a young, attractive blonde woman wearing a blue bathrobe and slippers. Hitchcock recognized her as Debbie, the barmaid at Charlie's Place.

She peered into the back seat.

"That's him!" she gasped, covering her mouth. "He was staring at me tonight while I was working. He stayed until almost closing. I was at home undressing when the neighbors' dogs started barking. I looked up and there he was, right outside my bedroom window, watching me."

Sergeant Breen arrived.

Walker briefed him.

"He could be our younger suspect," Breen said after he looked at Oldham "Roger, take him to the station and place him in a cell. Don't question him. If he starts talking on his own, just take notes. Leave the questioning for the dicks."

Hitchcock transferred Oldham to his cruiser and left for the station.

"Ira," Breen said, "get an impound on the way, seal his car, take a detailed statement from the victim, then follow the tow truck to the station."

# CHAPTER THIRTY-SEVEN
## The Interrogator

DETECTIVE LARRY MEYN drove through empty streets on his way to the station. His success as an interrogator was due in part to his disarming appearance. Everything about him was so average that people tended to underestimate him. His height, weight, and facial features were as bland and unassuming as a bar of Ivory soap.

What made the guilty buckle so often was his flat gaze. His eyes were wide and round, cobalt blue, questioning, demanding answers, unblinking. Even innocent people searched their souls for *something* to confess to, and sometimes all they had to offer was something like "I stole my teacher's pen when I was in fourth grade." But on the guilty Meyn's stare was judge and jury, hell and damnation.

Being the modest type who wore suits as bland as himself, Larry Meyn brushed off compliments on his unmatched record of interrogation-room victories, *"Just a humble seller of prison time,"* he liked to say.

HE GREETED ONCOMING first shift officers in the hallway as he opened the detective office and flipped on the lights. Sergeant Breen handed him a printout of Seattle PD's priors with the incoming prisoner.

He read the printout. "So, the boys caught a Seattle pervert prowling around Lake Hills, a block from a recent attack. Do you think this could be our guy, Jack?"

Breen shrugged. "He matches the younger one. He's from Seattle. No blue-hooded sweatshirt on him or in his car. Hitchcock put him in a holding cell. If you're ready he'll bring him out."

"And being a cab driver would give him access to our neighborhoods and who lives there, which occurred to none of us. And that's something," Meyn pointed out.

"Sure is," Breen agreed, thinking.

"Did he say anything to Hitchcock?"

"Roger says he kept his mouth shut."

"Let's get going, then," Meyn said as he swallowed the last of the stale coffee.

"Roger will bring him to you, then he has calls to take. You okay with that?"

"Sure," Meyn said with a nod. "Nice pinch on Walker's part."

"Work your magic, now, Larry," Breen said, not smiling.

THE INTERROGATION ROOM matched Detective Meyn's no-nonsense sterility and deliberate lack of frills. Except for a built-in one-way mirror, the walls, even the floor, were grayish-white and barren, nothing to distract. The three chairs and the table were gray plastic.

An experienced, trained interrogator who practiced his questions and facial expressions in a mirror at home, Larry Meyn sat in a chair, nothing between him and the door he faced. A stack of case files was on the table next to him. Printouts of Oldham's contacts with Seattle PD were on top for him to see when he walked in.

Terry Oldham appeared in the doorway with Hitchcock behind him.

Odors of cigarettes, beer and dirty socks preceded Oldham. His lime green, short-sleeve shirt was of the 50s bowling league type, loose-fitting, tails out, white T-shirt underneath. Below the shirt he had on grungy blue jeans and scuffed brown hiking boots.

Meyn dismissed Hitchcock with a lift of his chin.

"Have a seat, Mr. Oldham," Meyn said as he studied the SPD printouts.

Oldham sat with his feet crossed, hands folded, waiting, calm. Meyn kept studying the printouts, using delay to build tension before questioning began.

"I'm Detective Meyn," he said, extending his hand but not smiling. Oldham managed a nervous grin as he shook hands with Meyn.

"Have you been advised of your Constitutional Rights?" he asked.

Oldham's grip was firm. "Yes, sir. One of the officers—knew 'em by heart."

*He's articulate enough to be the one*, Meyn observed. "Good. I want to make sure you understand what's going on. Bear with me for a moment more—" He produced a statement form from his folder from which he read the Constitutional Rights and Warnings.

"Do you understand your rights as I read them to you?"

"Yes," Oldham said, leaning forward in his chair, making steady eye contact with Meyn.

"Fine. Print your name at the top of this form and then sign at the bottom. Then we can talk."

Oldham went over every line, then filled in the top and signed the bottom.

Meyn put the form in his folder. "Tell me about yourself, Mr. Oldham."

"Like what?" he asked calmly.

"Let's start with where you grew up, your current living situation, your work, are you married, any kids. Basic life-stuff."

Oldham squirmed under Meyn's unblinking, truth-demanding gaze. He looked down at the floor. Seconds later his hands and feet fidgeted. Long seconds later he lifted his eyes to Meyn's. "Grew up in the South End, went to Glacier High. N-never married. I'm a cab driver for Outwest. Wanted to do more—"

Meyn suddenly stopped Oldham by holding up his hand like a traffic cop. He touched his forehead and chuckled apologetically as he shook his head. "I did it again—forgot. My bosses are after me all the time for not doing this one little thing at the start of an interview."

Oldham seemed puzzled. "What?"

Meyn apologetically smiled again. "You see, you want to talk, I want to listen, but you'll need to waive your right to remain silent before we can. So, here's the same form again. Where it says, 'Waiver of My Constitutional Rights,' fill in the blanks and sign, then we'll talk."

Oldham signed the form and sat back, waiting.

"Let's continue. Who do you live with, Terry?"

"My parents."

Meyn went on alert. He knew from FBI studies that a significant percentage of serial sex offenders still live with their parents in their twenties and thirties.

"You're twenty-six and you live with your parents?" he asked in a polite, neutral tone.

"Yeah," Oldham replied with a shrug.

"What about the service?"

Oldham snickered. "Got drafted when I turned eighteen, but they gave me a general discharge 'cuz I couldn't keep up with boot camp training. Fallen arches—flat feet. My Army career ended after three weeks at Fort Lewis."

"Oh—okay," Meyn responded, giving Oldham his unblinking stare. "This is very interesting. How long have you been driving for Outwest?"

He paused. "Uh...almost three years, I think."

"Like it?"

"The tips are decent when I work the airport, but I don't like the hours."

"What hours?"

"Ten p.m. to six, Friday and Saturday off."

"How long have you had that schedule?"

"Since January."

"Do you have a police scanner in your car, Terry?"

Oldham knit his brows. "What's a scanner?"

"A radio to listen in on police radio traffic."

"Ah, a CB-type thing. Nope. You're welcome to check my car."

Meyn crossed one leg over the other and folded his hands in his lap. "What brought you to Bellevue at such a crazy hour tonight?"

"I got paid yesterday. I often go to the Bavarian Gardens on payday."

"Bavarian Gardens? The topless joint?" he asked, keeping his stare going.

Oldham couldn't look at him. He rubbed his hands on his knees over and over. "Yeah. I like the dancers they got there."

Meyn leaned forward, keying in on Oldham's nervousness. "Do you go alone or with your friends?"

"Once in a while with friends, fellow drivers, but usually by myself."

"Are you friendly with any of the dancers?"

"I wish," he snickered.

"Okay, so what happened last night that you ended up in Lake Hills–Bellevue?"

"Not much… Didn't like the rowdy crowd at the Bavarian Gardens, so I decided to try Charlie's before going home, and…and…"

"And what? Ever been to Charlie's Place before tonight?"

He shook his head. "Nope. Before tonight I had only driven by it a few times while taking customers from the airport to the Hilltop, but I never went in. I wandered in tonight out of curiosity."

"Then what happened?" Meyn probed, leaning forward in his chair.

Oldham rubbed his palms on his knees again and again. "Just wandered in, and uh, here was this beautiful barmaid, and I fell in love, or something."

"You 'fell in love or something'? Explain."

"I couldn't stop looking at her."

"What did you have in mind when you followed her home, Terry?"

"Nothing, really," he replied, leaning back in his chair, hands in his lap. "I wasn't going to come back or try to see her again. I was curious why someone so pretty would be working in a place like that."

"You've done this before, though, right, Terry?"

Oldham fell into a silence, his gaze to the floor.

"The Seattle PD's records show you doing this same sort of thing more than once," Meyn pursued. "A

Peeping Tom is what you are, Terry, aren't you?"

"Yeah... yeah," he said in a low voice, continuing to stare at the linoleum floor.

"Why did you run from the officers, Terry?"

"I just got off probation," he replied, nodding, hands clasped.

Meyn set the suspect statement form on the desk again. "Terry," he said, "I'm really glad you've been so honest with me. Believe me, it's rare."

Mallard grinned slightly. "I suppose so."

"Let's get this out in the open so nobody'll accuse you later of intending to do more than looking. You want to get that part cleared up, don't you, Terry?"

"Sure do," Oldham agreed, still staring at the floor.

"Okay, then. Write a page or two to explain what you did and why, and most important, just as you told me, state that you meant no harm, you just wanted to look because the girl is so pretty. Okay, Terry?"

Meyn handed him a sheet of blank, unlined paper.

Oldham took the pen from Detective Meyn. As he wrote, Meyn leaned forward and watched him write in barely legible scrawl, unevenly spaced.

*I, Terry Oldham, was blown away when I saw this pretty barmaid when I went to Charlie's Place. I followed her home just to be able to look at her some more. I meant no harm.*

"Excellent, Terry," Meyn said. "Now add your signature at the bottom."

Meyn shifted into interrogation mode as soon as

Oldham signed it. "Now, Terry," he began, "you may be wondering why all this intense interest over a little thing like prowling and peeping, right?"

"I was wondering about that."

"Really? Why?"

"Because you, a detective, was called out in the middle of the night. What I did wasn't right, I admit, but—"

"It so happens, Terry, that a man fitting your physical description has been entering women's bedrooms of women during the night and forcing them into sexual acts. Terry, are you the one who's been doing this?"

Oldham looked at Meyn as if he had been slapped in the face. "No! Absolutely not. Never," he said, leaning back.

"Terry, how do you feel about being interviewed about these incidents involving women?"

Mallard made eye contact with Meyn. "Now that I understand, I want to help if I can."

"Terry, did you ever think about doing something like enter a woman's home and have sex with her but never went through with it?"

"No way."

Meyn allowed a long pause to observe Oldham before his next question. "What do you think should happen to a person who would do something like break into women's homes and have sexual contact with them against their will?"

"Prison for life, no parole," came Oldham's prompt reply.

"Okay, Terry, it would help us to eliminate you from suspicion if you would take a polygraph test to verify you are telling me the truth. Would you do that?

"I want to clear my name."

"Terry, what do you think the results of the polygraph would be?"

"I'll do fine. I'll take one now if it will help."

"We'll schedule one for tomorrow. Say three in the afternoon?"

"Yes. Can I go now?"

"Not just yet. You must be booked before we release you, and we would like you to sign the voluntary search warrant for your car. It'll save us the time and trouble of getting one from our judge. Okay?"

"Sure."

A TOW TRUCK brought Oldham's car to the station. Meyn placed him in a holding cell after he signed the voluntary search warrant. The interior was cluttered with empty cigarette packs and food wrappers from drive-in restaurants, but nothing incriminating.

Meyn made plaster casts of Oldham's shoes for comparison to suspect footprints from other cases. He cited Oldham for prowling under the vagrancy ordinance and released him on signature.

"WELL LARRY, THINK you'll sell Oldham some prison time?" It was Sergeant Breen standing in the door of the interrogation room.

Meyn shook his head as he picked up Oldham's statements and files. "Physically and circumstantially, he could be the guy, Jack, but everything else points to his innocence. Either he's an innocent guy who was in the wrong place at the wrong time or he's the smoothest talker I've ever met."

# CHAPTER THIRTY-EIGHT
## No Stone Unturned

OLDHAM PASSED THE polygraph the following afternoon. Not completely satisfied, Meyn contacted Oldham's work supervisor in person, who supplied his timecards for the last nine months. They verified he was working in Seattle when each of the attacks occurred.

Captain Holland called Meyn and Sergeant Jurgens into his office. "Larry, how do you size up this Oldham character?"

"He's neither of the men we're looking for, Captain. He's too young to be the original suspect. He matches the younger suspect's description but reeks of cigarettes, bad breath and dirty clothes. His victims described the suspect as clean smelling. His responses to questions were consistent with truthfulness, he sailed through the polygraph, and his timecards show he was at work in Seattle when every one of the attacks happened. No blue-hooded sweatshirt was found on him, or in his car. We checked his bedroom at his parents' home with his permission. No hooded sweatshirts of any color."

"What do you make of him?"

"He's another passive non-achiever, typical of his generation, content to make just enough to squeak by and live in a fantasy world. He's a pervert, but he's innocent of attacking any of our victims."

"Okay, it *appears* Oldham is not the guy, but...," Holland opined when Sergeant Jurgens interrupted.

"But?"

"He's still a pervert who just *happened* to show up in the *same neighborhood* where a previous attack happened a few months ago. It's too much of a coincidence. We can't leave even one stone unturned. Before we let Oldham off the hook, let's consider the one aspect of the latest attack we withheld for security reasons: the suspect turned on the outside faucet before he entered the victim's residence. Let's ask SPD if they have any instances of this M.O. in any of their cases Oldham was responsible for."

Sergeant Jurgens spoke up. "I already did that at Larry's request. I called the SPD sex crimes unit this morning. No record of an M.O. like the one in our cases. I also called the Special Assault Unit at the Prosecutor's Office—same reply."

"Okay then. I guess we've done all we can."

"I'm thinking of one more thing we could do with Oldham before we move on, Captain," Meyn said.

"And that is?"

"A lineup."

"He's cleared himself of all reasonable suspicion already," Captain Holland said.

"Still, I think we should. It will satisfy any lingering doubts there may be."

"What if the victim identifies Oldham?" Jurgens asked.

"Then we have more work to do. A lot more," Meyn said.

"It's worth a shot," Holland said, "if Oldham cooperates."

THREE DAYS LATER, Detective Nate Williams and a uniformed police matron escorted Florence Abernathy into the witness section of the Seattle Police lineup room which was like a small stage theater. The barren, medium grayish-blue walls made for a gloomy setting in low lighting. The stage was about two feet above the floor. Beyond the stage were wooden bench seats, like church pews, for attorneys, reporters, other interested parties. All the way in the back was the victim and witness section, separated by a low wall.

"Don't be afraid, Mrs. Abernathy. The bright lights on the floor below the lineup prevents anyone in the lineup from seeing you, but you can see them. Are you okay?" Florence nodded as she fidgeted with her hands in her lap.

BLAZING CEILING-MOUNTED lights aimed down at the stage, and a row of floor-mounted lights aimed up blinded anyone on stage from seeing observers. Detectives Meyn and Small and two uniformed Seattle Police officers escorted a line of six men, each wearing a blue hooded sweatshirt with the hood up, to the stage. The line stopped and waited. On command, they turned and faced the blazing lights. Oldham was in third position. Hitchcock, Otis, Walker, and two SPD officers stood on either side of Oldham. Detective Meyn stood at the podium.

"Number One, step forward one step," Meyn commanded.

Hitchcock stepped forward. "Repeat after me, Number One: 'I don't want to hurt you any worse.'" Hitchcock repeated the phrase.

"Number One, repeat after me: 'I will come back soon.'"

In the witness section, Florence Abernathy shook her head no.

The process was repeated until all six men in the lineup had spoken the same phrases and turned in all directions. Florence Abernathy shook her head to each of them. Clutching Detective Williams's arm, she began crying. 'He's not any of those men. I can't do this again. Please take me home," she said.

Williams exchanged glances with the police matron, who touched Florence Abernathy's arm. "We'll get you home safely, Mrs. Abernathy," the matron whispered.

† † †

AT THE STATION, Sergeant Jurgens reported to Captain Holland. "The victim said it was none of the guys in the lineup, including Oldham, Captain."

Holland nodded. "Well done, Stan. I'll write a thank-you letter to Oldham for his cooperation which he can show to the judge to protect his name. And I'll recommend Ira Walker for a service commendation. He deserves it. I'll send copies to the Chief and the City Manager. This is the kind of police work that solves cases. Great work by everyone. Close, but no cigar."

# CHAPTER THIRTY-NINE
## The Original Returns

AS SOON AS his wife left the house, the oldest predator took a taxi to a restaurant in downtown Redmond. He went inside and waited until the taxi was out of sight, then he crossed the street to a storage facility.

The lock on the roll-up door of the large storage unit he rented hadn't been tampered with. The fine layer of dust on the exterior of his gray late-model Dodge sedan with oversized engine and Oregon license plates meant no one touched it during his absence. His blue hooded sweatshirt, rope, roll of duct tape and surgical gloves in the trunk were as he left them.

Conflicting emotions of fear of being caught and the urge to hunt for new victims swirled in his mind as he backed out of the storage unit.

The traffic was so heavy he had to wait to make a right turn to enter. A Redmond police car stopped in the curb lane. The officer behind the wheel gestured for him to enter.

*What if the Bellevue cops put out a bulletin on my car?*

To hesitate longer or refuse the officer's courtesy would arouse suspicion. With a lump in his throat, he faked a smile, waved thanks and entered the traffic with the police officer right behind him.

His hands were cold and clammy. Nausea filled his stomach for several blocks, wondering if this was the end of his freedom. The officer turned onto a side street. He made it the rest of the way home without being stopped.

He said nothing to his wife Mona who was watching soap operas in the den when he walked through the door. The pornography in his safe no longer aroused him, nor did the trophies he fondled—a hairbrush holding a victim's hair, soiled underwear, a bra. Fantasy wasn't enough anymore. Now he needed to touch his victims, feel their fear, their submission, he wanted them to touch him.

According to the local newspaper, his younger counterpart was going much farther with his victims. He wondered if the young man understood that the law of averages was working against them both. The police almost caught him last time. Certainly, the police were close to catching his young imitator. They will if he doesn't stop now. and what would happen to him when they do.

His thoughts returned to his second narrow escape. The blue-hooded sweatshirt he wore that night and the binding equipment in the trunk of his getaway car would have landed him in jail if not for his head start and fast car. *I've got to quit now, or the law of averages will get me,* he told himself. But dark urges overcame reason and survival instinct. He had no choice but to obey, to go on the scout again, to the same neighborhood where the cop spotted and chased him. And he'd strike twice, to get even for last time.

A familiar voice broke through his musings.

"Creighton, a man called while you were out. He was asking for you, wouldn't say who he was, said it was a private matter and he would call back," Mona called out from the kitchen.

Alarmed, he wondered who the caller could be.

# CHAPTER FORTY
## Not Quite Murder

ALLIE GROANED AT the third ring of the phone on the nightstand. She tapped Hitchcock's arm. "Answer it, honey. Only the station calls at three a.m."

He muttered drowsily as he picked up the receiver.

"Roger, it's Barbara. Randy's in the ICU at Harborview," she gasped, "heroin overdose again. Someone beat him up bad. He almost died! *Please* come. I need you."

† † †

INTRAVENOUS TUBES DRAPED over Randy Fowler like the tentacles of a baby octopus. Purplish abrasions, contusions and stitches covered his face and neck. His left eye was swollen shut. He opened his right eye as Hitchcock entered.

"Randy? It's me, Roger."

Randy barely shook his head once.

"What *happened*? You were doing so well."

"I'm sorry, Roger," he croaked. "I failed God and everybody. The ole devil's laughing at me now."

"Your mom called me. She said you got on heroin again and someone beat you up. The doc told her you would have died if you hadn't been brought in when you were. Tell me what happened."

"Everything's a blur, a blur," Randy replied, turning his head side to side, grimacing with pain at the slightest move.

"What *do* you remember?" he persisted. "Was it Mike Smith?"

Randy turned his head away at the name. "Yeah. Him"

"How did it happen?"

"He stopped by as I was getting off work. Offered to cut me in, to work for him, selling smack to kids. I said no, I'm a Christian now. He acted real interested, said, 'yeah? I've been thinking about that. You're the only Christian I know. Hop in and tell me about it.' So, like a dummy I went with him in his car, thinking I would convert him and the guy sitting behind me…"

Randy paused.

"Go on."

Randy's voice was raspy. Words came in a halting fashion. "We stopped. Don't remember where. He lit a joint and handed it to me as I was telling him about Christ. Something inside me screamed at me not to, but then Smith took a toke and blew the smoke in my face. He waved it under my nose until I let Jesus and everybody down and took a toke.

"I got high right away. I took another hit, then another. The big guy in the back seat was toking on a bong, and I took a hit on that too. I got *very* high. I didn't struggle when Mike stuck a needle in me. Next thing I knew, I was being beat up, but I didn't feel a thing. Then I woke up here."

"You recognized Mike Smith. Describe the other guy."

Randy turned his head side-to-side as though in the pains of heroin withdrawal. "He was big. Really big. That's all I remember."

"White? Black?"

"White. He was white."

"Now we're getting somewhere. Dark hair. Light hair? Bald?

"Dark...I think. Not short or long. Kinda curly. Like ringlets."

"Good, Randy. His name? Did you hear his name?"

Randy slowly shook his head. "Smith did all the talking."

"What else?"

"Nothing. I'm such a waste, Roger, such a waste," he said, moaning, fighting tears.

"Cut the self-pity. You're not a waste. You made a mistake. Everybody does. All is not lost. As a man what you do is you pick up the pieces and start over. Now tell me—have you seen this other guy who was with Smith before?"

"I don't remember, I tell ya! I don't remember! Oh God, I want to die."

"Knock it off!" Hitchcock demanded in a sharp tone. "You're not gonna die. By tomorrow or the next day, you'll remember more details and you're gonna tell me so I can get the bastards. Now, what car was Smith driving?"

"Blue Mustang."

"Not a green Firebird?"

Randy shook his head drowsily.

"You sure?"

"I know cars."

Hitchcock felt a tug on his arm. "Pastor Scratch is here, Roger," Barbara Fowler said.

Meeting Randy's mother in the hall, Hitchcock asked, "How did you find out about this, Barbara?"

"A deputy called me from the hospital. People at the Sammamish State Park found Randy lying in the bushes. They thought he was dead. An ambulance brought him."

"What did Randy tell you?"

"Not as much as he just told you. He's so ashamed, Roger," she said, her voice breaking.

† † †

HITCHCOCK LEFT HARBORVIEW Hospital in a dark mood. He saw Mike Smith becoming an underworld Pied Piper. He got Randy started on pot, then led him down the path to heroin addiction. After Randy refused Smith's offer to work for him, Smith tried to kill him the same way he killed Holly Gladwell—overdosing and dumping the body.

Smith was the suspect in two other overdose deaths of teenagers involving high potency heroin from Vietnam. Hitchcock guessed Smith decided to kill Randy because he knows too much and is friends with a cop.

*Randy's holding out on me. He knows more than he's telling me otherwise Smith wouldn't be trying to kill him. Once Smith learns that Randy survived, he'll try to kill him again. How can I find Smith when I don't have even one informant?*

ALLIE WAS IRONING when he returned home. "Randy overdosed. Heroin. Mike Smith tried to kill him by overdose," he announced bitterly.

Alle stopped her work. Her jaw dropped open in surprise. "No! He was doing so well! Oh, that poor family. Trouble follows them like a shadow."

He plopped into his leather chair, his face set and angry. "Randy almost died this time. He's recovering in Harborview. His family is with him, and a few church people too. He'll be okay, but he's got to undergo the whole rehab process again."

"Put your feet up. I'll get you some coffee," she said, heading for the kitchen.

Minutes later, Allie found him in the master closet, uniform on, doing his draw-and-dry-fire twenty-five times ritual. "Is Randy Fowler the reason you're going in to work an hour early?"

He didn't answer. He didn't need to.

She handed him his favorite mug. "Fresh made," she said.

He took the steaming mug as he lovingly touched her bulging stomach with his other hand and kissed her. He took two sips and handed the mug back to her. "A lot is going on now, baby. Gotta go."

# CHAPTER FORTY-ONE
## The Man in the Black Suit

THE JUKEBOX AT Charlie's Place just finished playing *Born on the Bayou* by Creedence Clearwater Revival when Hitchcock entered through the back door. He nodded at two young construction types playing pool, and noted three groups of couples sitting at tables with glasses and pitchers in front of them, chatting quietly Behind the bar, owner Wally Evans bowed and gestured welcome with his right hand.

"The man of the hour! Congratulations on your fantastic police work the other night for Debbie. Caught a creepy pervert in the act before she even called."

"The credit goes to my partner, Ira. Debbie lives in his district. I just happened to be his back-up."

Evans smiled amiably. "Either way, it was great police work. Who knows what might have happened if Walker hadn't been so alert? What did the guy have to say for himself?"

"I'm not allowed to say. He's been charged with prowling in our city court. You can call the court tomorrow to find out the date of the trial and attend, but I can't disclose full case details."

Wally nodded. "I'll be there so I can ask the judge to restrict him from here as well as Debbie's place."

"Good idea. You protect your people, even the divorced moms who moonlight with the truckers on weekends. I like that," he said with a sly smile.

Wally shook his head and chuckled. "Nice try, rookie. Back to our topic, can I see his mugshot in case he comes here again? If he does, I'll throw him out, headfirst. Debbie is like a daughter to my wife and I."

"I 'll arrange it," Hitchcock said. "The best time is?"

"Tomorrow, seven to closing. Debbie was one of many who was busted up about you getting married, by the way," Wally said with a sly smile of his own.

"She told me. Debbie's a looker. I was flattered."

HE HEADED FOR The Wagon Wheel next, hoping Gayle still worked there. Through her work he seized record amounts of hard drugs and killed or put bad people in prison. If her romantic interests hadn't become so demanding, she'd still be his informant.

Suddenly the same gut instinct that led him to dead bodies and dangerous criminals urged him to hang a U-turn and go back down the frontage road.

IT SURPRISED HITCHCOCK to see the dining area of The Great Wall filled with customers. *What they don't know won't hurt 'em, I guess,* he mentally joked, remembering the story of the cook taking a freshly killed cat into the kitchen a couple months ago.

The intensity of the urging to come to The Great Wall so suddenly put him on edge. *It's like a hand I can't see led me here. I'm here, now what?* Filled with anxiety and bewilderment, he didn't know what was so urgent, what to expect. He had no plan in mind except that he knew better than to mention Mike Smith's name.

A black full-size Jaguar sedan and a white Lincoln Town Car, both new, were parked by the back door but Juju's Cadillac El Dorado wasn't there.

He stepped into clouds of hissing steam, the foreign chatter of cooks and waitresses and the pungent smells of rice, meat and spices hanging thickly in the air. A male cook spotted him and ran from the kitchen to the cocktail lounge, speaking in Chinese with alarm in his voice. Seconds later, the cook hurried back, stood at attention with his hands at his sides and bowed deeply to Hitchcock. *Something is up, none of it good.*

Pressing his elbow against the butt of his service revolver to affirm its presence in his holster, he entered the darkened cocktail lounge. Four Asian men in expensive dark suits, kerchiefs in their breast pockets, white shirts, and neckties turned and stood shoulder-to-shoulder, facing him with hands clasped in front of them. The bartender faced him from behind the bar as if he expected to see something happen.

The sounds of customers in the dining area and normal clatter from the kitchen faded as if someone dialed down the volume. The smells of cigarette smoke and strange liquor replaced the smells of the kitchen.

With a friendly grin Hitchcock positioned himself so that his back was against an empty booth as he faced the four strange men, the bartender, and the entrance.

"Can we help you, Officer Hitchcock?" The one in the center asked. He was older than the others by a decade. He wore an expensive-looking black silk suit with red and black striped tie and matching red kerchief in the breast pocket of his suitcoat. The coldness beneath his smooth accent reminded Hitchcock of encounters during his second tour in Vietnam.

He nodded, keeping his eyes on his greeter and smiled thinly. "No problem, sir. Department policy is to visit bars often. Make sure everything is all right."

Black Suit returned the smile, hands still folded in front of him. The youngest and stoutest one, stood close behind, slightly offset from Black Suit, aiming an intense stare at Hitchcock.

The lounge was too dark for his uniform name tag to be read at this distance. "How do you know my name?"

Another brief, cold smile. "You are quite well-known, Officer Hitchcock. Miss Kwan, Juju, speaks very highly of you."

Hitchcock almost laughed in his face. *I'll bet she does!* He had to think fast. *Whatever business these men are in, rice or soy sauce it ain't. They're foreigners, they're big time, and my presence is unexpected and unwelcome.*

Playing the oafish country boy, he stepped into Black Suit's space with a broad smile and extended his hand.

"Well, goll-eee, I must say, that's *wunnerful* to hear! Any friend of Juju's is a friend of mine, Mister…"

Taken off guard, Black Suit forced a nervous grin as he took Hitchcock's hand. "I am Mr. Chen."

"And these fine men with you?" he asked as he nodded toward the others, smiling, pumping and squeezing Chen's soft hand; the hand of a man who gives orders which no one disobeys.

Hitchcock understood the stout young one close to Chen to be a trained bodyguard. The other two were corporate yes-men from the business rank-and-file, who were staying out of harm's way.

Hitchcock kept smiling, pumping and squeezing Chen's hand as his eyes warned the bodyguard not to come one step closer.

"My associates," Chen said curtly, drawing his hand back and putting it in his suit jacket pocket.

Hitchcock put on an ear-to-ear grin. "Well, shucks! I am *real* glad we met, Mr. Chen!" he gushed. "And, since all is well here, I must be on my way. Got other rounds to make, so good night to y'all," he said as he tipped his hat and left through the back door.

He wrote the plate numbers of the Jaguar and the Lincoln in his pocket notebook on his way to his cruiser.

Chen and his entourage emerged from the back door in single file. They looked around, speaking to each other in what sounded to Hitchcock like Mandarin. The two yes-men got into the Jaguar. The bodyguard opened the back door of the Town Car and bowed as Chen got in. Both cars took the short onramp to enter the westbound freeway toward Seattle from the frontage road.

# CHAPTER FORTY-TWO
## Instinctive Moves

SERGEANT JURGENS ARRIVED at his office an hour ahead of his overworked detectives. He sorted through the latest Case Reports and Field Interview Reports, hoping for new leads in the blue-hooded-sweatshirt cases.

One FIR that stood out was from Otis. At 3:00 a.m. a late model gray compact sedan with Oregon plates fled at a high rate of speed when he stopped and turned around. The car arrived ten minutes earlier. Jurgens wrote up and posted a BOLO (Be On the Lookout) on the squad room bulletin board, to be read at Patrol and Traffic briefings. He teletyped the details to Western Washington agencies.

Jurgens didn't envy Captain Holland, or the Chief. In the current cultural climate, their heads were constantly on the political chopping block. Complaints by pampered, privileged upper middle-class citizens about the boldness of the new crop of young veterans and two serial sex offenders ravaging women in their beds, among other issues, were fodder for the Department's political enemies.

He disliked and distrusted the news media, but they were the last hand in his deck of cards to play – the joker. Rape is one of the most underreported crimes due to victims' fear of retaliation by their assailants and the stigma of being a sexual assault victim. He drafted a press release, urging anyone who had been sexually assaulted and did not file a report to call the detective division. Jurgens knew that in doing so, he was putting himself and his bosses in the hot seat.

† † †

HITCHCOCK WAITED IN the library parking lot until he saw the Brass leave at 5:00 p.m. He didn't want to be seen in Records, nor did he want to compromise his boss, Jack Breen. Patty met him when he entered Records out of uniform.

"The Lieutenant stepped out, Roger, but he'll be back in a minute," she said softly. "What can I get you?"

"The newest mugshots we have of Michael Smith, D.O.B. 10/12/50. All vehicles registered to him, and a copy of his last arrest sheet."

"Leave it to me," Patty said. "Don't get caught in here. New rule."

Smith's mugshot was in his inbox when he came to work two hours later. He showed it to bartenders and barmaids at Charlie's and The Wagon Wheel, telling them the suspect is wanted regarding a death case.

Last stop was The Great Wall.

The same Lincoln Town Car and Jaguar sedan from the previous night were parked next to Juju's black Cadillac Eldorado in the back. An overwhelming sense of warning told Hitchcock not to get out of his vehicle.

He sat for long seconds with the driver's door of his cruiser open. This instinct, unseen hand, or whatever it was, had led him to evidence, dead bodies, and alerted him of danger about to strike. The alarm now was urgent as when he was on patrols in Vietnam. He knew he was not to enter the Great Wall now, but it went against his police instincts to sidestep danger. He opened the driver door and set his left foot on the pavement.

Butterflies filled his stomach. He had no peace about going in. The butterflies left when he drove away.

# CHAPTER FORTY-THREE
## Hunting the Pied Piper

AT THE END of his shift, Hitchcock waited in the parking lot next to Walker's Oldsmobile Cutlass, reading a map of East King County with the file on Mike Smith next to him.

Walker approached, wearing a black windbreaker over his uniform.

"Whatcha reading, Roger, *Under the Grandstands*, by Eileen Over?" he quipped, smirking at his own joke.

"You up for a trip to the sticks this morning, funny man?"

"Sure. What's up?"

"We've got to find Mike Smith."

"He's in town?"

"Nope."

"You know where he is?"

"Hop in."

There was silence between them until they were beyond Bellevue city limits, eastbound on I-90.

"What's the plan if we find him?" Walker asked.

"We're gonna arrest him under the authority of our county commissions, book him at the station, grab a black-and-white and take him to the slammer downtown."

Walker nodded his assent. "Then we'll go home and mail in our badges."

"You in, or not?"

"*Somebody's* gotta put the grabs on Smith," Walker muttered. "Nothing else is working."

† † †

IT WAS STILL dark when the headlights of Hitchcock's Jeep Wagoneer shone down the long tree-lined dirt driveway of Smith's last known address in Carnation. He stopped at the edge of the clearing when the house was barely visible in the trees.

"You sure Smith's here?" Walker asked.

"It was his address a year ago."

Hitchcock grabbed a hunk of greasy rag from under his seat and got out.

"What are you doing?" Walker asked.

"Get out and watch."

He covered the rear license plate with the rag. Walker started laughing. "Got another rag? I'll do the front."

They idled down the overgrown gravel driveway to a lights-out, white clapboard '40s vintage dump, black tarpaper roof, surrounded by knee-high weeds, rusted beater cars and trucks.

Walker looked around. "Uh, I must've dozed off. Are we in Appalachia?"

"See a blue late model Mustang anywhere?" Hitchcock asked.

"I left my machete in my car, but since we're here, let's get the plate number of every car if we can."

A brown medium-sized mutt began barking as they rolled into the front yard and stopped. Penlight in his teeth, Walker hurriedly wrote down six license numbers and descriptions as Hitchcock put his headlights on each and called them out.

"Got 'em all?"

"One more. The grass is hiding the plate of a blue sedan next to the carport. Get closer, Roger."

Hitchcock stopped close behind the blue sedan. It was an older Chevy Impala. "Mary Boy Charles Six Seven One!" He exclaimed. "Be quick! Lights came on inside!"

Walker repeated the plate number back. "Someone just parted the drapes. They're eyeballing us, Roger. More lights are coming on! I don't think they're happy! Make tracks!"

"Okay. If bullets start hitting the back, let me know."

"You'll be the first person I tell! Hoo-wee!" Walker chuckled.

Hitchcock spun a U-turn wheelie through tall wet

grass and mud. His Wagoneer bucked, lurched and splashed through water-filled chuckholes as he sped up the tree-lined driveway.

"Anybody following us?"

Walker looked back. "Other than that mob of angry peasants carrying torches and pitchforks running after us, all clear!"

Hitchcock stopped to uncover his license plates. "If the people in the house are crooks, they'll go ballistic over who entered their driveway at O-Dark-Hundred!"

"Maybe they'll kill their rivals trying to find out."

"We couldn't be so lucky. When we get to the station, I'll turn these plate numbers in, so we'll have the names of the registered owners and know if there are warrants out on them when we come back tonight."

"New rule, Ira. We aren't supposed to be in Records."

Walker snorted in disgust. "I'll make copies for us in case something happens and put the originals in a sealed envelope in Patty's inbox. She starts at four but arrives early."

Hitchcock suddenly took the Preston exit.

"What's going on?"

"A sudden impulse to take this exit."

"Hah! Last time that happened, Sherman was with you and three crooks bit the dust in a hail of bullets. This time I'm here, my gun is loaded, so follow your gut, Roger."

"Nothing out here but woods, an abandoned sawmill, a few scattered houses, but the draw is strong."

"You don't have to explain anything to me. My gun is loaded and I'm ready to pray and spray. Let's go."

"You don't pray and spray with a six-shot revolver, Ira."

By the time they reached Fall City, the instinct Hitchcock sensed was gone. Puzzled, he drove back the same way to the freeway. Again, nothing.

It was turning daylight when they returned to City Hall. Lieutenant Bostwick was preening and adjusting his uniform hat and tie bar in the reflection of a parked patrol car window in the parking lot.

Walker began snickering. "*Der veernerschnitzel*, little Heinie Bahstveetch is up to no good of some kind, *jah*?"

"Better wait until tonight to give those plate numbers to Patty, Ira."

They watched Bostwick enter the station.

"I'll come in early, so we'll have them by shift briefing tonight," Hitchcock said. "Patty will have checked all the registered owners for warrants. If it's quiet, we'll put on our detective hats. Catch you later."

Morning traffic began filling the streets and the 405 freeway below City Hall as Hitchcock watched Walker head for his personal vehicle, parked by the library. The upper City Hall parking lot would be empty for another half-hour.

His watch read 7:41 a.m. He wondered if Allie was

up, given that she is eight months into her pregnancy. Nothing had better disturb her now. She carried their son. From the station he headed west across the Main Street overpass, unaware of a tan early '60s Ford half-ton pickup following him.

# CHAPTER FORTY-FOUR
## The Tide Turns

ALLIE WAS RINSING dishes in the kitchen sink as Hitchcock slipped his arms around her from behind and kissed the side of her neck. With loving gentleness, he ran his hands over her swollen tummy and held her.

She broke into tears.

"What's wrong, baby?"

"The kind of world we're bringing our baby into, honey. Two strangers attack us at home because you're doing your job. Because they failed, one was executed and the other disappeared. That means they were hired killers. *Who* hired them? Your friend Randy becomes a Christian and someone tries to kill him with an overdose. On the nightly news, people burn the flag, bomb the Pentagon and ambush policemen."

He ran his hands over her arms and shoulders.

"I don't feel safe anymore, Roger," she sobbed. "People I know—my family—don't like what's going on either. They don't feel safe."

He held her in his arms from behind, his head next

to hers. "We've taken all the precautions we can."

She turned in his arms to face him, slipped her arms over his shoulders, tiptoed up and returned his kiss, long and deep.

"That was a long shift you were on, my man," she said, catching her breath.

"I want to sleep in. Unless it's an emergency, no calls, no visitors."

"Oh really? And what if a certain little blonde comes a-knockin' at yer door, laddie?"

He tilted his head back, laughing. "What is it with you Irish chicks?"

"Aye, we eye-rish gals gotta get back at you turrable Brits somehow," she said, rolling her r's in her best Irish brogue.

"Oh yeah? What's this bulge in your tummy then?"

"Ah! Go get your sleep, you *bloody* pirate you!" she said with a playful slap on his shoulder. "The surprise I have for you will have to wait."

He titled his head back again. "Ahh! Now I won't be able to sleep!"

Allie led him by the hand to the bedroom. "Come, my man. I order you to sleep now as best as you can."

He sat on the edge of the bed, faking a rueful expression. "Ah need hep, darlin'."

"With what?"

"Hep! Ah'm too tahrred to undress muhsef, ma'am," he said in his best Southern drawl with a wolfish wink.

Allie put her hands on her hips, smiling happily. "I'm almost past the point where I can do anything, mister! You got me into this, you know!"

Though exhausted, Hitchcock leered lustily at her, flipped his eyebrows up and down. "Did I hear you say *almost*, ma'am?" He beckoned to her, singing "*Little Red Riding Hood.*"

She laughed. "So that's what you do in your patrol car. Drive around, listening to Sam-the-Sham-and-the-Pharaohs. Well..." She turned to close the door as she sang, "*Little Red Riding Hood's gotta be everything a big bad wolf would want...*"

He threw his head back and let loose a wolf howl as Allie pushed him back on the bed. "*Ahh-ooooo!*"

† † †

AMID THE TYPICAL Bull Pen racket of clacking typewriters and overriding phone conversations, Detective Larry Meyn suddenly stopped typing, opened his desk drawer and again compared the writing on the note found in the pocket of the Asian suspect who attacked Hitchcock, to samples of writing he took from Bostwick's desk.

Meyn was no handwriting expert, but consistent similarities in letter and number formations led him to conclude Bostwick wrote the directions to Hitchcock's residence. Only the writing on the back of Juju Kwan's business card wasn't Bostwick's. Surely that writing is Juju's, which suggested a relationship, which raised other questions.

A side of him wished he hadn't found the evidence, let alone seized it. His discovery of the dark betrayal of an officer by a higher-ranking officer changed his life and probably his career path. If he blew the whistle, it would put him in the crosshairs of whoever Bostwick answers to.

Yet one of the two out-of-town thugs had written directions to Hitchcock's secluded, unmarked address at the end of an unmarked road, hid their car at a distant location and hiked through the woods to attack him and his family. Only a Department insider would know where Hitchcock lived, by personal knowledge or access to his personnel file.

A professional examination by a handwriting expert was needed to determine if Bostwick wrote the note, the writing was so similar to his, and his intense dislike for Hitchcock was no secret; only the reason was.

A man's hand waved in front of his face. "Earth to Larry, anyone home?" It was his sergeant, the square-jawed, clean-cut Stan Jurgens.

"Sarge, could we meet in your office for a minute?"

# CHAPTER FORTY-FIVE
## The Honeytrap

AT THE FAR end of the hall from the detective office, near the station door, Lieutenant Bostwick sat at his desk, pretending to be busy. He answered his phone on the second ring. From her first word he recognized Juju's voice, sultry, foreign-accented, alluring. "Rowlie, you come today. I need you."

His face flushed with excitement, His secret, exotic lover needed him. Maybe today would be the day she would tell him yes to his marriage offer. How it would play out with his parents didn't concern him anymore. All he knew was that Juju was his destiny.

He inspected his uniform in a mirror to be sure the creases were sharp, and the brass gleamed. He was unaware of the clerks and officers snickering and scoffing as he practiced his conquering-general walk in the station parking lot before he left.

A WAITRESS SCURRIED to the back as Bostwick made his usual grand entrance through the front door of The

Great Wall. Juju came out, her hand on the shoulder of a pretty, petite adolescent Chinese girl who was beaming at Bostwick. She kissed him, then gestured to the girl. "Rowlie-sahn, you meet my niece Pin-Yen, at my place before. You remember, yes?"

Playing the gallant warrior that he never was, Bostwick did his best imitation of the military officers he saw in the old black-and-white war movies on late-night television. He removed his hat with a flourish and tucked it under his left arm. The only gesture from the movies he missed was clicking his heels when he bowed stiffly like a German army officer as he took Pin-Yen's hand in his, and kissed it.

"Why yes, of course I remember Pin-Yen, how are you, young lady?"

Pin-Yen smiled shyly at Bostwick. Juju put her hand on Bostwick's arm. "You remember, Pin-Yen speak no English, Rowlie-sahn?"

Bostwick nodded and his thin lips curled up at the corners. "Oh yes! I remember now. Forgive me."

"Rowlie-sahn, Communists kill much of Pin-yen's family in China. They flee to Taiwan. Pin-Yen wish me to ask if you kill many Communists in Vietnam?"

The question caught him off guard for a moment. "Ah, Juju, my love, this you never ask war veterans. Even among ourselves, we never talk about what we did. Please tell Pin-Yen how sorry I am for the members of her family who were killed."

Juju almost laughed in his face. She who began life as an orphan on the run from Chinese Communists, grew up knowing war, poverty and prostitution in the new land of Taiwan before she was twelve, knew from first-hand experience what real veterans, real soldiers were like. She could tell if a man had served in the military. Bostwick wasn't one of them.

Skillful use of her beauty and cunning brought her from the slums and brothels of Taipei to America while she was still young, and her sensual mien enabled her to snare inexperienced men, young and old.

She communicated with Pin-Yen in Mandarin and with hand gestures. The girl nodded, bowed to Bostwick, and left.

With the practiced charm of a courtesan, Juju put her hand on Bostwick's chest long enough and gently enough with a hungry, pleading look up into his eyes that reduced him to putty.

"So sorry, Rowlie-sahn. Please forgive me. Come to my office. I make this up to you now, unless you want eat?"

"Uh, no, no. I'll have something later."

Juju took him by the hand. "Come."

Bostwick burned with boyish lust when she shut her office door and flipped the lock. "What did you want to see me about, my love?" he asked, his voice thick with desire.

She pressed herself into him and kissed him

forcefully. Breaking the kiss, she stroked his cheek with her hand. "You come my place tonight," she whispered. "Spesal dinner for you. Then I tell you what I need."

Minutes later, customers stared as Juju led Bostwick by the hand from her office to her private dining room, straightening his tie, his clothes and his thinning hair. She barked orders in Mandarin to her waitresses and sat next to him as a waitress brought him tea and a steaming bowl of won-ton soup, bowing as she left. Another waitress came with a platter of fried rice, egg rolls, and chop suey.

Bostwick ate hungrily as Juju watched. Lunch crowd customers stared as Juju escorted him out the front door. She watched him head west toward the station in his unmarked police car.

JUJU CALLED THE long-distance operator. Although the time in Taipei was twelve hours ahead, her instructions were to call no matter the hour. The phone was answered on the second ring. In Mandarin Juju confirmed the person on the other end was Mr. Chen. Translated, she said, "As you ordered, I started the process today. I will report on my progress in a few days."

Someone knocked on her office door as she hung up. "Come in," she said in English.

Pin-Yen entered. "What else would you like me to do?" Pin-Yen asked in perfect American English without a trace of accent.

Juju answered in Mandarin. "You will play my niece again tonight when Rowlie comes to my house. You will stay out of sight as you did before until I give the signal. Then do as before, I pay you and take you back to your parents in the morning."

"Was he really in Vietnam, Nuu-Shirh?"

Juju laughed out loud. "No, Hsiao Jie. We know everything about Rowlie. He lie. Never in military, never been outside America. Rich parents keep him safe, then got him police job. They have powerful friends. He no make arrest, never have girl before me. You saw his body. Is he the body of a soldier?"

"No, Nuu-Shirh! He's flabby like an old man. He's so ugly, but you are so beautiful. People everywhere gape at you. Why are you with him?"

"Shh! You are a child. Too young. Shh! No more questions!"

# CHAPTER FORTY-SIX
## The Closed-Door Inquiry

AFTER WHAT SEEMED like an eternity of staring in disbelief at the evidence on his desk, Captain Holland shifted his gaze to Sergeant Jurgens. Without saying a word, he got up, shut his office door, and sat down again. He picked up his phone and dialed zero.

"Holland here. Until I say otherwise, hold all my calls except for the Chief, or Erik Delstra."

His contemplative silence resumed. First and most damning was the note bearing Hitchcock's name, address and directions to Hitchcock's residence which was found in suspect Zhang's pocket during booking. Then there was the writing on the blank side of Juju Kwan's business card, which Detective Meyn found in Lieutenant Bostwick's desk. For comparison were five pages of Bostwick's known writing from his interoffice memos. Holland examined each one with a magnifying glass.

"Well, Stan, I'm not an expert, but it appears to me that except for the back of Juju Kwan's business card, all the writing is Bostwick's."

"That was my thought when Larry Meyn brought them to me," Jurgens said.

"The implications are enormous if Bostwick had any part in the attack on Hitchcock at his residence. As you know, both suspects disappeared as soon as they were bailed out. One is in hiding, the other was executed in the same place and in the same way as another failed hitman less than a year ago."

"Okay, organized crime has come to our squeaky-clean little town, so what do we do about it, Captain?" Jurgens asked.

Holland mulled the question for long seconds. "We get a court-qualified expert to determine if the writing on the note is in fact Bostwick's. If it is, we drag his butt through an internal investigation, guided behind the scenes by the Special Fraud Unit at the county prosecutor's office. The findings will determine our next steps," he replied meditatively.

Jurgens pondered. "The FBI lab follows set procedures," he said. "Bostwick and most everybody knows the directions to Hitchcock's home was on the note found in Zhang's pocket. How do we get him to fill out a handwriting exemplar without tipping our hand?"

"The element of surprise is crucial," Holland said. "We have so much of Bostwick's writing the lab might do the comparison without an exemplar. Call and ask. If they will, I'll send them as much as they need."

Sergeant Jurgens paused.

"Something else?" Holland asked.

"Larry Meyn is worried that he'll be in trouble for seizing evidence from Bostwick's desk."

The captain wagged his head. "Not a chance. I *ordered* him to use Bostwick's office to interview a rape victim because we had no other place available. When his pen ran dry, he naturally looked in the top drawer of a city-owned desk for another city-owned pen. Bostwick had no reasonable expectation of privacy; the desk and the supplies in it belong to the Department, not him."

"But Meyn is worried about Bostwick suing him civilly. His family has a lot of money and powerful connections and—"

"Bostwick be damned, Stan!" Holland shouted. "You guys forget how well the Department, as in Delstra and me, backed Hitchcock and Sherman after the shooting they were in last year. We fended off complaints and false accusations none of you ever heard about. We'll do the same for anyone else who gets in trouble for doing his job."

Jurgens pulled a pack of Lucky Strikes out of his shirt pocket. He offered one to Holland, who took it and lit it with his Zippo. They smoked in silence for a few seconds.

"There's a rat's nest in this building, Stan. We need to root it out. This investigation must be kept secret until we know if the writer was Bostwick," Holland said.

"Someone in our building tipped off someone else, who in turn warned Stanford we were coming for him. It's inconceivable to me that Bostwick isn't in this up to his eyeballs. If he wrote the directions to Hitchcock's home, he's the starting point of our investigation. If not, we will at least know what not to do or ask."

"The traitor's got to be someone else besides Bostwick, Captain," Jurgens said.

Holland gazed at his sergeant, a battle-tested veteran of Southeast Asia and along the U.S. border with Mexico. After eight years it still amazed him that Jurgens, with his background, could be content to work in such a city as Bellevue, let alone with its new and untested police department.

"I agree, Stan. But until we know who it was, I won't launch an internal investigation in the normal way. You answer to me and no one else. No disclosure to anyone, not even your wife, without my consent."

"Understood," Jurgens acknowledged.

"To prevent theft or tampering, store your evidence in our office safe, not the one the rest of the Department uses. Have Larry Meyn use one of the interview rooms to write a detailed statement about how and when he discovered the evidence in Bostwick's desk. Use my office to keep from being overheard when you phone the FBI lab and make other calls."

Jurgens snuffed his cigarette out in the ashtray on Holland's desk. "Captain, I've got to ask why you want to use the FBI Lab across the country in Virginia. They often take two or three months to release their results. Why not use the experts at SPD?"

"Two reasons: One, Bostwick is so hated here, and we have such a close relationship with Seattle that the impact of a positive identification could be clouded by claims of political spite and revenge. It would be hard to overcome a claim like that. I want to avoid that as many obstacles as possible," Holland said as he smoothed his tie. "Two, I want to protect Bostwick's reputation and ours if it turns out he's innocent. Just being investigated for something like this would stain his reputation and his career forever."

# CHAPTER FORTY-SEVEN
## Out of His League

BOSTWICK RETURNED FROM The Great Wall finally facing the fact that he was caught in a trap of his own making. All along, he had been afraid to ask Juju why she wanted Hitchcock's home address because he knew the answer. Such was his weakness for her exotic beauty and mysterious past. He not only gave Juju Hitchcock's address, but he also drove to the cabana himself, then wrote the directions.

Despite his risking everything for her, Juju kept pleading with him to dispose of Hitchcock in any way he chose. As always, he acquiesced without asking her the reason. It puzzled and frustrated him that every move he made against Hitchcock somehow backfired. Now, Hitchcock's profile and credibility are rising, making him a dangerous target.

Sitting at his desk, pondering his dilemma, an idea suddenly came to mind. It was so simple, he wondered why he hadn't thought of it before. Just then his phone rang. He smiled at the woman caller's words. He agreed to attend a confidential meeting next week. *Ten o'clock? Yes, absolutely.*

Bostwick tilted back in his chair at the end of the call. Things were finally falling into place–his ship was coming in. He felt smug for the first time in a long while. Tonight, he would tell Juju that in a few days, he would remove Hitchcock from her life, then he, not Juju, would set the tone and the terms.

EARLY THAT EVENING, he knocked on the heavy, ornately carved wooden door of Juju's custom home on top of Cougar Mountain, between Bellevue and Issaquah, with a sweeping view of Lake Sammamish. Juju opened, wearing a filmy, revealing purple dress. She grabbed him by his gun belt and pulled him over the threshold into her arms, the scent and sounds of rice, meat, vegetables and shrimp steaming and crackling in the air.

"Come. My cook fix spesa'l dinner for us." She said huskily as she led him by the hand into an ultra-modern kitchen featuring a fifteen-foot ceiling, polished slate floor, granite countertop, custom, oil-rubbed teak cabinets, wrought iron bar stools with dark brown leather seats.

Bostwick recognized the cook from the restaurant, an elderly Asian man, cadaver thin, gray wispy mustache, wearing a white linen cap, who bowed in deep respect to Bostwick.

Juju seated him at the counter and handed him a glass tumbler partly filled with an almost clear liquid and two ice cubes. "You try, I take one too."

A masculine, musky scent wafted up to him. He looked at her with a nod and raised eyebrows, questioning.

"Is Kaoliang," she answered with a lusty smirk before he asked. "Taiwan whiskey. Tunnel 88, number-one brand."

The fiery liquid tasted sweet, smooth and strong. It warmed his throat all the way down. He grinned and nodded his approval as he gazed at the murky liquid. After the second sip, he began to relax.

"I like you in uniform, Rowlie-san. Very manly!"

He blushed and took another sip.

"So, what you find out at po-lees station today?"

He gave a wary glance at the cook. Juju put her hand on his arm. "No, no worry, he no English. Him from Taiwan, him speak Mandarin only."

JUJU TOOK TWO clean glasses from her cupboard. She blocked his view with her body as she poured more whiskey into both glasses and emptied a small vial of clear liquid into his glass. Bostwick guzzled Kaoliang during and after dinner. Drunken logic told him now was the time to make his move. To impress her with his manliness, he woozily slammed his palm on the counter. She shuddered and smiled wonderingly at him.

"Juju, I'll be Chief of Police soon. Let's get married. I wanna shave you from all thish crime you're c-caught up in. Marry me and I'll shet you free."

The former bargirl and prostitute struggled to keep from giggling. She managed a credible expression of shock. "Crime, Rowlie-san? What crime?"

Bostwick cocked his drunken head to one side as he leered at her. "Hitchcock's address I gave you, my beauuuty," he slurred with a snort. "Those two you shent? That didn't pa–ann out, d–did it?"

"What mean *pan-out*?"

"The pan–the *plan* d-din't work. F-failed-they b-both failed. It didn't work!" he exclaimed, his head as wobbly as his speech. "They-they both wound up in the hoshpital–almost died, brain d-damage," he said tapping his head with his finger, "then j-jail. Ever-buddy who attacks H–Hit–chcock dies or needs a doc-doctor, bad–real bad! So, whut am I–to do, my Oriental qu–queen?"

Juju's eyes filled as she hugged him tightly and flipped the sobbing switch. "Oh Rowlie! Heetchcock ruining my business! I ask you–you say you help–but nothing happen!"

Physical contact with Juju caused him to forget about the attack on Hitchcock's wife and child, the sudden disappearance of the two men he knew Juju sent against Hitchcock, even the death of one of them as he held her in his arms. She continued sobbing and said,

"You get rid of Heetchcock, then yes–we make plans."

Delirious from desire, rich food, and alcohol, swayed by Juju's emotions and now her offer, Bostwick heard himself say: "I'll get rid of him for you."

Juju stepped back, surprised. "Promise?"

"I promise, if you promise."

She smiled as they clinked their glasses together. "To us, tonight," she said.

"And then?" he asked, his eyes moving over her, everything in the right place, to his delight.

"Drink up, Rowlie-sahn, and yes, later..."

UNAWARE OF HOW much time had passed or what went on after dinner, Bostwick awoke. His mind was fogged, he only knew he was in bed somewhere. He heard Juju slip out of bed and into her bathrobe.

Unable to move, he strained to open his eyes to slits, and through blurry vision he glimpsed Juju walk down the hall to the guest bedroom.

He thought he heard Juju say "Come, he sleep now. Move quickly. You know what to do," but maybe he was dreaming. Someone cuddled next to him. He heard a series of clicks. He couldn't tell what they were.

# CHAPTER FORTY-EIGHT
## Fireside Conference

THAT SAME EVENING and hour, in the high-ceilinged Colonial-style executive meeting room at Clinker-dagger, Bickerstaff and Pett's Captains Delstra and Holland met again. The eighteenth-century seemed to fit the two allies, who were at the top of their game, in their mid-thirties.

They had hired on the Department at the same time and rose through the ranks at the same time. Lounging in deep wingback chairs upholstered in dark brown brocade, facing each other across a hearty, dark wood coffee table, they waited in pensive silence.

A young waitress in a colorful colonial era costume set their whiskies on the table in front of them and left.

"It's too hot for a fire in the fireplace," Delstra said, the first to break the silence.

"Summers here are too short for my blood," declared Holland as he hoisted his glass of Maker's Mark. "To red-cheeked lads and fair maidens."

"May the lads be stout, and the maids have long hair

and soft bodies," Delstra returned as he clinked his glass against Holland's.

"How are your cases going on catching the two perverts?"

Holland chuckled and shook his head. "You need to work on your opening pleasantries and timing, Erik. But since you asked, we're sweating bullets. We're closer to identifying one suspect as a result of the latest attack even though the prints were smeared. The blood type of the younger one is O Positive. The older one, the original, is A Positive."

"Both types are universal donors, which is discouraging," Delstra observed in a low voice.

"It's next to nothing, all right," Holland allowed.

"I have it on good authority that people upstairs are sharpening their swords over these cases not being solved," Delstra said. "You and the Chief are standing on political gallows with nooses around your necks."

"I don't doubt it," Holland said. "I'm losing sleep, but not over what the City Manager will do to me or the Chief. Serial homicides will happen if we don't catch them both. The younger one's moved to rape rather quickly. Murder is next."

"Do you think they know each other?"

"Unlikely," Holland said.

"The CM and his crowd don't care about the victims. They conveniently ignore this sort of thing unless they can use it for political advantage," Delstra said.

"Nipping this in the bud is all that matters to me," Holland said. The Zodiac killer in the San Francisco area is an example of what can happen when predators aren't caught," Holland said. "Five women dead so far, most of them were in the suburbs. The cops there are in the same boat as us: exhausted all leads, neighbors, former tenants, roommates, and fellow employees of the victims."

"Now what?"

"You have some ace patrolmen who have worked the same districts so long they know the people who work and live there, who the bad guys are, what's in all the nooks and crannies. Like when Ira Walker spotted a car in a neighborhood at night that he knew didn't belong there and caught an out-of-town Peeping Tom on the prowl, *before* the victim called in."

Delstra nodded. "I'm putting a commendation letter in his file."

"He deserves it. Whatever you do, don't move them around to districts they aren't as familiar with, at least until this is over," Holland said.

"Agreed. What else?"

"Better have another drink before I tell you why I called this meeting."

"Twist my arm."

The waitress brought fresh drinks and left.

Holland leaned back in his chair. "I can't risk talking about this at the station. When I learned about it, I started a secret internal investigation on the spot. Jurgens is the lone handler for now. I can't inform even the Chief because of where this could lead."

Delstra's eyes locked on Holland's, waiting.

"Someone in our building tipped off someone who alerted Stanford that we were on our way to arrest him — within minutes of our meeting."

"One of our men?" Delstra asked, surprised.

Holland nodded.

"Tell me."

"I sent Joe Small to get the description of Stanford's house for our warrant affidavits," Holland began. "Joe arrived in about thirty minutes. Stanford's car was there when he arrived."

"That's enough time for the alarm to be passed to several intermediaries," Delstra remarked.

"Seconds after Joe radioed the house description, Stanford dashes out, carrying an armload of stuff and splits in his car. Joe followed him to the downtown where Stanford spotted and ditched him. The Seattle PD found his car hidden in the brush under the West Seattle Bridge a week later."

"I didn't know about that," Delstra said.

"Stanford turned up dead a couple weeks after his car was discovered. The autopsy report indicated his time of death was shortly after he fled from Small."

Delstra set his drink on the side table. He leaned forward. "So, we've got a leak. What else?"

"The landlady told my detectives that Stanford split right after he got a call from a man with an accent that sounded Oriental."

"No one in our building has an accent. What about Bostwick?"

Holland shook his head.

"No?"

"We've accounted for his whereabouts. He wasn't in the building the whole day.

"Who, then?"

"I think I know. But you better have another drink first, Erik."

# CHAPTER FORTY-NINE
## Another Missing Girl

THE HOUSE WAS a typical Lake Hills split-level with white wood siding, large front windows to allow in as much weak Northwest sunlight as possible, and a two-car attached carport. Officer Jason Allard rang the doorbell.

A balding man in his middle forties answered the door, medium height and build, horn-rimmed glasses, white dress shirt, holding a meerschaum pipe in his hand, opened the door. He had crisis written all over him.

"Mr. Waters? Good evening, sir. I'm Officer Allard. How can I help you?"

"Please come in, and thank you for coming so promptly."

The living room smelled like aromatic pipe tobacco as Allard stepped inside.

"I'm Henry Waters. Our sixteen-year-old daughter, Julie, is missing. This morning my wife took her to work at the Eastgate Dairy Queen. When she went back at five to pick her up, the manager said Julie left around noon with a guy and never came back. This is not like her."

A rail-thin, brown-haired woman in her forties wearing a blue gingham dress, entered the living room from the hall.

"You say this is not like Julie, sir. Do you mean she's never done this before?"

"*No!*" The woman exclaimed. "I'm her mother. Julie was *never* in trouble until she got involved with a man we said is too old for her."

"Who is this man you are talking about, ma'am?"

"Julie didn't want us to meet him. She did tell us she met him at Robinswood Park. Mike was the only name she gave us. He seemed to drive a different car every time he picked her up or brought her home."

"What kind of car did you see him driving last time?" Officer Allard asked.

"A blue Mustang. Late model," the father cut in.

"What does this Mike look like?"

Waters looked his wife as he shook his head. "We've never seen him, actually. He's always in a car."

"Well, is he white, black, brown or–"

"Of *course,* he's white. We've raised Julie better than that," the mother said.

"On one occasion I saw he has long blond hair," the father added.

"Tell me more about Julie and this Mike guy."

Waters turned to his wife. "You know more than I

do, Joan."

Mom was too stressed to remain standing. She sat on the couch. She was Kansas-plain, early forties, thin mouse-brown hair tied in a bun, sallow complexion. Stress over her missing child was etched into her face.

"Before this Mike came along, Julie was a solid student, As and Bs in her junior year at Sammamish," the mother said. "She participated in girls' basketball and softball and Job's Daughters. Other than those, she was content to have very little social life. She dated only a couple times for school dances, always boys from our neighborhood.

"But as soon as she met this Mike character, she became increasingly disconnected from us. Even when she was home, she holed up in her room, we hardly saw her at all. But this is the first time she hasn't come home."

Allard took notes on his metal clipboard. "Does Julie drive?"

"She's almost seventeen but she's never wanted to get her license," the mother replied.

"Any siblings?"

Mom shook her head, hands fidgeting in her lap. "Julie is our only child."

"What are Job's Daughters?"

"An international order for girls between ten and twenty years of age," the mother answered. "It's sponsored by the Masonic Lodge. Girls must be related to a Master Mason to belong. Julie's grandfather, my father, is a Master Mason. The men in *my* family were *all* Masons going back to *George Washington*," she said, shooting a sneering glance at her pipe-puffing husband. "Our Julie's belonged since she was ten. Why do you ask?"

"Maybe Julie told some of her friends in the group more about Mike."

"No need, officer."

"You've already alerted the other parents that Julie is missing, ma'am?"

"We don't want them knowing about it. Bad for our family reputation, you see," she sniffed.

"What else do you know about Mike, ma'am?"

Mom began gently rocking back and forth on the couch, clasping her knees with both hands, staring into space. "Not much, I'm afraid. After Julie met him, he hung around her while she was working at Dairy Queen…" Her voice drifted off.

"Then what happened?" Allard prompted.

"Several times Julie called me saying Mike would be bringing her home from work. He always brought her back an hour or so late. We didn't like his manners. He just let her out and drove away before she reached the door. Julie didn't want us to meet him. She told her father Mike is twenty-five and lives with some other guys out in the woods in Fall City–"

"No, Joan," the father interrupted. "Julie said Mike

is from Carnation and Fall City and lives somewhere near Preston," the father corrected.

Mom and Dad began arguing. Allard stopped them.

"All right, Mrs. Waters, you said Julie left this morning. What happened?"

"As I was starting to say, as a result of seeing this Mike, we saw dramatic changes in Julie; she would be awake all night in her room, wouldn't communicate. She lost a lot of weight because she hardly ate. My husband put his foot down this morning. Other than her job, she was grounded until we could meet Mike."

"How did Julie take it?"

Mom gave a solemn shake of her head and looked down at her hands, still clasping her knees. "She became enraged and wouldn't come out of her room. After Henry left for work, I took her to her job at the Dairy Queen."

"That was the last time you saw her?"

"Yes." Mom answered, her voice a whisper.

"What time did you drop her off?"

She wiped tears from her eyes. "Just before ten."

"Did you check her room for drugs or paraphernalia?"

"Oh no. We would never violate Julie's privacy. She has her rights, and we're not the police," she said.

Allard hid his dismay as he probed further. "Help me understand. Your underage daughter became involved with an older man. Then you saw sure signs she was involved with drugs by the changes in her appearance, health habits and behavior, but you didn't intervene, even though as her parents you have the legal right to look in her room?"

The father stood over Allard, his arms folded across his chest, holding his pipe. "That's right, officer. We're people of principle."

"Principle?"

"Just because Julie is a minor doesn't mean she doesn't have rights. She is *entitled* to her privacy."

"Did she start insisting on her privacy more after this Mike guy came into the picture?"

The mother looked at the father, who shrugged. "Looking back now, I would have to say yes," she said.

"Mr. Waters, Mrs. Waters, since you won't, will you allow me to search her room for evidence which might help us find Julie?"

The father hesitated. "I would feel better if you got a search warrant, officer.

The mother erupted, tears filling her eyes. "For God's sake! This is our *daughter,* Henry! Can't you get it through your thick head that we're in a *crisis?* The police are here to *help!*"

"All right then, officer," the father said snappishly. "We give you our permission if it will make you happy. You won't find anything, but follow me."

Allard was perplexed. Julie's bedroom was too barren for a teenage girl. Nothing on the walls, no photos on her dresser. He wondered if the parents cleaned up the room prior to his arrival.

"I will leave you alone to do your search," the father said. "The missus and I will wait in the living room."

Minutes later the parents' jaws dropped when Allard went to his patrol car and returned carrying a camera, paper sacks and large evidence envelopes.

Twenty minutes later he came down the hall carrying two paper sacks, one having what appeared to be baggies of marijuana, a bong, a length of surgical tubing, two used hypodermic needles and an empty plastic baggie with traces of white powder in it. The other sack held two spiral notebooks and a small address book. He filled out a receipt, detailing the items as suspected drugs and drug paraphernalia and gave a copy to Julie's speechless parents.

"One more thing, I'll need your most recent photo of Julie. I'll return it after we make copies for our bulletins," Allard advised.

The parents were too stunned to move or reply. Finally, the mother went down the hall and returned with a color portrait of a slim, pretty brunette in her teens. "This was taken a month ago," she said.

Allard headed to the station. He didn't tell the parents that Julie's journal contained information about Mike Smith, including where he lived in Preston.

# CHAPTER FIFTY
## A Foiled Attempt

LIEUTENANT BOSTWICK WENT home two hours early. He needed to rest before he launched his plan tonight. Minutes before 8:00 p.m., he left his parents' home in uniform, driving his unmarked departmental car. He recognized Hitchcock's voice among the third shift officers reporting themselves in service when he set his radio to monitor both frequencies.

He saw Juju's Cadillac El Dorado and other cars parked behind The Great Wall. He hid his vehicle among heavy construction equipment behind the rear parking area, which gave him a clear view of the open screen door as he waited for Hitchcock.

To his surprise, he heard Hitchcock call out on a bar check at Charlie's Place first. Bostwick left The Great Wall and set up in the dark at the farthest edge of the back-parking lot, facing the rear entrance to Charlie's. He spotted Hitchcock's black-and-white cruiser in the parking lot. He checked his watch.

Bostwick listened to radio traffic as he waited; a

shoplifter being held by store security at the Jafco store, a dine-and-dash at Sambo's, an unwanted guest refusing to leave The Gas Lamp steakhouse downtown.

Envy and hate filled Bostwick nine minutes later as he watched the cause of his misfortunes walk amongst parked cars, shining his flashlight into each one. He felt a flicker of fear when Hitchcock twice looked in his direction. *Is he on to me? Being caught would be disastrous.* He decided Hitchcock was too aware of his surroundings to risk following him.

A minute later Hitchcock called out at The Wagon Wheel. Bostwick positioned himself among the used car section of the Cascade Ford dealership next door, with a visual on Hitchcock's cruiser.

He saw Hitchcock return in eight minutes, heard him call in, and head east. A minute later he called out on another bar check, at the Hilltop Inn.

Bostwick followed.

A powerfully built black man in a black leather coat walked across the parking lot of the Hilltop with his arm around a hard-looking bleached-blonde white woman as Bostwick arrived. Seeing an interracial couple made him feel utterly out of his element. He feared and disliked people of color and despised whites who associated with them – like Hitchcock.

To avoid being seen, he backed out of the parking lot. He checked his watch as Hitchcock came back on the air. Like Hitchcock's other bar checks, this one lasted ten minutes. The next stop had to be The Great Wall. Bostwick returned to his vantage point.

The back door was still open. He could see and hear through the screen door. His headlights off, Bostwick listened to radio traffic as he waited for Hitchcock, his nemesis, his hated enemy, the man he would be if only he could.

Hitchcock's cruiser appeared a minute later. Juju's Cadillac hadn't moved, so she would be inside when Hitchcock walked in. As he did at other bars, Hitchcock parked at the rear, called out, slipped his baton into the carrying ring on his duty belt, put on his eight-point billed hat and locked his cruiser.

Bostwick crept, bent over among silent bulldozers and backhoes, and hid behind a road grader to hear what would happen when Hitchcock walked into the kitchen. His knees and back ached from remaining crouched, but he dared not risk standing up.

Friendly foreign-accented voices other than Juju's in the kitchen exclaimed, "Hi Boss! Po-leese-man! You good tonight?"

He felt betrayed when Hitchcock returned eight minutes later amid cheerful farewells from the same voices inside. Then he heard Juju's voice. She was chatting with Hitchcock, and Hitchcock was chatting with her. Bostwick felt his face flush and his heart race as he moved closer through the shadows of silent road graders and back-hoes to see through the screen door.

Juju's voice sounded friendly and inviting as she spoke with Hitchcock—the same tone as when she talks with him.

Burning with jealousy, Bostwick crawled on his hands and knees through gravel and shadows cast by heavy construction equipment until he came within ten yards of the back door of The Great Wall. He laid on his belly on the dirt and gravel under a dump truck.

Like film on an old home movie projector, a hundred emotions flickered though Bostwick's heart as he watched Juju, the love of his life, in the doorway, standing close to Hitchcock, inches from him, smiling up at him, presenting herself to him, dressed provocatively. He saw Juju put her hand on Hitchcock's arm as she said, "I like you in uniform, Heetchcock. Very manly!"

His heart pounded even harder when he heard Juju saying the very same words to Hitchcock she said to him the night before. He covered his mouth, curled into a fetal position in the dirt and sobbed in silence. Juju did almost all the talking. He couldn't make out what Hitchcock said to her. It didn't matter. Hitchcock was stealing the only woman he had ever known, laid with, loved. Bitter hatred engulfed him as he laid in the gravel, listening to Hitchcock return to his cruiser. He craned his neck to see his Juju, so beautiful, standing at the back door, watching Hitchcock drive away.

Juju went back inside. Bostwick strode to his car, his

chest heaving, tears running down his cheeks, crying, oblivious to the dirt on his uniform. He hunted all over Eastgate for Hitchcock, intending to shoot him. If he could get Hitchcock alone, he could get away with it. No one knew he was out and about. No one would suspect a police lieutenant. His hands shook and butterflies fluttered in his stomach as he cruised the streets of Eastgate. The calls coming in from Dispatch were few, and none involved Hitchcock.

Unable to find his enemy, Bostwick mused on other ways to make a permanent end of Hitchcock as he headed for home. By the time he reached his parents' house, he had a new plan.

# CHAPTER FIFTY-ONE
## The Raid at Dawn

AN HOUR BEFORE end of shift, Hitchcock parked under the lights of the Sunset Bowl. He opened the manila envelope Allard gave him.

"This is a runaway report I took tonight," Allard told him earlier. "Julie Waters, age sixteen, Mike Smith's latest squeeze. I found his current address in Preston, along with dope, possibly heroin, in her room. I made copies for you, plus her photograph."

"Preston?"

"Yeah. The old Preston Mill. It's abandoned now."

"The sawmill right off the highway exit?" Hitchcock recalled. "What would be there for anyone to live in?"

"I worked there the summer after high school. The full-time guys lived in shacks on the property. It's been abandoned for years. If the shacks are still standing, she's in one of them, and not alone. The weekend starts tomorrow. The Juvie dicks won't receive this until Monday, and they probably won't read it, let alone act on it until later, given their caseload. If she was my kid,

I'd want us to act right away."

"Thanks. Walker and I'll follow up on this."

Julie's notes were wistful introspections of a lonely young girl yearning for a taste of life. Pages of intense, heartfelt, romantic and navel-contemplating prose. She described Mike Smith as the love of her life, with descriptions of his hideout in the woods, and his two friends, unnamed.

He radioed Walker to meet him.

"How do you think we should handle this?" Walker asked after he read the runaway report and the missing girl's notes.

"First, we tell Breen, then either Breen or one of us calls King County for assistance. It's their jurisdiction."

"No present like the time," Walker quipped.

Hitchcock keyed his radio mic. Breen answered quickly.

"Contact us in front of Sunset Bowl, please."

† † †

A KING COUNTY Sheriff's deputy met them at the Highway 10 Preston exit. He fit the Hollywood image of a rural lawman; tanned and tall, cowboy lean, high cheekbones and square-jawed. He embodied rural authority in his green and tan uniform and gold sheriff's star. Hitchcock noted with envy the deputy's six-inch barreled .357 Magnum in his holster as they shook hands.

UNFINISHED BUSINESS

"Dale Hastings. How can I help?"

Walker handed him the reports which he quickly read.

"The Preston Mill's been closed for years," Hastings said. "I've met the owners many times. The property is posted No Trespassing. Only two of the old workmen's shacks are still standing. Most of the trespassers I've caught were armed, wanted and on drugs. The owners gave us a standing order that anyone on the premises without written permission is to be arrested for trespassing."

"The latest information about Mike Smith is that he's carrying a revolver in his waistband. Also, the prosecutor's office says there is PC to arrest him on investigation homicide," Hitchcock said.

Hastings nodded. "Good to know that. Follow me."

THE NIGHT WAS yielding to another gray day when the two marked cruisers rolled into the weed-infested graveled grounds of the Preston Mill. Engines and headlights were shut down. Except for the entrance, the property was surrounded by an impenetrable wall of Douglas Fir trees and a steep, rocky hillside.

The muffled murmur of the Raging River beyond the trees, and the morning fog gave the property an aura of mystery. Across from them by thirty yards was a huge empty lumber yard and a cavernous sawmill, built during the 1930s. It was open on two sides, wooden, dark, abandoned and rotting. With the background noise of the river, the fog, and the low light, the mill seemed to Hitchcock to ooze a brooding sense of grief, a brokenness over its abandonment.

To the immediate left, at the edge of the gravel driveway, two remaining workers' shacks stood about ten feet apart. The other shacks laid in heaps of decaying wood. Two beaters, a yellow Dodge Dart and an oxidized black Chevy K-5 Blazer were parked side-by-side in front of the closest shack.

Deputy Hastings got out of his car. "I called in the plate numbers," he said in a low voice. "Results should be back in a minute. Each cabin has a front and a rear door. The windows should be boarded over. This driveway is the only way in or out."

Hitchcock and Walker nodded as they scanned the property.

"The people inside are probably asleep," Hastings said. "we'll move fast to gain the advantage of surprise. Park your vehicle behind theirs to prevent their escape. One of you covers the back, the other goes with me through the front. They'll panic if they hear us when you pull up, so we must be quick. These are one-room shacks with no electricity, so use your flashlights. Assume the guys inside are armed."

"I'll know her if she's there," Walker said," I used to see her walking home from school."

Hitchcock handed his cruiser keys to Walker. "I'll

cover the back."

Hastings went to his patrol car and returned in seconds. "No warrants on either car or the registered owners. Let's go."

Hitchcock ran to the back as Walker pulled the patrol car inches behind the Dodge Dart and the Blazer, blocking them in.

Walker and Deputy Hastings burst into almost total darkness, flashlights on, revolvers in hand, to find three sleeping bodies in two sleeping bags on the floor. "Police! Don't move! You're all under arrest for trespassing!" Hastings shouted.

The shack stank of rotting wood. In one sleeping bag was a thin youth with shoulder-length red hair and beard stubble. In the other was an overweight man with dark curly hair, appearing to be in his in his late twenties to early thirties. The young girl with him was thin and gaunt, dark circles around her eyes, her long dark hair was matted and tangled. Both were naked. Walker shined his flashlight into her face.

Her eyes squinted as she raised her hand to shield her eyes from the light. "Hey, don't-who-what?" She stammered.

"Julie Waters, I'm Officer Walker, Bellevue Police. You're under arrest as a runaway juvenile. Get up and get dressed."

"Please hand me my shirt and jeans, Officer. They're on the couch."

"Who's the guy?" Walker asked as he checked Julie's clothes for weapons or contraband before tossing them to her. He noticed needle tracks on the inside of Julie's left forearm. She turned her back to Walker and the deputy to dress.

"Um, Bill, I think. He's a friend."

"Bill, *you think*? You sure he's not Mike Smith?"

Julie stopped cold. "No, he's Bill, Mike's friend. Mike isn't here."

Walker handcuffed Julie as soon as she was dressed. He made sure Deputy Hastings had secured his prisoner before he nudged Bill with his foot. "Wake up, inmate!"

Bill rolled over on one side. "Aww, poor Bill's awake, he just doesn't *feel* like getting up, Walker said as he grabbed a thirty-two-ounce plastic 7-11 cup of melted ice on the floor and emptied it on Bill's head.

Bill sat up, sputtering and shaking his head, cursing. He sprang to his feet, buck naked, hands clenched into in fists, ready to fight. Walker shined his flashlight on his badge then into Bill's face.

"Don't try it, sonny."

Bill sat down and covered himself.

"You're under arrest, Inmate! Grab your undies and get dressed."

"What did you call me?" Bill asked, a confused scowl on his face.

Walker, holding Julie by the arm, pointed at her as he said, "I'm speaking future tense. The girl here is sixteen—jailbait, and that makes you a future *inmate*!" he shouted.

Deputy Hastings added, "It's ball-and-chain time for both of you. You're under arrest for Investigation Statutory Rape and Contributing to the Delinquency of a Juvenile."

"Keep your hands where I can see 'em as you roll outta that sleeping bag. Do it before I shake you out," Walker ordered.

"My name is Bill, officer. Would you please hand me my clothes? They're over there," he asked, pointing to a rusted chrome frame kitchen chair.

Walker ordered Julie to stand aside while he read the driver's license he found in the wallet in Bill's filthy logger-style jeans. "William Goforth, age *twenty-six*! Must be you, huh?"

Goforth nodded and mumbled and extended his hand for his clothes. Walker fished a marijuana pipe and a small baggie stuffed with what looked like marijuana from the pants pockets then threw the jeans at Goforth's face.

"Possession of Marijuana will be an additional charge. Get your duds on, Inmate Goforth. From here you will 'go forth' to the county tank where you will stay until a judge has time to listen to your lies."

Deputy Hastings found a loaded .38 revolver of South American make on Paul Kirby, the other male suspect. A search of his person yielded a small plastic baggie having ten unidentified white tablets. Hastings stood Kirby with Goforth as he informed them that they were both under arrest for Investigation of Statutory Rape, Contributing to The Delinquency of a Juvenile, Investigation of Violation of the Uniform Controlled Substance Act, and Criminal Trespassing. He read them their Constitutional Rights.

Hitchcock came in. "Is Smith here?"

Walker shook his head. "The other shack, maybe?"

"Both doors are padlocked on the outside and the windows are boarded."

Hitchcock shined his flashlight on Goforth. "Ah, Goforth, people have been telling me about you."

Goforth shot a frightened glance at Hitchcock. "How's that?"

"A little birdie told me everything," Hitchcock said.

Deputy Hastings took both sleeping bags for lab analysis as evidence of statutory rape. "Let's get these people downtown."

† † †

A BLUE LATE-MODEL model Mustang fastback burst into the driveway as Hitchcock and Walker were loading the two men into the back of the county patrol car and Julie was about to be seated in the Bellevue cruiser.

"Run, Mike! Run! They're after you!" Julie screamed.

The Mustang spun a full circle, engine roaring,

spraying the county car with gravel as it headed toward the paved road.

Hitchcock shoved Goforth face-first against the county cruiser, drew his gun, cocked the hammer, aimed and tracked the Mustang with a two-hand grip.

The Mustang fishtailed, screeching, smoking tires as it returned to the paved road. Hitchcock kept it in his sights as it roared through the trees, but a clear shot never came.

"Did either of you guys get the plate number?" the deputy asked.

Hitchcock's pulse raced as he holstered his gun, shaking his head.

"All I saw were the last two numbers, six-eight," Walker replied. "At least we got a brief look at Mike Smith. We better take Julie to the Youth Center. She's got fresh tracks on her arm. She might be in early stages of withdrawal."

"She won't die in the next few seconds," Hitchcock said, gripping Goforth by the arm.

"What are you doing?" Walker asked.

"This is the one who was in the sack with Julie, right? I think he wants to tell me something. Back in a minute." He marched Goforth back to the shack. Alone with him in the semi-darkness and nostril-piercing stench, Hitchcock, backed him against the wall. "Start talking."

"About what?"

"Mike Smith. Where would he be going?"

"That was him in the Mustang. He moves around a lot."

"How long have you known him?"

Goforth shrugged. "A year or so, maybe."

"You're the one who bought the Mustang for him, aren't you?"

Goforth's eyes widened, surprised. "How'd you know that?"

"Like I told you, a little birdie told me."

"Don't matter. No crime in buying a car for someone else," Goforth shrugged.

"That's right. Even if it was, it wouldn't compare to what you're facing, big man."

Goforth scoffed. "Yeah? Like What? A little catnip in my jeans?"

"The underage girl makes for a serious felony, but you're looking at another felony besides her, Goforth."

"Yeah? What would that be?"

"Accessory to Attempted Murder."

Goforth's jaw went slack. "How so?"

"Accessory to Attempted *First Degree* Murder, actually."

Goforth's mouth fell open. His eyebrows raised. "Come on! You're scarin' me!" he sputtered, red-faced.

The absence of denial gave an open door to Hitchcock.

"Tell me about Randy."

"Don't know Randy," Goforth mumbled, looking down.

"No? You tried to kill him. I've got witnesses who saw you and Smith leave him for dead at Lake Sammamish State Park," Hitchcock bluffed.

Goforth turned his head fully left and held it there, saying nothing.

"Tell me the truth, Goforth," Hitchcock pressed. "Life won't be worth living if you don't, because Randy's alive."

Goforth's head snapped around. He stared at Hitchcock, questions in his eyes, but saying nothing.

"That's right. Some people at the park found him. I talked to him in the hospital. He told me everything. From the back seat of Smith's car, you shared a bong with Randy. There's a lot more. Believe me now?"

Hitchcock could see Goforth's heart pounding, moving the fabric of his shirt. His forehead and bare chest glistened with sweat despite the cold.

"Ever hear of a girl around Smith named Holly?"

Goforth gulped as he shook his head. "Mike's always got women. Holly? I might've heard him mention her. Why?"

"Holly was with Mike when she died last year. The prosecutors' office wants Mike for her murder."

"I didn't know, officer, honest," he said, his voice shaking. "I want nothin' to do with murder."

"No? Then why did you go along with Smith in

trying to kill Randy Fowler?"

Goforth turned his head, shook the greasy curls out of his face, stamped one foot and exhaled sharply. "I got nothing more to say."

"Did you meet the girl you were sleeping with through Mike Smith?"

"Maybe," Goforth replied with a quick smirk.

"How did you get her? Did Smith give her to you?"

Goforth cracked an involuntary smile. "Maybe."

"You like girls, do you, Goforth?"

"Yeah," he said, grinning again.

"Do you like boys too–guys?"

Goforth scoffed and shook his head. "Whatever you might think of me, Officer, I ain't no queer."

"Where you're going, there ain't no women, only guys. Guys who'll use you as a woman whether you like it or not."

Hitchcock tapped Goforth's meaty chest with his finger. "The lifers in the joint will love having a big fresh boy like you. If you tell me all you know about Mike Smith, how I can find him, who supplies him, I can help you through the prosecutor's office. Deal?"

Goforth scoffed. "You want me to snitch for you? Hey, I'm sorry about the Holly chick, but I never knew her. If I helped you on the Randy thing, it'd be a death sentence for me–no thanks–I'd rather do the time."

Hitchcock spun him around and slid his left sleeve up. "Some of these track marks are old. Been getting smack from Smith for a long time, Goforth?"

"No deal, Officer. The longer the other guy sees I'm here with you, the more I'll have a snitch jacket on me. Take me to jail."

"Listen, Goforth, you need help. I'm offering you legal help where no one can hear us. I can protect you if you accept."

"Take me to jail."

"What about this Kirby guy?"

Goforth looked up at the ceiling. "Take me to jail."

USING HIS REARVIEW mirror, Hitchcock kept an eye on Julie in the back seat as he entered the freeway. She was quiet, staring solemnly out the window. He glanced at Walker in the passenger seat. "She seems all right, but I don't think we should take her home," he mumbled.

"We don't know when she last used or how much."

"Which hospital, then?"

Walker glanced back at Julie. "You okay, Julie?"

Julie looked at Walker and nodded.

"Youth Center," Walker said under his breath. "I'll have Records notify her parents."

TWELFTH AVENUE WAS void of traffic when they arrived at the King County Youth Center. Hitchcock led Julie to a bench at the front counter. Walker started to fill out the admission form when Julie began fidgeting.

A social worker rushed from behind the intake desk and shook Julie's shoulders. "Talk to me, Julie!" Julie's eyes rolled up into her eyelids. She collapsed from the bench to the floor and curled into a fetal position, writhing and moaning.

"Call an ambulance! She's going into withdrawal!" the social worker ordered the clerk at the front desk. Two ambulance attendants arrived in ten minutes.

Julie's mother had a complete emotional breakdown when she saw ambulance attendants strapping their daughter's squirming body onto a gurney. Her husband caught her as she collapsed to the floor as their daughter was taken to the Harborview ER.

† † †

A SULLEN SILENCE hung over Walker as they drove back across the Floating Bridge. Hitchcock finally asked, "What's bothering you?"

"Why you didn't shoot Smith when you had the chance."

"I didn't have a clear shot."

Walker scowled, staring out the windshield. "We've gotta catch this guy, Roger. He's killing people."

Hitchcock said nothing for over a minute. "Smith crossed the line a long time ago. He won't go down without a fight. He won't stop killing, either—he likes it too much."

# CHAPTER FIFTY-TWO
## Moves and Countermoves

*The Squad Room*
*Saturday, 7:40 P.M.*

BOSTWICK STRUTTED INTO the squad room as shift briefing was in session. He avoided eye contact with Hitchcock as he approached the podium and handed a typed directive on Department letterhead to Sergeant Breen, who read it quickly.

"What's the meaning of this, Lieutenant? District assignments are decided by the sergeants."

"Well, *Sergeant* Breen," Bostwick sneered, "*I* have observed that patrol officers aren't as familiar with the city as they should be *because* they work the same district year after year. Rotation will round them out a bit. Beginning now, move officers who work the west side to the east, and vice versa,"

THAT NIGHT, JUJU was surprised to see a different officer walk through the lounge in The Great Wall. "Hi," she said with her seductive smile. "You not Heetchcock.

I am Juju, owner this place. Heetchcock off today?"

"I'm Officer Brooks, Ma'am," Clive smiled, tipping his hat. "Officer Hitchcock is working the downtown area now. I'll be here from now on."

† † †

THE NEXT MORNING Juju put in a call to Taiwan from her home. A man's voice answered on the fourth ring. "I must speak to Mr. Chen, now. This is Juju, in America," she said in Mandarin.

A long minute later Juju heard a man's voice she recognized. "I have good news, Mr. Chen. As you instructed, the officer, Heetchcock, is gone." She paused, listening. "Yes, I have confirmed it. The official I own did it for me. I will reward him, and we are free to do business again. More than before. We are ready, Mr. Chen. I wait for your instructions." Juju smiled as she ended the call, then dialed again.

† † †

*Shift Briefing*
*Monday, 7:45 P.M.*

THE ENTIRE SQUAD was in an uproar. "I know they're ugly, but we better not complain too loud, or the City Manager will come up with something worse for us," Sergeant Breen warned.

"Black-and-white cruisers always distinguished us from other departments. Why doesn't the Chief stand up to him?" Hitchcock asked.

Breen held up a newspaper. "All right–pipe down. The Chief folded, is the only way I can say it. Here's the write-up from today's *P.I.* with the Chief standing by one of the new cars."

He put on his reading glasses and began to read. *"'Police cars in Bellevue are taking on a new look, part of the Bellevue Police Department's move for modernizing its image. The familiar black-and-white, which has traditionally marked police cars here, is being replaced with all-white vehicles that include a multi-colored city seal accented by blue striping running from the rear fender to the front fender.'"*

"What does the Chief say?" someone asked.

"I'm coming to that," Sergeant Breen said.

The officers groaned and swore.

Sergeant Breen held up his hand. "Hold on, here's the headline. *'Bellevue Chief Sean Carter said the new design will serve several purposes, including a softening of the police image in the community.'* Here's more," Sergeant Breen said. *'In considering the design change we looked for something which would be distinctive and yet at the same time be less brash than the traditional black-and-white.'"*

"I don't like this any better than you do," Breen said. "Even worse, the new cars are Ford sedans without the Police Interceptor package. I take this as another gesture of contempt from the third floor. The City Manager would put us in pink leotards and carrying slingshots instead of guns if he could, and several members of the

City Council feel the same way."

Breen continued. "There's a continuum to the anti-police attitude. At the extreme end are groups like The Weatherman Underground. They attack symbols of the Establishment. They bomb government buildings, police stations, banks and corporate offices. Last March, they bombed the U.S. Capitol to protest the bombing of Laos to stop the North Vietnamese army from launching attacks on South Vietnam.

"The FBI predicts more groups like them will form. Attacks on police officers as symbols of established society will escalate. Seattle is not immune – last year the Seattle Weather Underground Collective was formed. So far, we have seen very little violence here, but the crime wave is headed our way.

"Small departments like ours will be targeted because we're less prepared than big-city agencies. That's it. Be alert, know the condition of your weapon, take nothing for granted. Hit the bricks, boys. Disss-*missed!*"

"I got something to say before we go," Hitchcock said.

"Say it, but be careful," Breen nodded.

"You just read the latest on people out there who want to kill us for no reason other than we're cops," Hitchcock said. "We used to think the City had our backs while we're taking risks on their behalf. But now we see they don't back us up at all. We're on our own."

A murmur of anger and cursing rumbled through the squad. The men filed out, headed to their cruisers.

† † †

CAPTAIN DELSTRA FOUND a sealed envelope the next morning marked ERIK under his office door. The handwritten unsigned note inside said:

> *Wednesday at 10:00 a.m. this week, a*
> *closed-door meeting will be at the city*
> *manager's office to discuss the next move to*
> *take about further changes they will make to*
> *control and diminish your department.*
>
> *Lt. Bostwick has accepted their invitation*
> *to attend.*

Delstra recognized the writing. He gazed out the window, thinking. He couldn't fathom why the writer would risk a promising career and a bright future by informing to protect the Department.

The Department's Press Information Officer poked his head in. "Got a minute, Erik?"

Delstra gestured to the chair in front of his desk.

"You didn't hear this from me, but with the latest batch of new officers coming on the street, the City is authorizing the creation of two slots for the new rank of Major."

"I'm surprised. This is the first I've heard of it. Why the secrecy?"

"A few of my contacts in the press, friends of mine

for a long time, knew about it before I did. They told me that you, Erik, are one of the reasons for the secrecy."

Delstra knit his brows, staring hard at his visitor. "I am?"

"My sources tell me Bostwick is telling certain reporters that he expects to get the new position, and later become chief, as a result of his reorganizing shift assignments, which he claims has revitalized Patrol. They also say Bostwick is saying *Sunrise 71* violated the civil rights of young people and that he fueled the negative publicity the Sunrise 71 action got in the Seattle papers and was part of the basis of the ACLU's class-action lawsuit against Grant County. This is third hand information, but it comes from experienced, credible newsmen on condition of anonymity. The consistent thread is that Bostwick is helping the very people who oppose us."

Delstra struggled to keep his rage in check. "Thanks. We never had this conversation. I will not forget your loyalty and your confidence in me."

# CHAPTER FIFTY-THREE
## "Do You Want to Die?"

THE ABDUCTION, TORTURE and execution of a Texas deputy with his own gun by two prison escapees from the Georgia penitentiary haunted Joel Otis.

Recent information from the FBI had it that both Lonnie Slocum and Virgil Howard were still in the Puget Sound area.

The information agreed with Otis, who was well-known for his uncanny ability to be at the right place at the right time. Acting on his sixth sense that the gang would return, Otis redistributed copies of the wanted posters of the gang to gas stations, fast food joints and 24-hour restaurants, telling employees that the gang of cop killers is still in the area.

Otis also learned the FBI named the third gang member as George Robert Udall, WMA, 6'0", 220 lbs, brown hair, brown eyes, prior convictions for armed robbery, kidnapping and assault, currently wanted for assaulting a police officer in Nevada.

THE DAY WAS cool and cloudy, dry and windy a week later when, at 1:00 P.M., Otis got a call. *"Contact Gary Griggs at Midlakes Chevron. Says situation is urgent. Wouldn't specify. We asked if it was a robbery in progress, he said no."*

"I'm a block away, ETA one," Otis replied.

Hitchcock, across the freeway in the downtown, came on the air: *Two Zero One will assist.*

Griggs, a timid, lanky nineteen-year-old wearing the uniform of the white short-sleeve shirt with the Standard Oil logo and gray workpants, was stuttering when he came out to meet Otis. Shaking, he held a paper in his hand.

"Th-thanks for getting here so f-fast, O-Officer Otis."

"I was just up the street when I got the call, Gary. What's up?"

"R-remember you g-gave us wanted posters of three guys wanted for killing a c-cop in Texas?"

Otis nodded.

"Well, a-a moment ago I w-walked across the s-street to pick up a b-burger to go at Sambo's. I saw this-this guy parked in the back, facing the b-bank next to Sambo's, the one on the corner..."

"Go on," Otis urged, listening intensely.

"Well, uh, he was just sitting in his c-car, watching the bank. When I came out, he-he was still there. He seem-seemed familiar, like I had seen-seen 'im b-before.

So, uh, when I got back, I ch-checked the poster you gave us."

Hitchcock arrived as Griggs handed Otis the wanted poster. "Th-that's him-the b-blond g-guy," he said, pointing to Lonnie Slocum's mugshot.

"Car description?"

"B–blue Ch–Chevy Malibu," he stuttered.

OTIS BURST INTO Sambo's back parking lot from the south side, which faced Rainier Bank on the corner. He blocked the blue Chevy Malibu from behind. Lonnie Slocum bounded out of the driver's seat, facing Otis, his hand disappeared under his green and white flannel shirt as Hitchcock rounded the north corner of Sambo's and bailed out of his cruiser, his gun already drawn. At the sight of a second officer, Slocum sprinted toward the freeway.

The freeway noise was deafening as Otis chased Slocum across the uneven, uncut grassy median toward the 405 freeway, gun in hand, Hitchcock close behind. A six-foot chain-link fence forced Slocum to a halt. He reached under his shirt again as he turned to face his pursuer.

"Do you want to die?" Otis shouted over the roar of freeway traffic as he aimed his service revolver at Slocum's head.

Slocum's hand froze on the butt of the gun under his

shirt. He stared at Otis, who was calm, purposeful, businesslike and had the drop on him.

Slocum didn't move.

"Goodbye, then," Otis said as he cocked the hammer and aimed at Slocum's eye. Slocum's empty hands went up in the air.

Hitchcock circled wide around Otis and came up behind Slocum, gun in hand. "On your knees, keep your hands in the air," he ordered. Slocum kept his eyes on Otis as he slowly squatted, then knelt in the grass.

Otis kept his gun pointed at Slocum as Hitchcock cuffed and double-locked Slocum's hands behind his back. He removed a blue steel revolver from his waistband. "You're under arrest for the murder of Deputy Cunningham." Otis declared.

Slocum was still kneeling when Otis pressed the muzzle of his revolver against Slocum's forehead. Over the roar of freeway traffic, in a calm voice, Otis asked, "Tell me, Slocum, are you the one who pulled the trigger on Deputy Cunningham?"

No answer.

"Was the deputy kneeling like you are when you killed him?"

Slocum confessed with a slight nod, then he looked down, expecting to die the same way.

"Did Deputy Cunningham beg for his life?" Otis demanded tersely.

No response.

"Well did he, dirtbag?"

The left side of Slocum's face began twitching. Hitchcock wondered if he should look away before Otis pulled the trigger.

Otis holstered his revolver. Relieved, Hitchcock stood Slocum up and felt along his waistband.

"What's this I feel?" The small, hard object was a handcuff key, taped to the back of Slocum's inside waistband.

"You'd have more of a chance if you'd gone for your gun, Slocum," Otis said. "You're a dead man now. They use the death penalty in Texas; especially for cop killers."

Otis stood back a step and glanced at Hitchcock. "Take him in, Roger. I'll stand by for the impound."

† † †

THE STATION WAS electric with excited activity as Hitchcock arrived with Slocum in custody. Calls from nervous citizens reporting officers holding a man at gunpoint next to the freeway poured into the State Patrol and police emergency lines. Television news desks lost no time calling and showing up at the station, swooping in for the scoop.

Otis followed the tow truck bringing Slocum's car to the station. A detective sealed it with evidence tape, and another went upstairs for a search warrant. Otis met Hitchcock in the booking room, where Slocum sat on the bench, silent as a stone.

"Guess what, Joel?" Hitchcock asked.

"What?"

"The gun we took off Slocum was Deputy Cunningham's weapon."

Otis approached Slocum. "Do you want to die alone in Texas, or would you like some company?"

Slocum barely glanced at Otis. "Whatya mean?" he drawled.

"Tell us where Virgil Howard and George Udall are."

Slocum shook his head.

† † †

THE LOCAL FBI liaison phoned Captain Delstra to confirm the arrest. The Sheriff of Deputy Cunningham's county publicly praised the Department and Chief Carter on national television for their "fine police work." Local television stations broadcast details of the daring capture of Slocum as "Breaking News."

The dramatic arrest brought an avalanche of congratulations from across the country, got Chief Carter temporarily off the political hotseat and skyrocketed the credibility of the Department overnight.

Hitchcock went home at the end of shift, feeling triumphant that he helped Otis capture a cop killer. Allie was in the kitchen, popping popcorn on the stove. She was heavy with child and past her due date by two days.

The television was on in the living room.

"Hi, honey. How was work today?" she asked with a loving smile. *Obviously, she hadn't heard the news,* he realized as he wandered into the living room and turned the television off.

"Same-o, same-o," he fibbed.

"The popcorn is ready, but I have to check to see if Trevor is asleep," she said. "There'll be re-runs of *Rawhide* tonight, with Clint Eastwood."

# CHAPTER FIFTY-FOUR
## A *Coup D'état*,
### and
## The Third Man

*The Station*
*Wednesday, 9:45 A.M.*

CAPTAIN DELSTRA LEFT his office door open to keep an eye on Lieutenant Bostwick's office across the hall and down one door. As his confidential informant said, Bostwick stepped out of his office, a folder in his hand at 9:50 a.m.

"Where are you off to, Lieutenant?" Delstra asked.

Bostwick froze, then gulped. "Oh, uh, just checking on something upstairs in Records, Captain," he lied.

As he hustled down the hall to the staircase, Delstra picked up his phone.

By five minutes after ten, Bostwick was seated in the third-floor conference room with a few key officials. The meeting call to order was interrupted when Lydia, Captain Delstra's loyal, steel-eyed, no-nonsense administrative aide strode through the door uninvited, unannounced. She headed straight for Bostwick.

Bostwick's jaw dropped as Lydia took his folder and set another folder on the table in front of him and tapped the first page with her forefinger. "Captain Delstra orders you to read this file, and bring it with you when you report to him *at once*. Without delay. You are not authorized to attend this meeting."

Lydia left the room, leaving the door open.

Bostwick gasped when he saw Mark Forbes's statement to Hitchcock. Worse yet was his own memo to a City Manager's aide, outlining his scheme to fire Hitchcock and other officers, mentioned by name.

He shut the folder and stood up. "You will h-have to ex-excuse me," he said as he bolted to the men's room.

A young man from the administration came in.

"Can we help you, Lieutenant?" he asked.

Bent over a toilet, vomiting, Bostwick could only speak between retches. "No–no. I–uh–tell them-tell them I-I can't make the meeting."

Ignoring the flecks of puke on his uniform, Bostwick splashed cold water on his face and headed downstairs. For him it was a death march; every step seemed like a year of his life taken away. He appeared at last, ashen faced, at Captain Delstra's office door. He knocked. He felt his blood run to his feet when the door opened, and he saw Captain Holland also waiting for him.

THE NEXT MORNING, an internal memo was posted in the squad rooms of Patrol and Traffic, the Bull Pen, and Records:

> *Lieutenant Rowland Bostwick has accepted a demotion to the rank of sergeant. Sergeant Bostwick will manage the new property and evidence facility. He will assume his new responsibilities at once.*

Captain Delstra ordered all Patrol sergeants to immediately return all officers to their usual district assignments. "They will use their familiarity with their beats to detect suspicious persons who could be the sexual predators we are seeking."

THREE DAYS LATER, a postman delivered a cardboard box wrapped in brown paper to the property room. It was addressed to "Sergeant Bostwick." Bostwick opened it to find a rabbit fur cap, mittens and mukluk booties. Puzzled, he read the card inside.

> *Dear Sergeant Bostwick,*
> *Congratulations on your new post. As it is bitterly cold in Siberia, you will need these to keep from freezing.*
> *Warm Wishes,*
> *The Boys in Patrol*

Screaming, spittle rolling down his chin, Bostwick ran around the cavernous room, smashing and throwing property. Two hard-hat mechanics from the adjacent City service shop peeked in. "Whatsa matter, Bub?" one of them asked.

† † †

TWO DAYS LATER, Hitchcock received an internal memo from Sergeant Jurgens:

> *Roger,*
> *The State Patrol Crime Lab determined the saliva on the Salem brand cigarette butts is from someone with Type O Positive Blood.*
> *Andrew Stanford's blood type was Type O Positive. Jinjie Zhang is Type A Positive.*
> *The saliva on the Marlboro brand butts is from someone who has Type B Positive blood.*
> *Crime Lab technicians lifted prints off the roll of duct tape in the bag found behind your home. Two prints were Stanford's.*
> *A thumb print on the same roll of tape has been sent to the FBI for identification. If no record is found, the Bureau will search military service files.*
> *I will keep you posted.*
> *Stan Jurgens, Sgt.*

HE DECIDED NOT to tell Allie about the report. He

wanted her to remain calm during the final stage of her pregnancy.

He shared the memo with Sherman, Otis and Walker at the Pumphouse Tavern after work.

"It turns out the memos and FIRs I've sent in regarding drug trafficking and shipments coming in at night at the airport were intercepted," he said.

"Bostwick?" Sherman asked.

"I can't think of anyone else. There is evidence of a third man who was with Stanford when he spied on me and Allie. Whoever he is, smokes Marlboros—Zhang doesn't smoke, neither did Bostwick, Stanford smoked Salems."

"Don't count Bostwick out yet," Walker said. "He still has influence and a following on the Department and in the City."

"Bostwick was working with Frank Kilmer in the photo lab all day on a project for the City," Otis reported. "Frank verified that Bostwick never used the phone and worked with him all day. Whoever started the chain of calls to warn Stanford to flee is someone else."

The ever-upbeat Tom Sherman raised his glass. "At least the little Nazi is innocent of something! A toast to finding the third man, boys. May we get the bastard in a dark alley soon!"

United by the strong bond of the badge, the four clinked their glasses together and drank to the dregs as one.

Before he left, he called Allie from the payphone by the restrooms. "I'm on my way home. Had a brew with the boys," he said. "Are you okay?"

"I'm fine, honey. My mom's here. The baby's moving around a lot today."

He felt a strange anxiety. "Do you need anything from the store?"

"A gallon of milk from the Milk Barn on your way home."

"Anything else?" he asked.

"Yes. Jamie's been on full alert all day for some reason."

"What's he doing?"

"Pacing the house, checking the windows and doors, he growls, keeps a close eye on me and Trevor."

*Not good.* "I'm on my way. Keep the doors locked."

Hitchcock unlocked his Wagoneer, unaware of the non-descript, middle-aged man in a tan early '60s vintage Ford short-bed half-ton pickup watching them from an adjacent parking lot of the lumber store next door.

The ends of the driver's thin lips curved up into a cold smile as he started his engine and entered heavy traffic, two cars behind Hitchcock…

# ACKNOWLEDGEMENTS

The events and characters in *Unfinished Business* have been brought to life with the help of former Bellevue Officers Robert Littlejohn, Al Ward, Jim Hassinger, Gary Trent, Mike Beckdolt, Craig Turi Bob Phelan, and certain officers at the Seattle Police Department with whom I had the honor and pleasure of working with during the '70s and '80s. Thanks for the memories.

# ABOUT THE AUTHOR

JOHN HANSEN draws from personal experience for most of his writing. Between 1966-1970 he served as a Gunners Mate aboard an amphibious assault ship that ran solo missions in and out of the rivers and waterways of South Vietnam, the militarized DMZ and other places, often having detachments of U.S. Marines and Navy Underwater Demolition Teams on board.

While a patrol officer with the Bellevue Police Department following military service, his fellow officers nicknamed him "Mad Dog" for his tenacity. After ten years in Patrol, he served eleven years as a detective, investigating homicide, suicide, robbery, assault, arson and rape cases.

As a private investigator after retirement, his cases have taken him across the United States and to other countries and continents. His cases in the public and private sectors have been featured on television, newspapers and magazines. He is the winner of several awards for his books, short stories and essays.

Made in the USA
Middletown, DE
12 February 2022

60624315R00236